BEYOND ILLUSIONS

BEYOND
ILLUSIONS

·

DUONG THU HUONG

·

TRANSLATED

FROM THE VIETNAMESE BY

NINA MCPHERSON AND

PHAN HUY DUONG

HYPERION EAST

Nina McPherson wishes to thank the author for all her generous help in discussing the work and answering questions regarding the translation. The translation is from the original Vietnamese manuscript and has been edited with the author's permission.

Library of Congress Cataloging-in-Publication Data

Duong, Thu Huong.
[Bên kia bờ ao vong. English]
Beyond illusions / Duong Thu Huong ; translated from Vietnamese by Nina McPherson and Phan Huy Duong.
p. cm.
Novel.
ISBN 0-7868-6417-6
I. Title.

PL4378.9.D759 A213 2002
895.9'22334—dc21
2001039868

Design by Abby Kagan

FIRST EDITION

10 9 8 7 6 5 4 3 2 1

BEYOND ILLUSIONS

1

HOW COULD I HAVE LOVED HIM LIKE THAT? She stared at him in the green glow of dawn. Still sleeping soundly, he was both strange and familiar to her, like a waxen effigy. That face. The curve of the nose, those earlobes. He was the same man, the same flesh, that had once been a beacon inside her. Now, he no longer radiated life, love.

The man rolled over, his beard grazing her cheek. Repulsed, she sat up.

Odd, how his beard has thinned.

She stared at her husband again. Bewildered, she slid her back up against the wall. Outside in the corridor: footsteps, the clatter of a pail on the ground.

"Who's making such a racket? It's not even dawn!" a woman's voice shrieked. It was that harpy, Tong, who terrorized the building.

"Sorry, sorry, the handle of my pail just broke," replied a timid, male voice.

Tong didn't reply. Professor Le descended the stairs, the shuffle of his sandals fading in the distance. Then all was quiet again. It was about four o'clock in the morning; the city hadn't awoken, yet already the dawn rays spread through the gardens, filtering through the streets. A poisonous light, late spring's potion of fog and sun.

She shuddered as her husband's head emerged from the covers. Like a wooden statue in a museum, inert, utterly alien in the pallid, murky light.

Liar, hypocrite. To think I was once madly in love with him.

They had met during her sophomore year of college, in the suffocating heat of a June morning. Nguyen had been assigned to teach literature to her class. Most of the students were young women. Educated, romantic, they had a sense, early on, of their own worth. And they were all curious about their young professor, known for his prodigious intelligence, and dreamed of attracting his attention. Nguyen was medium height, with sparkling eyes, jet black hair, and a confident voice. But he was a bit aloof; he didn't so much as look at the girls in Linh's class, who were renowned for their beauty and talent. He used to stand in front of them in his crudely cut suit, hands smeared with chalk dust, fingers stained with ink, oblivious to the dandruff on his jacket, or the top button missing from his shirt. Everyone was captivated by his passion for the classics. He would lecture on the Italian Renaissance, the progressive aspects of capitalism, the flaws that had shaken the foundations of feudal society, the power of individual aspirations—all the noble forces that promised to lead mankind up the luminous steps to a more humanist culture. Linh was in awe of the range and depth of Nguyen's knowledge. His aloofness only fanned the flames of a love that she had felt from the moment they met. She had been nineteen years old at the time. Beautiful, gentle, she dazzled men. The previous year, on the advice of an aunt who had raised her since childhood, she had become engaged to a neighbor boy who had fallen madly in love with her when she was sixteen. Linh's fiancé was handsome enough, soft-spoken, and eager to provide for her. If she hadn't met Nguyen, her life would have followed its due course. But she *had* met him and to be with him she had endured her family's rejection, the snide mockery of the neighbors, and her ex-fiancé's hatred and contempt.

My God, I loved Nguyen more than my own life.

If she hadn't fallen so madly in love with him, she might have led a rich, comfortable life. Her fiancé had promised to wait for Linh to finish her studies to marry her. But his family had already given them a big house filled with expensive furniture made of precious wood, the kind of comfort and luxury that most people only dream of. He was always switching motorcycles when he took Linh out. He wore smart clothes and dressed her up in all the latest fashions. When she broke off her engagement, Linh had to work nights as a seamstress to repay her aunt for the returned wedding gifts. Exhausted, she would often fall asleep between classes, even in the middle of conversations with friends. How many times, on those icy winter nights, as she studied, had she felt hungry, craved a bowl of cheap Chinese noodle soup or a pork sandwich. But instead of going through with her planned marriage, she had waited for Nguyen. During their early years together, she had grown accustomed to hardship, to meals of not much more than pickled vegetables.

Yes, I loved him with all the love a woman has to give.

She remembered all their trysts in the empty classrooms. How one summer, in the shade of a tree, he had explained Dante's *Divine Comedy*, saying in his deep, serious voice: "Why are you always surprised that events change people, the course of their lives? Stop thinking of them as saints. Saints only exist in the imagination of primitive man. Today, people are intelligent enough to know that great men are thirty percent talent and seventy percent vulgarity. That's why they suffer when their interests are at stake, make mistakes in judgment, in their actions."

Nguyen had toppled Linh's most revered idols from their pedestals, but he himself had taken their place. Linh found confidence and strength in the slight smile that curved his lips, in its hint of irony. In the depths of his eyes, she sensed the experience of a compassionate soul.

Linh shivered. Memories of her passion for him flooded back. One evening, in the darkness of a movie theater, he had stroked her fingers. They were watching a film, *Robinson Crusoe*. His caress had bewitched her, and he had whispered into her ear: "Robinson is a hero from a bygone age. Being a hero now is much more difficult. There's no quest more complex, more perilous, than a man's struggle with his own soul."

Startled, she remembered staring at him in the darkness, how his eyes had sparkled, tender, and yet distant. The beauty of the intelligence in his gaze: those eyes, like two mysterious flowers floating on water. She had squeezed Nguyen's hand, secretly yearning to smother it with kisses, to tell him that she adored him.

They had lived blissful years together. Then, one day, she discovered the lies he had published in his articles, the contempt of his colleagues, the jokes that circulated after his trips, the reason behind the promotions and salary raises. "No quest is more complex, more perilous, than a man's struggle with his own soul": The person who had uttered these words had compromised himself. The man with the sparkling eyes, the pensive, gentle air about him, had submitted, surrendered. He had shattered everything she had believed in, killed their love in a single blow.

Why, why?

Linh couldn't explain how it had happened. Terrified by the pain of this lost love, by a future that threatened to evaporate, she latched on to the secret hope that she could preserve the peaceful, happy life they had shared. But the lucid, skeptical woman in her knew she had already left Nguyen. Now that she saw him clearly, her hatred was tainted with disgust, like the revulsion she felt when the stubble on his chin grazed her skin.

Wretched liar. How can I still share your bed?

Nguyen rolled over, stretched, and yawned. Linh turned away, and looked outside. She noticed that the flowering tree in the front yard was grimy, covered with dust. It is a horrible moment when you suddenly see your own home as a filthy, miserable hole, when your idol is torn from the altar's sacred darkness, no more than a piece of moldy wood in the harsh light of day.

"Linh, sweetheart, is it light out?" Nguyen asked sleepily.

"Probably," Linh replied.

Nguyen opened his eyes and smiled. "You still want to argue, don't you, my complicated one?" He reached out an arm and clasped his wife's head against his chest.

"Let go of me."

"What's the matter?"

"Nothing, but I want to get back to what we talked about yesterday."

"Again?" Nguyen smiled fondly at his wife. "Let's not talk about it. It's not worth it. The world, success, failure, truth, falsehood—let's leave all that on the doorstep, outside our home. Here, there's only you, me, and our little Huong Ly."

Nguyen kissed Linh, nuzzling his head in her bosom. She noticed that his hair had started to go white. *How can a man have white hair at age thirty-two?*

When she fell in love with Nguyen, his hair had been black with iridescent blue highlights, like bird feathers. Each time a lock of hair fell on his forehead, he would brush it aside with a slow sweep of the hand. Linh liked that gesture. How many times, waiting in front of the university gate, had she seen him run his hands through his hair that way?

Nguyen took her in his arms. Ever since they had lived together, his love had only deepened.

"Man needs a family like an animal needs a burrow," he said. "Bears take shelter from the winter cold in caves, sucking grease from their palms to survive. We're no different. When I want to forget life's hardships, all I have to do is shut the door, take you and Huong Ly in my arms . . ."

She pitied him, but winced in disgust. His face seemed so old, wizened, wretched. She closed her eyes to blot out this vision. Suddenly, she asked him, "Why are you so hot? Are you feverish?"

"No. I'm as healthy as a bear, and I love you."

Linh pushed his hand away violently, but he took her in his arms, passionate, insistent.

"Stop it, Nguyen, it's daylight," Linh snapped.

"There's no day and night here. This room is a world apart that belongs to us alone."

The stubble of her husband's beard grazed her cheek again. This time, the feeling of estrangement was unbearable. She let out a gasp. Startled, Nguyen lifted his head and looked at his wife's pale face. "What's the matter with you, sweetheart?"

Linh couldn't speak. Her eyes brimmed with tears.

Who would have thought we would reach this point? Nguyen thought. He tossed off the covers, got up, dressed, and pulled the curtains. A dazzling blue spring sky appeared outside the window.

"Don't go barefoot, you're going to get a sore throat. Your sandals are under the table," Linh said mechanically, through tears. Nguyen turned and looked at her. The beauty of her face still overwhelmed him. On their wedding day, she had looked exactly the same—young, radiant, a face that refused to submit to time.

Nguyen sat down in a chair, fumbling for a pack of cigarettes. "Go ahead, speak."

"Ever since this incident, you disgust me."

Nguyen lit a cigarette. Linh watched him and repeated: "You disgust me, do you understand?"

"I understand."

"But I don't understand."

Nguyen flicked the ashes from his cigarette into an empty seashell. "You've lost respect for me, haven't you?"

"No, no," Linh protested, but he at least had dared to speak the truth. She burst into sobs. Nguyen put out his cigarette. He wanted to console her but realized it was useless. He lit another cigarette. "Please don't cry, my love. You've got to stay calm to talk. I've lived in fear of this for so long. With a woman like you, this day would have come, sooner or later."

"So it's my fault?"

Nguyen shook his head. Before he could reply, Linh continued: "No, no, don't blame it on me. Listen, since last summer I've heard all sorts of rumors about you. And not from Trong, or Nam, or Miss Tram, or even Phuc. From people you wouldn't even think of, who I run into on the street. They snicker about the articles you wrote, about your loyalty to the editor-in-chief, your trips to Europe, the lavish ceremonies you organize everywhere you go. I'm no girl anymore, no starry-eyed Young Pioneer in a red scarf. I did my homework, through different sources. That's why I finally confronted you, because I wanted to know the truth. Oh, you had your explanations. You laughed. You mocked people. The slightest gesture from you—a nod of the head, a wave of the hand, an eyebrow raised—was enough to make me forget all the rumors. All you had to do was frown disdainfully and I was convinced it was all pettiness, jealousy, lies. I believed in your integrity; I tried to imagine the pain you must have felt, having to endure such slander. I believed in you all along."

Linh stopped, her voice choking. Tears welled up again, cascading down her face. Nguyen bowed his head. His hands were shaking. "It's my fault, and I know it. But to be fair, part of the blame is just life."

"That's a cowardly excuse. Say it, you acted like a . . ." Linh stopped, unable to find the words, her eyes squinting in anguish. Nguyen took a puff of his cigarette and lowered his head. Staring at the floor, he noticed an overturned cockroach. The insect spun in circles on the flowered tiles, its feet flailing in the air. "Listen, Linh, I'm going to tell you everything. Not to beg your forgiveness, but so you will judge human beings with more objectivity." Nguyen threw his butt into the shell. He raised his head. Linh watched him, waiting anxiously for him to speak. Her eyes shone, clear and cold as crystal shards. But behind that gaze, those rosy cheeks, lay a naive, implacable soul. Nguyen shivered. He slowly placed his foot over the cockroach, and held it there for a few seconds before speaking. "I won't try to defend myself, as I did last night. I love you. I've always asked my colleagues not to discuss work with you. I didn't want to burden you with something you'd never accept. Now, it's too late."

Nguyen lifted his foot. The insect spun on itself, trying to gain momentum. "Can't you understand the psyche of a man who must provide for his family?"

"Psychology is no excuse for writing lies."

"Before we were married, I was a student. A free man. Aside from the time I spent with you, I read books. Week in and week out. All I needed for food was a bit of bread. Then we got married and Huong Ly was born. Life was fuller, happier, but more stressful. Suddenly, I was at the ship's stern, and I watched, terrified, as other families sunk all around us."

Nguyen fell silent, his forehead creased with worry lines. "I don't want you to go without a new blouse. I don't want my daughter to long in vain for a pair of new shoes."

Linh turned away, her nostrils burning. Nguyen continued: "When I finished my studies, I was as zealous as a knight putting on his armor before battle. Maybe not as impassioned as you. But like you, I was determined to live with dignity and integrity. I imagined my writing serving the Revolution, helping in the fight for justice, extolling progress, denouncing the ugliness, the baseness that still poison our society. I wasn't alone. Many of my colleagues shared my ideals. But little by little, I came to see that the space and time that separated us from our aspirations overcame our willpower. They sent me all over to do reporting. Everywhere, people are eager to greet us, eager to vaunt their inflated, fabricated statistics. Everywhere, success is exaggerated; failure and defeat hidden. Everyone suffers from the same pathology. Our obsession with results and performance masks the reality, whitewashes the dangers that loom for our society. Who has the courage to stand up against old habits, rooted in our compatriots for as long as you and I can remember? In a society where individual rights don't amount to much, individual actions are swayed by the tide of the community."

Nguyen stopped for a moment, lit a cigarette. Huong Ly rolled over in bed, murmuring in her sleep. Outside, a bird let out a sharp cry.

"The first few times I wrote those articles I felt remorse, doubt. I rebelled and protested. Then I started to see that this cult of success served the interests of certain people, that they cultivated it with shameless lies. Each time someone gets a bonus, society is pushed further into the abyss. But to fight back and overcome them, you'd need an army, armored tanks, and missiles. I'm only a foot soldier; all I've got is a CKC rifle and a few bullets."

Nguyen pursed his lips as if to smile, but it never came. Linh watched her husband in silence.

"Little by little, I got used to the situation. What else could I do? I'm an intellectual, but I'm also a civil servant. And as a civil servant, I have to carry out my duties to get my salary at the end of the month. Life isn't perfect. What we believe in today may turn out to be false tomorrow."

"How skilled you are at consoling yourself," Linh sneered. "I don't even recognize your voice."

"It's all been for your sake."

"Oh really? Is it always someone else's fault?"

"Don't shout, Linh," said Nguyen, frowning. "People can hear us. We've always been the closest family in the neighborhood. I love you, I want to take care of you. But at heart you're still a college student. Reality for you is only written in romantic, purple ink. And you won't tolerate a single exception. You're as naive as a child and as intransigent as a queen. That's why I've kept things from you."

"Like what? The reality of your lies?"

"There are two realities: There's the reality of human ideals, and then there's the harsh reality of life."

"An honest journalist has no right to trick people, to confuse ideals and reality."

"But what if this suits everyone?"

"We don't live to please other people. We live by our convictions." Linh glared at her husband in silence, her cheeks scarlet.

"But I'm not the editor-in-chief, and you forget that..." Nguyen paused, snuffed out his cigarette and lowered his voice. "Even in everyday life, who has the courage to tell the truth? In this building, we know that Mrs. Hong's child is ugly, deformed. He has a harelip, a sixth finger on one hand, a huge head on a wobbly neck. But to her, he's the most precious treasure on earth. You, who are so adamant, so uncompromising about telling the truth, would you be so brutal as to tell her: 'Your son is a cripple?' "

"A child's not an industrial or agricultural product. He's not the result of a mode of production, a work method."

"But what a man believes in—his ideals, his aspirations—have as much value as his life. Sometimes, it is even more important than a child."

"You *lied* . . . You make me sick," Linh rasped, her voice cracking. Nguyen started to reply, but stopped. Huong Ly had woken up and she stared at her parents, dazed.

A few seconds passed, then a woman's voice shouted outside the stairwell: "It's your turn to sweep the stairs today. Don't forget to return the duty roster to Mrs. Hong."

THE RAIN wove silver threads in the window frame. Sometimes, on those final days of spring, a strange rain fell, a mixture of the Tet lunar new year drizzle and summer's sudden showers. Nguyen and Linh faced each other in silence across the table. Huong Ly was with her paternal grandparents. The couple hadn't spoken for days. They had nothing new to say to each other.

Cigarette butts and ashes piled up in front of Nguyen. His hands were yellow from the smoke, his tongue bitter. He couldn't even taste the tobacco anymore. He listened in silence to the falling rain, recalling the rainy season right before their marriage. Back then, the drizzle had lingered from one week to the next, leaving the streets boggy with mud. At the time, he didn't even have a raincoat. When he picked up Linh, he used to cover himself with a torn plastic sheet. They were young at the time—too young. Love had blinded them to life's deprivations and misery. For them, a few dumplings were a feast. Linh had been able to put a little money aside, but it had been stolen just a few weeks before their wedding. In the end, she fell ill from overwork.

"Make me a bit of rice porridge with some sugar. When Mama was alive, she loved that more than anything."

That was the way Linh used to speak, stretched out on the bed, her face pale. His heart tight, Nguyen would find a tin lunch pan, gather whatever small change he had left, and go out to buy her a *pho* beef soup. Once he had forgotten to take the plastic sheet. Halfway there, it had begun to pour and Nguyen arrived at the *pho* vendor's stall. A scaling old mirror tacked to the wall reflected the faces of the customers. He remembered glimpsing himself in it: a pale, thin young man in patchy pants and an old shirt, rain streaming down his face and hair. He pulled his change out of his pocket, counting and recounting it to find enough. The owner tilted his chin in Nguyen's direction, "Hand me your bowl," he scowled. Nguyen felt his face burn as he set his mess tin on the table. Everyone ignored him and slurped their soup noisily. And yet all around him he felt dozens of eyes staring at him. These people were well fed, smartly dressed. For the first time, in a flash, he felt the humiliation of being poor. *Never let yourself fall into poverty, never,* he vowed to himself.

He had struggled, had done everything in his power to build a comfortable nest for his family. Linh's soft skin, her fresh, rosy cheeks, her shiny hair, her radiance—all this he had struggled to defend, to preserve. And now, suddenly, all this was slipping from his grasp, and precisely because he had been willing to do anything to hold on to them. He had published short, superficial articles and insipid, generalizing features. Only every now and then was he able to slip in a critical piece, one that reflected reality, though always within the authorized limits. This type of article would only really be allowed when society had evolved to a certain point. In the meantime, how was he supposed to make a living for his family? He couldn't just live for himself, blindly defending his ideals. No, Linh was just too intolerant, too unfair.

In the early days of their marriage, when Nguyen was still just a humble staff reporter, they both had only three changes of clothing. They used to store canned food in a chest they had cobbled together out of old crates. Linh never asked for anything. She lived happily with a bit of rice, watery broths masquerading as soups, and a few pickled eggplant. With her savings, she bought some fabric to make pants for Nguyen. She put aside the cigarettes she was given at various official ceremonies for him. Her shabby clothes clashed with her beauty. Yet she had never breathed a word about a single yearning, even a hankering for a pair of shoes, or a flowered blouse, or a stylish pair of pants. Their life of deprivation and their poor diet had left her skin sallow and discolored. Nguyen had seen it most clearly when she was pregnant with Huong Ly, and one day he decided that he couldn't bear it any longer. He couldn't afford to keep writing articles that never made it past the censor. So he surrendered, bent to life's constraints, conformed. At the time, it was easy for him to be successful using just a fraction of his talents. Materially, their life improved overnight. Linh welcomed this new existence as naturally as she had accepted past miseries, without resentment or suspicion. She had trusted him. Now, she condemned him and despised him. Nguyen looked over at her. She still had the same rosy, childlike lips, the same radiant, bewitching gaze.

Linh turned, just then, and glared at him, furious, disdainful. He felt his heart twist. Yet he knew at that moment that he still loved her madly, anxiously.

Like him, Linh had said nothing all morning. They had stayed up late into the night talking. After that, she hadn't slept at all. When she realized her love for him had died, terror and emptiness had begun to gnaw at her soul. A home razed by a storm, a ravaged land, and in the middle, a yawning chasm. She was like a fortress that bore his seal on every door. Her parents had died a long time ago. They were no more than shadows now, floating in the fog of the past. The tenderness she felt for them was only a dim glow. Nguyen had become her only reality, and she lived her life with him fully, passionately, his every word resonating within her. She remembered his first promises to her like a sacred mantra:

"The moment a man becomes infatuated with worldly possessions—the opulence of his rice paddies, his house and its vast courtyard—fate has already chosen the day that it will all turn to dust. To me, the drive to acquire material wealth is pitiful. Once you've learned this, you can live a full, peaceful life, in harmony with your dreams, your conscience. I've never tried to sell myself to anyone, least of all to you. I can't offer you riches, or guarantee we'll have a comfortable life, free of need. Life changes, and everything will change with it. But I will do everything to keep my promise, to give you love and dignity."

In the cool shadows of the university auditoriums, she had laid her head on Nguyen's shoulders, and she had believed in him. From the day she met him, space and time, her whole life ceased to be so cold and deserted. He was her anchor in this world, her safe haven, the summit of everything she had aspired to. With him, the world seemed beautiful, majestic, filled with infinite possibilities. And so, in his fall Nguyen had pulled her with him into an abyss.

What insanity. How could I have loved him that much?

Suddenly, the wind lifted the curtains to reveal pearly clouds drifting across a patch of blue sky. This simple image calmed her. The silky curtain rippled and danced like sea foam. Their living room was lovely with its high walls, pale blues, and embroidered carpet. The glass buffet table reflected the gold rims of the porcelain cups, the crystal wine glasses, the sparkles in the hair of a Japanese doll, the gold key in the alarm clock. Objects, souvenirs they had collected together as their life had become more comfortable. Linh shuddered: Perhaps she was too innocent, indifferent to life's constraints. Perhaps life was much harder, much darker, than the ideals that had inhabited her soul. The cuckoo clock on the wall chimed; a wooden nightingale chirped a staccato song. Then the room fell back into silence, stillness. Linh contemplated the clock that Nguyen had brought back from a trip to the Soviet Union, the embroidered Uzbek tablecloth draped over the television, the tape recorder above the bookshelves, the plaster Venus de Milo. These objects now seemed to stare at her, sad, jeering.

Linh's heart raced. Had it really all been for her and Huong Ly that Nguyen had built this well-feathered nest? During the years she had lived with him, she had yet to see his eyes gleam at the prospect of a new motorcycle, or a television, or an expensive meal. Comfort was just a means to an end for him, a way to please Linh, to see her delight and keep the glow in her cheeks, or to hear his daughter break into peals of joyous laughter. Linh remembered how he used to come home after his long trips abroad, his soft, tender smile, his contented look when he gave her the gifts. Perhaps she was cruel, unjust, to condemn such a loving man.

Silent sobs rose in her bosom. Tears rolled down her cheeks. Nguyen dropped the cigarette he had just pulled out of a pack and rushed over to his wife. "Don't cry, Linh. What do you want?"

"I don't know."

"Are you going to leave me?"

"No, but I have no more love to give you."

"How are we going to live?"

She said nothing.

"I love you. I'll always love you," Nguyen said softly.

"But I can't love you anymore. From now on, we'll just be acquaintances."

"And our daughter?"

"She'll sleep with me. I'll put a mat in our bedroom."

"No. I'll sleep on it. You stay in the bed with Huong Ly."

"I couldn't sleep on a bed bought with dirty money."

Nguyen stared at his wife, speechless. *She's a fanatic, intoxicated by her adolescent ideals. And she spares no one . . .*

He cleaned the room and spread the mat in the corner. Then, he pulled the mattress off the bed to put it on the mat. But Linh said, "Take that mattress off! I don't want it."

Nguyen paled, frozen in horror at the harsh rasp in her voice. He placed the two pillows on the mat and wrung his hands, frantic. Linh's full, soft thighs brushed against her thin silk pants. He felt desire rising in him, and yearned to rest his head in her lap, to get it back again, the feeling of peace and ease that lulls the sailor returning home after being marooned on a desert island.

LAN, LINH'S PATERNAL AUNT, often praised the soup vendor on Ly Quoc Su Street as having the best snail soup in Hanoi. She had taken Linh there several times. The words "Hot Snails" were scrawled on a signboard outside the stall. The interior was hardly luxurious, with rickety tables and low wooden stools teetering on their legs. But the rice noodles were always pearly white and the snails deliciously plump. Their famous chilies fried in oil and vinegar—the kind that stung the tongue—drew Hanoi women like a magnet. But today, they were out of luck: The sign to the restaurant read Closed.

"Where should we go now?" asked Lan.

"Wherever you like. I'm not hungry," said Linh.

"Let's go have a cup of hot chocolate. I know a café near here."

They cycled side by side near the edge of the street. It was cold out, but teenagers were still showing off their fall clothes. Lan smiled at her niece. "Look at those silly kids. We wore clothes like that too in my day."

"Mmm," Linh sighed mechanically, her head empty. Lan glanced at her. "What's the matter with you?"

"Nothing," she said listlessly.

Dead pancovier leaves fell to the ground. A young hood-lum, about eighteen or nineteen years old, rode by. "Well, old lady, you're still full of spunk. And you, miss, you're gorgeous. Why such a cold look?"

Linh kept silent. The kid muttered something between his teeth and raced off. Lan sighed. "What times we live in. The streets are swarming with these young toughs."

The two women turned a corner and arrived at a back alley. There was no sign, not even an arrow to mark the spot. Lan guided her through the street. They passed several *chè* pudding stalls, where groups of the city's black marketers were squatted down to eat. They slid under a low door, through a back en-trance, and climbed up a crumbling staircase in the dark.

"Here, take my hand, careful not to trip," Lan called to Linh, who stood in the corridor, coughing from the thick smoke that filled the place. It took her a few minutes to get used to the suffocating atmosphere, the reek of old cigarettes and coffee. The café was small but unusual, with tables and chairs made out of varnished tree trunks and roots. The lacquered brown ashtrays were enormous. On the wall hung a frenetic, modern painting in which an impaled deer stared stricken out at the world. On both sides of the deer, facing each other, were two vases filled with bellis vines. Linh rarely went out to such places. She and Nguyen had all the imported alcohol she could want at home. Because she never frequented such places, she felt something like repulsion, even when she went into a res-taurant for a glass of lemonade or a *pho*. The lack of hygiene shocked her. Even more unsettling to her was this atmosphere, all these people fleeing the normalcy of family life.

Lan whispered into Linh's ear. "This café is really *in* at the moment. Lots of famous people come here."

Lan turned, smiling, to greet the owner. Pressing his hands

on the glass counter, he cocked his head, flirtatiously. "What can I serve you, Mrs. Lan?" He was about fifty years old, tanned, with twinkling, mischievous eyes.

"Two cups of hot chocolate with a bit of butter would be perfect."

"Any pastry, Mrs. Lan?"

"Please."

"Same as usual?"

"Yes. Is the butter fresh?"

"Of course. My cakes are the finest in Hanoi," the owner replied. "Your composer friend says he'll probably come by later and have some too."

"Oh, really," said Lan, blushing to her earlobes. Just then a girl appeared with two steaming cups of hot chocolate.

"Drink up, while it's hot," Lan urged. "It smells delicious, real cocoa smell."

"I put a lot of effort into that," the owner boasted. "The old aluminum cocoa tins were high quality. But now, they pack it in paper. If you aren't careful, the cocoa goes stale, loses its aroma. It's happening all over the world. Standards are slipping."

Lan laughed. "So it's only in your café that luxury doesn't go stale, eh?"

The owner laughed, contentedly.

A new customer entered, about the same age as the owner, but gaunt, with an artistic, bohemian air about him. With his dirty, patchy clothes, and sad, defeated face, he could have been a bum off one of the park benches, or one of those beer drinkers who loitered in front of the fried squid and shrimp stands.

"Hello, old friend," said the man, tossing his dirty satchel on the ground and settling on a stool, his back to the wall.

"You still haven't left for Saigon?" the owner asked, puzzled.

"Oh, everyone dreams of going to Saigon. Except me. I've been five times since Liberation. That's quite enough."

"But Saigon is a hundred times more beautiful than Hanoi."

"Yeah, maybe. It's all in the eye of the beholder. This ceramic vase is lovely here on this rustic wood table, but put it in a Saigon hotel room and it'd look ridiculous. The same goes for people. They've got to be in the right setting."

"Well, if I were you, I'd go without a moment's hesitation. A three-story villa! You wouldn't dream of finding that here."

"True, brother. People say I'm nuts. But I have no roots there. Saigon is a place I visit, not a place I can live. Here, tell me what I owe you . . . Ah, eight thousand *dong* exactly. Add a pack of Samit cigarettes and a cup of black coffee."

The man ripped open the pack, lit a cigarette, and inhaled, his eyes half-closed in pleasure. Suddenly he saw Linh, and for the space of an instant, his eyes looked troubled. Linh had noticed him too, but looked away. But just then, two new customers entered the room. One was a tall man whose age was difficult to judge. He could have been fifty, or older, or just over forty. The stranger's movements and gestures were rapid and abrupt. He was accompanied by a young but already plump woman, heavily made up, her eyebrows elongated with liner all the way to her temples. Barely inside the door, the man saw Lan and froze in embarrassment. "Lan, Lan . . . how are you?"

"Fine, thank you." Lan's voice was polite, but full of innuendo. In an instant, she had sized up the flashy young woman—the leather boots, the scarlet lipstick and nail polish, her tight, hip-hugging jeans. Lan pursed her lips.

"And you? You look well."

"Thank you, Lan."

"Yes, you've still got your aura." Lan laughed mockingly, but her eyes glistened strangely. "Well, let me introduce you to my niece, Linh. This is the composer Tran Phuong, the one who writes the songs you love so much."

Linh was surprised. *So this was the artist of the famous lacquer paintings, the composer of the songs admired all over Asia?*

"Hello, sir," she said, in a cheery voice.

Ever since the stranger had entered the room, he had kept his head bowed. It was only at this moment that he looked up at Linh. His cold, somber face suddenly lit up. But it dissolved just as suddenly in the smoke that surrounded him. Linh was instantly struck by his mysterious, smoldering eyes and long, bushy eyebrows.

"Hello, miss," the composer said almost shyly.

Before he could say anything more, the young woman accompanying him pulled him by the sleeve of his shirt and introduced herself: "I'm Ngoc Minh, a journalist at *Musical Studies* magazine." She pulled up two stools for herself and the composer. Tran Phuong sat down on one obediently.

"Bring us a pack of cigarettes and two coffees," she said, turning to the owner. "Why are you so grumpy today?" Ngoc Minh asked. "I just found a divine pastry place on Buom Nhuom Street. You really should make them your supplier. Everyone I've recommended it to just adores it."

"Thanks," the owner said tersely as he served the coffee and cigarettes himself. Tran Phuong gazed out the window at the alley of pancovier trees, trying to hide his emotion. Seen from the side, his eyelids seemed bordered by a dark mauve line. An unfathomable solitude lurked behind his gaze.

Linh suddenly felt uncomfortable. This man must get no pleasure from this flashy woman's chatter. He seemed to hide a deep sadness within him. She felt like telling him something.

"I know your songs by heart," Linh suddenly blurted out.

"I'm flattered. They don't deserve it," the composer replied modestly. He lowered his head, carefully flicking his ashes into the ashtray.

"I also like your paintings," Linh continued. "Though I can't say I know much about art."

"Well, I painted them a long time ago. To be fair, they're not bad." Tran Phuong smiled, appreciative. When he smiled, the white sheen of his teeth made him look youthful.

Lan, it seemed, couldn't take her eyes off him. "My niece, like many women, admires your talent. I'm sure life still holds much luck for you," she quipped.

The composer's face clouded over.

"I've kept some old photos," Lan said. "Do you remember our friend Hoang?"

"Yes," Tran Phuong said softly. "When you see her, send her my regards. She's a very strong-willed woman."

"And you're a very strong-willed man," Lan replied.

"I don't claim that nobility, that character."

"You claim even nobler qualities, don't you?" Lan chuckled and left her question hanging. Tran Phuong said nothing, as if he had decided to patiently submit to her haughty, sarcastic jabs. Bothered by her aunt's tone, Linh could no longer contain herself: "What's with you, Aunt Lan? Tran Phuong has a fine reputation."

Lan burst out laughing. But Tran Phuong had already turned to Linh. His eyes were dark and stormy. "Thank you, young lady, very kind of you."

Lan looked at her niece dreamily, then her face froze. She had felt a kind of premonition. "Let's go. I've got things to do," she stammered, getting up to leave. When she didn't see the owner, she hurried toward the register to pay. In the other corner of the room, the man with the dirty satchel drew long puffs on a bamboo water pipe. He watched Linh with barely concealed sadness. The journalist stood up and began pacing, her hands stuffed in the pockets of her jeans.

"Through the days, through the nights, we cross the land of Africa," Ngoc Minh recited. "Magnificent. Tran Phuong, do you remember those verses from 'The Island of Venus'?"

Tran Phuong didn't reply.

2

MARRIAGE CAN BE HEAVEN OR HELL. Ever since Linh had learned that Nguyen had built his career on dishonest articles, their relationship had disintegrated, tumbling as inevitably as pebbles down a steep slope. Nguyen tried to endure his wife's coldness and contempt. He did everything to help her with the daily chores. Huong Ly slept with her mother, but clung to her father. At meals, she sat between her parents, chattering away, as they tried to keep up an appearance of harmony.

But at certain moments, Nguyen was overcome by shame, and Linh by self-loathing. And this was nothing compared to the pain they felt when the memory of their past happiness surfaced.

One morning, instead of writing an article tailored to the directives of his editor-in-chief, Nguyen went to Dong Xuan Market and bought a crab to make fried *nem* spring rolls and sautéed crab with rice vermicelli. Linh returned just as Nguyen had finished preparing the meal. Huong Ly scampered up to her mother, waving a crab claw.

"Mama, quick, go wash up. Dinner is special today."

"You eat with Papa. Mama's not hungry."

"But you have to come eat. Or else, in class, they won't give me points for being a model child."

Linh took her daughter in her arms and smoothed her hair. Her little girl was intelligent, with a good memory. She was only five years old, but she had already learned entire passages from *The Tale of Kieu* by heart.

"I've got a headache. Papa is here. He's going to eat with you."

"You're silly. Papa is Papa. But Mama is Mama. I need Papa on one side, Mama on the other. I'll give you each a crab claw, okay?"

The little girl stared at Linh, trying to convince her. Linh struggled to hold back tears, her nostrils stinging.

"Eat something, Linh," said Nguyen. "Otherwise, you're going to get sick." He stopped, then added: "For the last few days, your face . . ." But he didn't have the heart to finish the sentence. That week, Linh had lost weight and her cheekbones stood out. She didn't answer, just shivered and sat down at the table in silence. At the end of the meal, Linh opened a cabinet, took out an orange, and peeled it. She stared at the peels as they unfurled, fanlike, on the table.

"Aren't you going to have some?" Nguyen asked.

Linh took a piece, chewed it mechanically. She hadn't peeled the orange as carefully as she always did, but she didn't even notice. Suddenly, a spring storm lifted the curtains on the window. Linh started and came to her senses. She angrily tossed the peels into a wastebasket in the corner of the room, and stared out the window at a dark patch of sky. The first spring rain fell in a slanting weave of crystal threads through the light of the street lamps. A sudden flash of lightning illuminated the leaves of the pancovier trees. Thunder rumbled on the horizon.

"You seem tired," Nguyen said meekly. "Go rest. I'll put the little one to bed later."

Linh didn't reply. Nguyen had decided to endure this icy atmosphere in hopes that Linh would reconsider. He would wait—one year, two years, three years or more, whatever it took. Nguyen still believed he could rebuild their happiness.

Linh didn't reply. She brushed her teeth in silence, then lay down on the mat. The monotonous drumming of the rain lulled her and she drifted, half asleep, half awake, listening to the crackle of the storm outside, the shrill voice of a singer on the radio. In her mind, she surveyed streets, houses, lights, familiar faces that had retreated behind a dense curtain of fog. Someone murmured words she couldn't seem to make out. A long road, littered with purple bellis leaves, choked with vines, stretched out before her.

"Do you have a fever?"

A voice echoed somewhere in the distance. A hand touched her forehead. Like her mother's hand. Linh had been seven years old when typhoid fever had carried her away forever.

"Linh."

Who was calling in such a tender voice? Ah, Nguyen. He was standing in front of the door to the university dormitory. He slipped Linh a sliced meat sandwich, still piping hot. It was chilly out, barely eight degrees. The dinner ration, two bowls of rice, was always finished at exactly seven-thirty. "My little brown-eyed fairy. My God, you've cut your hand. Here, I'll bandage it for you." He had the pained, paternal look of another time. A bit of the lost authority of a father, a bit of brotherly love, and the desire of her twenty-year-old heart.

Sleepy, Linh circled her arms around Nguyen's neck. He leaned down and covered her with kisses. In the lamplight, he could see each hair of her eyelashes. And yet, he was gripped by fear. Had she forgiven him? A warmth rose from their past love, surged in their veins, transporting them. A long shared intimacy guided them down old, familiar paths. Nguyen turned off the lamp. Lightning flashed in the distance.

Around three in the morning, Linh woke to the screech of a train siren at the nearby Hang Co Station. She stretched and her arm brushed Nguyen's warm, naked chest. She sat up with a start. Nguyen still slept soundly, his hair scattered on the pillow. His breath smelled slightly of the cheap tobacco he smoked to save money. Linh realized what had happened. A wave of shame seemed to wash over her. She'd slept with Nguyen, not out of love, but out of habit, in a moment of oblivion. Only animals groped for each other, following their instincts, the moans of the opposite sex, she thought with disgust.

Waking, Nguyen saw Linh seated, motionless in the flickering light of dawn. She looked at him, dark purplish circles under her eyes. From the expression on her face, Nguyen guessed her thoughts. "Please, forgive me."

Linh, despondent, said nothing.

Nguyen took his pillow from the mat and returned to the bed. He felt Linh's vacant, pained eyes following him. He picked up a pack of cigarettes on his way.

"If you want, from now on I'll keep my distance," he said softly.

Linh seemed not to hear him. "First, I disdained you. Now I disdain myself."

"Don't say that, Linh. It doesn't matter. You think too much, and you're too harsh."

"Right, it doesn't matter. At least not for other people."

Linh knew he was right: It didn't matter for others. Everyone in the building respected Nguyen. He was a talented young intellectual, cultured, earnest, and generous. Not to mention a loving husband and a good father. He had climbed too high too young. Was she just impossibly demanding? Or did real life just involve more shadows and illusions than she had imagined?

Linh closed her eyes. She could see a seaside landscape. Clean roads baking in the sun, roadside stands filled with tourist souvenirs, and boats, and above them flocks of birds hovering above the blue-green water ... All you had to do was return to those places off-season, to see the garbage, the oil slick floating on the water's surface, the knots of rotting algae, the fish scales littering the beaches. And the smell. The stench of fishnets laid out to dry, of junks being scrubbed down.

Should she forgive him? Linh looked at her husband. He lit a cigarette, his forehead creased with tiny wrinkles. A few flakes of dandruff rested on his shoulders. In a way he was a man who truly lived for his work. But what purpose had it served? Linh choked back her rage as she thought of the absurd distortions in the articles he had written. Nguyen was intelligent, but he hadn't had the courage to live by his convictions. He had compromised himself to carve out a secure place in society, to reap all the material benefits, the advantages. This room. The beautiful carnations in the crystal vase. The fine wool carpet embroidered with giant roses. The polished wood furniture. Even the silk nightgown she wore. Comfort. He had acquired all this. But he had lost the aura he once had for her.

Linh belonged to the generation born after the Revolution, but her soul was steeped in its myths and the ideals that had won her over as a child. No doubt, none of life's uncertainties could crush or efface them. Sincere, earnest, she could never admit compromise. On a purely intellectual level, she had begun to see the complexity of life, and to forgive Nguyen. But in her soul, the shimmer of those adolescent ideals had reduced her image of him to ash. Her love was dead. Nothing could bring it back.

After a moment of silence, Linh announced: "I'm leaving this house."

"Please. We have to protect our reputation, for ourselves, for Huong Ly. I swear I won't touch you, not a single hair, unless you permit me."

"I can't stand it anymore, to see your hypocrite's face, day after day."

"Linh, for most woman the fidelity they want in a husband is sexual. I'm faithful to you, even in my thoughts. But I guess that's not enough for you to—"

"But you haven't been faithful to your own dignity. I can't love a man with no sense of honor."

"You're ruthless, Linh. Don't you think I haven't thought about all of this, that I suffer from the memory of it? Do you know how many times I've tortured myself about that last investigation in central Vietnam? When I saw those pale, emaciated women pretending to rake the grass on a potato field for the photographers, my stomach was in knots. But I'm a man after all; I wasn't going to burst into tears. I chased after the photographer. I went up to one of the old women and asked her, 'Auntie, that field you're weeding, does it belong to your production brigade or to your family?' She turned to me, her face gaunt and miserable, and said, 'What field would be mine? Everything belongs to the collective.' So I asked her, 'Why are you weeding here?' She threw the spade on the ground, panting, and said, 'The leaders of the commune ordered us here for the photographers, for their newspapers. Our rice paddies are parched. The ground is cracked, the furrows are so deep they come up to your knees. There's not a drop of water left in the ground. How can they talk about planting potatoes and rice? It's been two months now since we've eaten a grain of rice. The other day, when they heard you were coming, they went to the district to ask for sticky rice and distributed four and a half pounds of it and ten and a half ounces of pork to every household.' She wiped the sweat dripping down her face and urged me, 'Quick, take your photos so we can go home. We can't stand it anymore.' At the time, I couldn't even think. My eyes clouded over. I was about to open my mouth to tell those poor women to go home when a silent form blocked my voice. My civil servant's conscience forced me to remember the photographer. He whispered to me, 'These people are starving, brother. I don't dare take clear photos. I'll have to blur them. How dare they try and pass off this district as a model of economic success?' I didn't reply. I knew that the party secretary of the district was an ignoramus. After a few totally random successes, he was promoted from the direction of some tiny, godforsaken commune up North to the position of political director for the entire district. He took himself for a genius, believed that his mission was to guide the people toward radical revolution. So he decided to transform the district into a model for the entire country!"

"How can such imbeciles, such vain opportunists of his ilk come to power?" Linh snapped.

"Sometimes the promotion of one individual or another depends on a whole series of random events. But let me tell you the rest of the story. With the grandiose ambition of becoming the flag-bearer for the entire country, this man launched a comprehensive plan of public works designed to improve production and reform the irrigation system. This kind of task requires great minds, a mastery of science, people with experience in development. The party secretary only had a grade school certificate. With that level of education, he should have been happy just raising a family, managing his wife and seven or eight kids, maybe five acres of rice paddies and a little garden. How could he possibly organize the lives of millions of people in such a complex region? Ambitious, with absolute power, he obviously launched risky projects, random production targets that weren't based on any scientific criteria. He forced the population to cut down pine forests to grow rice. Where they had traditionally grown rice, he made them plant vegetables. Then he mobilized fifty thousand people to improve the irrigation systems. Rice paddies that had once been fertile started to dry up and crack. Even the water buffalo couldn't walk through them. In other places, fields rotted in pools of stagnant water. It's horrifying to see what happens when ambition and power bloom in the brain of an idiot. Destruction can reach a scale and a depth that go far beyond the ravages of bombs."

"And the journalists? Were they so easily fooled?"

"No one was fooled. Everyone knew what was happening. But when the machine is switched on, it's dangerous to move in the opposite direction. The brakes, the steel threads that pull them, are worn by use, have to be constantly replaced. It's the same when the editor-in-chief summons me and says: 'This district is well managed, it's the standard bearer of the revolutionary movement. The Counsel of Ministers has already decided to give them a medal. Go investigate and write a report for next month's issue. Hurry, don't let the other journalists scoop us.' I hit the road with a mission. And then I observe the bitter truth. But I've never had the real story, all the pieces of a puzzle needed for a real article. It's in no one's interest to let me see the big picture. What use would it be to throw myself, a mere pebble, into the gears of this machine running at full steam? I'd be reduced to dust in the blink of an eye. The first person to turn on me would be the editor-in-chief himself. He wants the newspaper to attract the attention of the leaders, to build his reputation. Now, suppose I do the opposite: deny a publicly acknowledged reality and put forward my own observations. I would still be throwing myself into the path of an oncoming train. And let's suppose the train slows down, my fate is the same. I will still be reduced to pulp, smashed to pieces."

"So you've played it safe," Linh said. "That's precisely why those farmers are starving. By the time the authorities are informed, and realize what is happening in that godforsaken place, the damage is irreversible. It's a catastrophe!"

"Yes, it's deplorable. But we can't do anything about it."

"Crime really pays for intellectuals, especially those of your ilk!" Linh screamed at him. "If you were uneducated, ignorant, I'd understand. But you're too intelligent, too reflective. You're like a murderer—one who kills, not out of insanity, but in premeditation!"

"Are you crazy? Why are you screaming like this? Linh, you must understand. Even if I did try and stop the machine, the result would be the same. Can't you accept even this basic reality?"

"But you never *did* oppose the machine!" Linh shouted.

Nguyen heaved a long sigh and lowered his voice. "I'm just a speck of dust, Linh. If I were still single, I might have been tempted to take my own life. But ever since I've been with you, since little Huong Ly—"

"I'm not eating your rice anymore. I'm leaving. Now." Linh stood up.

Nguyen rose too, frantic. "I thought that by telling you this I could—"

"You were mistaken," Linh said, opening an armoire and pulling out her clothes. She took out the little suitcase Lan had given her when she had been accepted at the university. For several years, she had stored things there: a mosquito net, a flowered bedspread from her student days, old shirts kept as mementos. The odor of mothballs mixed with that of the musty old clothes. Slowly, reluctantly, she picked up these objects, one by one.

Nguyen was still standing in a corner of the room, taking drags from his cigarette. His hand shook violently. He didn't dare look at Linh. Wind swept through the room, scattering the cigarette ash onto the flowered tiles. Carnations were strewn across the table. Linh hadn't changed the flowers for days. She was the center of this room, of his happiness. If she left, his life would go with her. But what could he do to stop her?

Nguyen gazed at the shiny, flowing hair on Linh's neck, her firm, full thighs. She was beautiful, seductive. Her soul was even more magnetic, like the beauty of a diamond, hard, shimmering, razor-sharp. Linh just didn't know how to forgive.

If only I could beg, Nguyen thought to himself. He would have knelt before her and pleaded with her to reconsider his sentence. But he realized it would be useless. He remained standing, sucking silently on his cigarette. An orange-winged maybug flew into the room, and its noisy buzzing woke Huong Ly. The little girl sat up.

"Mama?"

Linh turned around.

"Here, sweetie, I'm here."

Huong Ly glanced at the open suitcase.

"Why are you putting clothes in there?"

"To take them to Grandmother's house."

"Why?"

"I'm going to live there."

"Where are my clothes?"

"In the closet. You're staying here, with Papa."

"No, I'm coming with you," she cried, throwing herself into Linh's arms, clinging to her neck.

"But it's too cramped at Grandma's house. There are uncles, aunts, Hung and Bao."

"So let's stay here. I don't want you to go!"

Huong Ly turned to her father. In her daughter's silence,

she sensed the unhappiness that lay in store for her. Huong Ly burst into tears: "You stay here, Mama, stay."

She cried harder, and Linh covered the little girl's mouth with her hand.

"Calm down, Huong Ly, be a good girl."

The girl's hair covered Linh's face like a silken veil. Linh sniffed the sweet fragrance of Huong Ly's skin, and felt her stomach knot.

Nguyen opened the door and went out. He walked to the end of the street, wandered through the stands of cigarette vendors, and bought a pack of Song Cau. When he returned, he found mother and daughter sleeping in each other's arms, tears still moistening their cheeks. Nguyen knelt, inhaled the perfume of his wife's hair, overjoyed to feel his beloved's face so near his.

Linh slept deeply. She fell into an oppressive, anxious nightmare. A strange beast chased her through a field. The animal's head was half cow and half lion, spiked with the flaming red hair of a goat. Its bulging eyes flashed, threatening. The field was parched, riddled with deep cracks and furrows that formed arabesques in the dirt. Suddenly, Linh's foot sank into a furrow; she gritted her teeth and pulled her leg with all her strength, trying to free her foot and flee. But the beast came nearer and nearer. Linh was incapable of screaming. The broiling sun seared her face. Beads of sweat dripped down her forehead, stinging her eyes. Suddenly, she saw a house rising up from the deserted fields and ran toward it to take shelter. But the shutters on the door slammed shut. Against its whitewashed walls, a row of women appeared, black veils draped over their heads. Their dull, yellow eyes stared at Linh.

"Please, don't look at me like that . . . I haven't done anything wrong," Linh wanted to cry out, but her tongue stuck to the roof of her mouth. The women clutched their rakes and rose in silence. The cracked earth spread all the way to the edge of the horizon. Wind blew in gusts, whipping up tornadoes of dust. Linh collapsed on the ground. The beast had vanished, but just then two eyes appeared, gazing passionately at her through the smoke: *Thank you, young lady, very kind of you.*

3

AFTER THE SUDDEN SHOWERS, the sun returned. The leaves on the trees, cleansed by the rain, glistened in the dawn. Here and there a flame tree blossom, heavy with rain, splashed a kiss into the air. Tran Phuong gazed dreamily at the grass.

He liked coming here early in the morning to admire the little garden in the octagonal courtyard, to listen to the bamboo hedges rustle and murmur in the wind. Here, he met eager young composers clutching their first compositions. The young female singers were beautiful in their glittering white *ao dai* tunics. They gathered here like a flock of birds in the rice paddies near harvest time. One and all were in awe of Tran Phuong's talent, his imposing stature, his passionate intensity, his proud, melancholy gaze. Often, Tran Phuong himself had been surprised by how easily he attracted women.

Lying against the stone bench, Tran Phuong gazed up at the sky. The secretary of the Musicians' Union came over to him.

"The Soviet Musicians' Union has officially invited you to participate in a conference on the music of the Orient."

He was about to take the envelope but changed his mind, thrusting his hands into the pockets of his jacket. "Thanks. Tell the comrades that I'm very tired. Have them send someone else, anyone will do," he replied, dismissively.

"But this is a personal invitation."

"Oh, really?" Tran Phuong affected a smile, took the envelope distractedly, and thrust it into his pocket. A group of young music students sauntered across the courtyard, greeting him respectfully. To them, he was a god; to him, they were pathetic.

As the musicians disappeared up the staircase, a chauffeur came scrambling down. He started the car and waited. A stranger appeared, probably a visitor from the South, and got into the car. The door slammed shut as the car rolled toward the gate. Tran Phuong remained silent, motionless, for a long time. He felt utterly empty. Once, this car had accompanied him wherever he went. Once, it had been his car; it had been for him that the chauffeur had started the motor, opened the door, waited.

Vanity.

He felt his gut twist. The wound, still stinging, had refused to heal. The composer stood up and started pacing, trying to chase away the memories that haunted him. As he counted his steps all the way to the second courtyard, he heard the strains of a piano coming from the concert hall on the second floor. Suddenly, he saw a young woman's silhouette flit past the gate. His heart leapt. He had to stop himself from running across the street: It was her, the young woman who had so captivated him in that café. He stopped, looked beyond the wall to follow the direction in which she was heading. He ran back to the parking lot, hopped on his Honda 50, and drove straight for the exit.

Linh walked slowly along the sidewalk, pushing her bicycle. A nail must have flattened one of the tires. She headed toward the home of a friend to get help. Sensing someone behind her, she turned around. "Ah!" she exclaimed, surprised.

Tran Phuong smiled at her affectionately. "Hello, kind-hearted woman. You've been in my thoughts since we met at the café the other day."

Linh was dumbfounded. After a moment, she regained her composure. "Oh, hello, where are you headed, uncle?"

"The office. Do you have a flat tire?"

"Yes."

"My motorcycle has an ignition problem. I'll go with you to get it repaired," Tran Phuong said softly. His voice was warm, and his eyes twinkled.

"Are you tired?" Tran Phuong asked.

"No."

"We're almost there. It's pleasant out today. In a few weeks, though, it's going to be sweltering."

"Yes."

"We're so crowded here in Hanoi. Who knows when this old colonial town will become a civilized place? Where were you born, Miss Linh?"

"In the hospital on Hang Ga Street."

"A real Hanoi girl. Have you ever traveled abroad?"

"No. And I probably never will."

Tran Phuong shook his head. They arrived at a bicycle repair shop where Linh knew the owner.

"Bring in your bicycle, young lady."

"Yes, uncle, yes."

Suddenly, Linh felt embarrassed addressing Tran Phuong as "uncle." Even more so since Lan wasn't present and there was no longer a precise relationship between them. The composer looked at her and smiled, "Oh, stop calling me uncle. You're obviously not a girl anymore."

Linh's cheeks burned. She felt as giddy as the first time her mother fed her fermented sticky rice.

They went into a nearby café. Tran Phuong pulled up a chair for her and hung her bag on the wall. "Could we have some music?" he asked the café owner.

The composer sat down next to Linh: "What would you like to hear?"

"I don't know. Whatever you like," she replied, sincere, a bit flustered.

"Put on a Mendelssohn barcarole. It's calm here. It'll be perfect."

He stood up and took a few steps, as regal as a lord surveying his lands.

"Do you like music?"

"Yes."

"Music refines humanity, makes it purer. In the past, the great dynasties founded their governments on respect for rites and music. That's the gentle method of governing. Have you ever been to a midnight mass in a Catholic church?"

"Once. But I was too little. I don't remember anything."

"Pity." Tran Phuong squinted again. A dense tide seemed to flood his gaze. Linh looked at him in silence.

"Of all the spiritual values that men have created, music is the most important. It is so universal, so deeply human."

Linh knew that Tran Phuong's paintings were also famous, that they had been reproduced many times, all over Asia, that the state bank had offered to build a villa for him with the revenues it had earned from sales of his works.

"Have some coffee," Tran Phuong said. As he pushed the cup toward her, his hand grazed hers. In that moment they understood, knew already that they belonged to each other. Linh lowered her eyes. The composer looked at her fresh face, her glowing skin without a trace of makeup. Her large eyes were chestnut brown, and behind her gaze as clear as autumn water was the soul of a defenseless child. Tran Phuong remembered the women who had fallen into his arms, their gaudy clothes, their heavy makeup and heady perfumes. They seemed to strut and parade before his eyes, tossing their heads proudly, impulsively. Suddenly, this staple food, having nourished him for too long, nauseated him. This young schoolteacher was so wholesome.

"You are like music."

"What did you say?"

"You have music in your soul. And you're a teacher. Two priceless qualities."

"You flatter me . . ." Linh stammered, flustered.

Tran Phuong poured more coffee. Linh looked at his thick, shiny beard. She found his face even more handsome this time.

"Taste, see if it's sweet enough for you."

"Thank you, big brother," Linh said, slipping into a more familiar form of address.

Strains of Mendelssohn filled the café. The high and low notes of the barcarole alternated like the rocking of a boat.

Tran Phuong sat down next to Linh, resting his elbows on the table.

"Can you stay on here a bit longer with me?"

"Yes."

"This is a magical day for me."

"For a famous man like you?"

"A lonely man."

"I thought someone like you was always—"

"There are many kinds of loneliness. The worst is the kind you feel among your own kind."

The composer bowed his head, propping his chin on his hands. His cheeks were crisscrossed with wrinkles and there was a sad glow in his eyes. Linh felt her heartbeat quicken. *He must be thinking of his failures. He has the face of an exile, a condemned man.* An almost maternal instinct rose in her, a longing to console and protect him.

"When will I see you again, little sister?" Tran Phuong whispered.

"I don't know. Whenever you like."

"Tomorrow, at three o'clock in the afternoon, here. Okay?"

"Okay."

The sun licked the corners of the tiles on the floor. Linh cycled home, pedaling rapidly. Tran Phuong followed her with his eyes until she had disappeared around a corner. Suddenly, the café seemed empty to him.

Tomorrow afternoon, at three o'clock.

It had been a long time since he had felt this impatience. It was as if he were twenty years old again. Those chestnut eyes had just opened a vast, entirely new horizon for him, a sky filled with light.

"AH, TRAN PHUONG, big brother, there you are. I've been looking for you everywhere!"

Ngoc Minh's booming voice startled the composer, even in the middle of the bustling street. Passersby turned to stare at him. He blushed, felt like pretending he didn't know the woman facing him. She was dolled up in such garish colors that she looked like a parrot. But he reminded himself that she was his most loyal fan. She had moved heaven and earth trying to reinstate him to his former position. Everywhere she went, she sang his praises, especially in the corridors of power, among the high-ranking party cadres. She leapt like a tigress at every possible opportunity to promote him.

"My God, I've been all over Hanoi looking for you. You must give me, immediately, a photo of yourself at age sixteen."

"Tomorrow morning, okay?"

"No. *Now.*"

"Well, then you're going to have to come to my place."

"No problem, unless your wife throws one of her jealous fits."

Ngoc Minh also drove a Honda 50. As she passed him, the multicolored braids of her epaulettes fluttered in the wind, making her look like some kind of folk dancer.

Fortunately she's not driving beside me. That would be too embarrassing.

When Tran Phuong reached the gate to his house, he saw that Ngoc Minh was already waiting for him at the foot of the stairwell. "Please understand, my wife's home," he said, grimacing. He left her there and climbed the staircase. Tran Phuong and his wife inhabited three rooms on the second floor of an old colonial villa. The spiral wooden staircase was creaky and slanted, but the building superintendent kept postponing repairs. After about a quarter of an hour, Tran Phuong returned with a photograph.

"Sorry, but this had slipped somewhere between some old music scores. I had to rummage around for a long time."

"You're so scared of your wife you don't even invite me up for tea?"

The composer winced and said nothing.

"Just teasing," Ngoc Minh giggled. Then she mounted her Honda and took off at high speed.

Tran Phuong watched the smoke spew out of her tailpipe, the multicolored tassels flapping at her shoulders. Suddenly, he felt bitter, weary. He looked up the staircase anxiously. Who awaited him at the top? A wife who bored him, who he had detested for twenty years. He placed his hand on the railing of the decrepit old staircase. This French colonial style of architecture was for old ladies in green seersucker and princes with their hair coiffed in chignons. The steps were made out of thin strips of precious wood, now worn as shiny as buffalo horn. The banister, just a bit thicker than a flail, twisted in an elaborate spiral. The elements of the staircase were all intact, but the links that held them together were already in a state of advanced decay. They reminded him of all that had been rotten, for so long, but that continued somehow to survive. The staircase was deserted. No one was there to see the expression of defeat on his face. A slight gust of wind spread the dusty, moldy odor of the walls through the air. He remembered a traveling theater troupe he had loved as a little boy and that from time to time used to come through his tiny provincial town in a ramshackle caravan, or a few old covered wagons. Around three in the afternoon, the youngest, most beautiful actresses would put on their makeup and then parade around town in a rickshaw. Another rickshaw would follow them advertising:

Here, here—Come see the play tonight!
A Debt of Love Unpaid
Performed by the Le Thanh Theater Troupe

In the center of the huge banner the actors had painted a huge bleeding heart pierced by a sword. Hunched behind the banner, beating a drum, was a man as thin as a hungry cat. People would rush out of their houses to watch them. Children scampered after them, shrieking and mimicking the drum rolls. Tran Phuong had always been part of the gang. His parents, who owned a pastry shop, belonged to the city's upper class, and they forbade him to go fishing or to the theater, occupations that they considered beneath them. Fortunately, Tran Phuong was protected by his paternal grandmother, a plump, imposing woman who doted on him. Thanks to her purse, which was always full, Tran Phuong had his fill of everything he loved. At night, he would ask her for money to buy a *pho*, and then sneak out to the theater. Perched on a rickety wooden stool, he used to stare, transfixed, at the actors. Without their powder and rouge, their rhinestones and sequins, they were just a haggard bunch. Their faces were sullen, their clothes wrinkled and patched. Hunched over a wooden crate that doubled as their table, they ate their dinner: a few slices of tofu sautéed in onions and a plate of boiled duckweed. He could see the bloated stomachs of the pregnant actresses under their *ao dais*. The actor who beat the drum wore a pair of shorts that exposed thin, bowed legs. The ammoniac stench of the nearby outhouse flooded the cheap makeshift stage, mixing with the smell of betel nut juice people had spat on the walls. As a boy, Tran Phuong never tired of watching them, observing the misery and deprivation of their vagabond lives with a mixture of curiosity and fear. A few hours later, when night fell, floodlights would illuminate the stage and the poor people who he had seen eating duckweed and tofu with onions would vanish. Under the stage lights, they became princes, gallant knights, and elegant princesses. This life was dazzling, mysterious, and it beckoned to him like some beautiful siren from her ocean rock. As a six-year-old boy, he had lost himself in this miracle, held his breath, watched how the men brandished their swords and sliced the air, how a wooden skull rolled noisily on the ground. He had dreamt of queens with pink cheeks, sultry eyes, and shimmering costumes. The image of their miserable, itinerant lives merged with these moments of breathtaking glory captivated him and burrowed into his memory, entered his blood. Truth and falsehood mingled there until there was no longer any boundary between them, only moments when they were temporarily arrested from a shifting, continual movement. He had submitted to this world of artifice and had lived this way, from the age of sixteen, without ever realizing it.

AFTER THE JOURNALIST HAD LEFT, Tran Phuong stood motionless in the darkness of the stairwell. He suddenly felt exhausted, defeated, like the old actor fed too long on duckweed and tofu who had to dance night in and night out with a fake sword.

Enough. I'll pretend I don't see her when I meet her in the street.

The composer mounted the stairs, muttering to himself,

yearning to sleep. He opened the door, tossed his coat on a chair, and lay down on the bed.

His wife Hoa shouted from behind a screen. "Come see if you like this outfit." She had just had a new pink silk blouse made for the official ceremonies.

"It suits you," Tran Phuong mumbled, his eyes shut.

"How can you know without seeing? You're really rude!" she shouted, her shrill voice heavy with reproach. The composer heard his wife push over a chair. He felt like slapping her, but he played the supplicant:

"I've already seen it. Please, leave me in peace for a moment."

"You're just an ingrate! You never pay any attention to me!" Hoa whined. "When a man loves a woman, a new blouse is a source of shared joy."

"I know, I know."

"Oh, I'm so unhappy. I'm so unlucky with you," Hoa moaned, slumping into a chair, her tears overflowing. She launched into the litany of her misfortune. "I trusted you. I made a mistake. To think of all the handsome, talented men who were in love with me!"

Tran Phuong closed his eyes. *God have mercy!* It had been the same refrain from her for decades. More than twenty years ago, he had met Hoa in the mountainous, liberated zone up North. At the time, his artistic troupe had left for the front to entertain the soldiers. He had fallen ill and had to stay back, bedridden, at an inn on the edge of the jungle. He remembered lying there with the covers pulled up to his chin, how the owner had brought him a steaming bowl of rice with stir-fried bamboo shoots and chilies. How when he had finished, he sat up, leaned against the wall, and watched the monotonous jungle rain whip the trees. From time to time, the cry of a lost doe pierced the curtain of rain, echoing in his ears. Wind howled through the mountain passes. Never again would Tran Phuong know such hardship. That was when Hoa had entered his life. She had a flat, ruddy face, a stub nose, and short hair, but she was young at the time—the age that makes any woman seem attractive. But she was not beautiful. She did, however, have a comfortable house right near the inn. Her mother worked hard raising chickens, tending a vegetable garden and a small retail business for soldiers passing through. Mother and daughter offered their hospitality and they spoiled him like a prince. Tran Phuong was used to being spoiled, so he fell right into their trap. When he came to his senses, it was too late. What's more, Hoa had an uncle who was a prominent statesman, the great oak tree that would later cast its protective shadow over Tran Phuong's career.

"Come, stop crying," said Tran Phuong.

"You're an ingrate. I'm so unhappy!" Hoa continued to weep and count her sorrows. Tears rolled down her puffy red cheeks.

"Please. Let's stop this farce."

On their wedding night, his mother-in-law had blown out the gas lamp, and left only an oil lamp burning. He remembered seeing Hoa's flat, plain face, almost without eyelashes, in the flickering light, how he had been overcome with revulsion. This feeling had never left him, through their entire life together, poisoning moments of tenderness and indifference alike. Now that it was mixed with hatred, it made him crazy, tempting him to end his life of suffocating hypocrisy. *Whether she dies, or I do, it's all the same. Everything would be easier.* But suddenly he saw a white Moscovic sedan cross the octagonal courtyard, a chauffeur opening the door, waiting for him. His heart froze. From the other side of a black sea, a voice shouted: *No!*

JUST AS A GREEDY PERSON is drawn to a pile of gold coins, Linh was dazzled by Tran Phuong's talent. This new love pulled her out of the chasm of her own despair. Her vision of this exceptional man, this noble soul, so obsessed her that the outside world was a blur. It was as if he were everywhere, all the time, in everything from the reflections of her daughter's smooth hair to the dark shadows of the trees on the road to her school.

Tran Phuong . . . Tran Phuong.

From time to time she caught herself murmuring his name. She saw him, his dark gaze, his full beard. Compared to him, Nguyen was just a vulgar journalist, a miserable liar. Twenty-seven hours lay between their last meeting and their next, twenty-seven hours of anxious waiting. Linh counted the minutes, even in her fitful sleep. She didn't know even the most basic truth: The intelligent woman makes her lover wait. So, the next day, at three o'clock in the afternoon, when Tran Phuong walked into the café, she was already there, pale and anxious.

"You're here?" he noted, beaming.

"Yes," she said, her voice shaky.

The ironic glint in the man's eye faded when he saw Linh's sincere, chestnut brown eyes. *My Young Pioneer has just taken off her red scarf*, he thought. With this young woman, it would be a crime to make use of the experience, the savoir faire that he had acquired in his countless affairs. No one had ever loved him so purely. Suddenly, he was overcome by nostalgia, re-membering himself at twenty: the orange trees in bloom in the garden of a small town; the first kiss on the lips of a woman that he desired but didn't love; the long, empty months and years spent in an unhappy marriage; all the clandestinity, the infidelities. If only the past would dissolve like a wisp of smoke, if only he could start over, give her all the passion of his youth.

He gazed at her intently. "Forgive me."

"Why?" Linh asked, surprised. "You haven't done anything wrong."

Tran Phuong discreetly squeezed her hand in his. "I have no youth to give you."

"No, no," Linh shook her head. "Please, there's no need to . . ."

Just then, the café owner arrived with their coffee. Strains of Mendelssohn played again. They gazed at each other in silence. They could have stayed there together forever. New customers arrived, a public security officer among them, followed by two young men. All three were dripping with sweat. With a toss of his head, the officer signaled to the two young men to sit down. He turned toward the owner. "Three cold lemonades, please."

He took off his cap and fanned himself with it. His damp, matted hair stuck to his skull. Only then did Linh notice that the two young men were attached to each other by a chain. The first one must have been about twenty-five; the other looked younger. They were both well dressed. Had they just been arrested? The tallest one had a mustache, almond-shaped eyes, and a straight nose. The shorter one had white skin, rosy lips, and an actor's long hair. They didn't look like killers. These were the kind of young men you could imagine pleading with their mothers for money to buy a pair of fashionable shoes.

"What's their crime, officer?" Tran Phuong asked, offering him a cigarette. The man turned around and his jaw dropped, his eyes opening wide.

"That's it!" he gasped. "You're Tran Phuong, the famous composer!"

Tran Phuong forced a smile: "Have we met?"

"You don't remember me? I was in Camp 27. Last year, the head of the camp invited you to lecture about music."

"Forgive me. I've got a terrible memory."

"You should come back and pay us a visit. Many journalists responsible for propaganda have come to see us, but no one spoke as well as you did. We just loved your stories. Guarding

prisons like we do, why, we almost become prisoners ourselves. We don't see the city streets for an entire year."

Tran Phuong pulled out his lighter and lit the young man's
cigarette. He smiled to himself. This earnest young officer
seemed ill-suited to his line of work. The composer turned toward the two young men chained together and asked, "Some
new guests for the camp?"

The sergeant suddenly came to his senses and stood up.
"Well, I've got to be going, sir. I have to take these two escapees
back to the prison. They've been caught twice now breaking
into state warehouses to find goods to sell on the black market."

The two prisoners turned their heads away, their defiant
looks fading. Tran Phuong took a drag on his cigarette, pensive.

Linh watched the men as they left: "They seemed well
behaved enough. Greed makes men into monsters. If only we
knew how to rid ourselves of desire, society would be so much
better."

Tran Phuong looked at Linh and chuckled. His eyes twinkled. Linh blushed. "Why do you mock me?"

Instead of replying, he gazed at her silently, even gentler,
more loving.

"You were looking at me as if I were a little girl who still
smelled of mother's milk, weren't you?"

"Exactly," he said, slowly taking Linh's hand in his. "I
didn't realize you were so naive. Do you really believe all we
have to do is get rid of desire? The premise is all wrong. Society
is a machine and passion is what makes it run. Eliminate human passions and you destroy the very force that drives society, that makes it evolve."

"But desires and passions also incite us to crime," Linh replied, hesitant.

"Of course. Every human being has two faces, black and
white, light and dark. The key is not to suppress human desire
and passion, but to channel them for the good of the individual

and the community." Tran Phuong fell silent for a moment, then sighed. "And that's the crux of the problem. As for the solution, well, we're going to be searching for a long time."

If she had really thought about it, Linh might have recognized the same old discourse she had heard in countless discussions with Nguyen and other young intellectuals. But somehow, the same words uttered by this man that she was falling in love with held a new, transcendent meaning. She watched him in silence, mute with admiration and respect.

4

THE BOAT slowly ascended the river. Only a few miles separated the Bac Giang Bridge from this area. And yet it had taken them several hours to come this far. The boat driver was in no hurry; he stared at the water, paddling as slowly and methodically as if he were an artist. Trong, a journalist in Nguyen's party cell, whispered to Nguyen: "Looks like we got a dying boatman. In his previous life, he must have been the indolent son of some minister at the imperial court."

"It doesn't matter. We're in no hurry," Nguyen replied. They had been sent to write a long historical series for the magazine on the insurrection of the province of Yen The led by Hoang Hoa Tham. They had taken the train and gotten off at the Bac Giang station. First, they made a stop at the cultural offices of the town to gather some documents and letters of introduction for the district cultural bureau. The deputy chief, responsible for the provincial museum, had assured them that he had notified the district authorities by telephone. The journalists were expected at Bo Ha. Taking their leave of the deputy chief, the two men went to the market to eat. This was by far the best way to eat for a journalist on the road. A plate of steaming white rice, two huge pieces of fried tofu as big as your hand, a few chunks of caramelized pork, and some pickled vegetables made for the perfect meal when you were far from home and your pockets weren't full. While they savored this simple meal, they were surrounded by private food stalls, drivers, traveling salespeople, and suppliers of construction materials. "What's it going to take, when are we going to live like these black market people?"

"Stop brooding, Trong. We are just cogs in the machine. Wherever it goes, we go. The little people, they're free. They're driven by other forces. It's all about choices. You've got to accept the tradeoff, what you lose, and just let go without looking back."

"That's weak," Trong said, shaking his head.

"I'm not as modern as you young people."

"Right. But you're smarter than anyone at the newspaper. A guy could use up seven pairs of shoes trying to keep up with you."

Nguyen smiled. He had always known to keep his silence at the right moment. They finished their tea, then walked toward the station. A bus was scheduled to take passengers to Bo Ha at about two o'clock. Faced with the crowd in line in front of the station, Nguyen suggested renting a boat. Trong agreed.

"Let's go. Let's not hassle over the difference of a few *dong*," he said. "I'm going to suffocate in this station."

They jumped in a cyclo and headed toward the banks of River Thuong, where they rented a boat. The boat pulled up anchor and they set off just as the sun was setting. The owner rowed peacefully. In the prow, his wife was laboriously scaling a huge fish. Her daughter, twelve or thirteen years old, tanned as black as charcoal, was roasting peanuts. The two journalists observed the boatman's taut, muscular arms gripping the oars, his rippling, glistening muscles as intricate as roots. In front of them, the sunset gilded the waves a coppery brown. Stands of reeds on the sandy banks were covered with fine dew. Water buffalo nuzzled the water, shattering the sun's reflections into a thousand shards of light. As they watched, the boatman's arms slowly darkened, silhouetted against the scarlet backdrop of the water. Each slice of the oar seemed to release waves of blood, as if gushing from the throat of some sacrificed beast. The luminous glow of sunset flickered out and the surface of the water turned to the deep purple of the water lilies. The boatman's wife popped her head out of the cabin, her back still crouched in the low doorway, "Dinner is ready. Come to the stern."

The boatman didn't even stop to turn around. "Go ahead and eat with Thu. Come take over from me when you're finished." The woman silently obeyed, returned to the cabin, and moved toward the stern. There, in the darkness, mother and daughter ate their dinner. Nguyen heard the clicking of chopsticks and bowls, their murmuring.

"Another bowl, Mother?"

"That's enough."

"But you didn't eat at noon."

"I've got to keep my stomach light to row. Otherwise, your father's going to yell at us."

She slipped into the prow and stood like a shadow in back of the boatman. "I've finished. Come eat or the rice will get cold."

"Did you roast some peanuts?"

"Yes. I told Thu to keep them warm in the teapot. The bottle of rice wine is in the corner, in the chest."

The man stood up and passed her the oar.

"Row slowly, you hear. The current is mounting."

With these imperious instructions, he turned toward his two passengers. "Care for a drink with me?"

The journalists thanked him, but declined. The boatman returned to eat in the stern. The pungent smell of rice wine drifted toward them. The boatman's dark silhouette was etched against the sky. The oar beat in cadence with the water. To the west, the first stars appeared against the darkening azure of the sky. Nguyen could smell the woman's acrid sweat in the wind.

"Do you know how to row?" he asked Trong. "Go give her a hand."

"Row? I don't even know how to swim."

"Shame. I don't know how to row either."

The wind blew hard from upstream and the boat pitched with each stroke of the oar. You could hear the woman panting in the wind, the smack of the oar against the water. "She's thirty years old. At most. Probably not even," Nguyen mused. He had studied her face that afternoon. You couldn't say she was beautiful, but she was attractive with her tanned skin. Her long, shiny black eyebrows curved over eyes shaped like persicaria leaves. She possessed a natural, simple beauty, the kind you would see in the popular theater, in some godforsaken part of the countryside. She couldn't have been much older than Linh, and yet she lived with a man who must have been fifty, a real brute. What did this young woman dream of? A few kind words, a handkerchief, a new blouse for the coming spring? In this monotonous, nomadic existence that followed the current of the water, the daily struggle to survive, what pleasure lit the dull succession of her days? What made her happy to be alive? Compared to this peasant woman, Linh led the life of a princess. A selfish, fanatical princess. What more did she expect of him? He was a devoted, faithful husband, who had provided for them in difficult times. He had sacrificed many a man's vice to ensure Linh and Huong Ly's happiness—all those bottles of European wine, the luxury of foreign cigarettes, wild evenings out with bachelor friends trawling for affairs. He had forsaken all that for her. And she couldn't forgive him? *Linh, you are the most extremist woman. You only know how to adore the great men of your childhood, ideal beings invented to feed your imagination. I was once your idol. But how would we have survived if I had remained as pure as you wanted me to be?*

"Let's borrow a sleeping mat from the boat owner," Trong said. "My back hurts from sitting. What are you thinking? You look dazed."

Nguyen leaned into the cabin to call the boatman. The man was seated, motionless, a bottle of alcohol by his side. "Thu, bring the mat," he ordered his daughter. "Spread it out for the gentlemen."

The girl emerged from the darkness of the cabin, a mat under her arm. She climbed toward the stern, ducked behind her mother's back, and unrolled it. Still silent, she returned to the stern and disappeared into the cabin. She had probably slipped between the sacks of manioc to sleep. Without waiting for Nguyen, Trong slumped down on the mat.

"It's so cool, Nguyen. Look, the moon is beautiful."

Nguyen lay down next to his friend. The sky seemed more distant, more threatening from below. The vast, infinite space was as if strewn with celestial rocks, stardust ready to tumble on his head. At any moment, fire could shatter the empty sky. A few lives buffeted by the waves would disappear in the ruthless chaos of nature.

"What are you thinking, Nguyen? Why so silent?" Trong asked. "When I was little, I loved Thach Lam's writing. This setting is right out of one of his novels: two human beings dreaming on a boat adrift."

"I didn't know you were such a romantic. But it's true, this night, this moon—it's magnificent."

A full moon floated above a mountain range that loomed on the horizon. Between the mountains and the river stretched the mirage of the plain. On both sides of the river, the sandy, grassy banks had vanished, replaced by marshy stands of bamboo. From where they were lying, the thick crisscross of the bamboo wove a curtain against the moon. The boat wound its way through this surreal cavern born of the play of the night and the moon. The woman had stopped rowing. Leaning on her pole, she guided the boat through the thickets of bamboo. Birds awoke, startled, and scattered. One of them, blinded, fell under the boat. Trong reached out his hand to grab it. But it slipped from his grasp.

"Stunning," Nguyen murmured. But beyond the halo of the moon, he could already see the town, a room with faded, cut flowers, a blue curtain rippling in the wind at down, the spring that Linh had stopped loving him.

"Will we get to Bo Ha by tomorrow morning, Nguyen?"

The woman pulled the pole from the water, replying for him. "We'll get there by ten o'clock, at the latest. Don't worry."

"We have to go on to Wooden Bridge," Trong explained.

The woman leaned down to pass under an arch of bamboo.

"Don't worry. From Bo Ha to Wooden Bridge, it's quick. I go there sometimes to buy charcoal. On foot, it only takes a couple of hours. But you'll take a car. Don't worry."

"Have you been to the local museum?" Nguyen asked.

"Venerable De's temple? Of course, people here have started to observe the anniversary of his death every year."

"Who started the ceremony?"

"No one. It's always existed, since the time of my great-grandparents. Destiny weighs heavy on our people. We must honor his memory; he will protect us, liberate us. From the time of the anti-French Resistance, we have won every battle led by troops from this region. It's heaven's will, Buddha's will. Venerable De's soul is miraculous."

She stopped speaking and threw her weight on the oar. The boat slipped through the bamboo and glided toward the middle of the river. The banks, illuminated by the full moon, were no longer covered with trees and vegetation. The mat was chilly.

"The mat is damp from the fog. If you want to get some sleep, go back in the cabin," Nguyen said to Trong.

"No thanks. It's strange, but I don't feel like sleeping. Ordinarily, in the evening, as soon as the hens go back to roost, my eyelids start to droop. My wife always teases me, calls me a lazy intellectual."

"I can't sleep either."

"What time is it?"

"Eight forty-five."

"Days are longer in the city."

"Yes, but here it's the night that lasts longer. The further you get from the big cities, the slower the rhythm. Last year, I visited a seaside commune. There were a few thousand inhabitants scattered over three small islands. They got around in small boats. Almost every family still cooked rice in clay pots. Even the ladles and spoons were made of clay. Can you imagine? I later found out that their cooperative was barely able to furnish the islands with fuel, needles and thread, notebooks for the schoolchildren."

"Ah, that's because there's a fuel shortage. But tell me, Nguyen, were you able to buy the Paustovsky short stories?"

Nguyen said nothing.

"Hey, Nguyen, why don't you say anything?"

"I was thinking about you, about everything that makes you who you are. How can you jump from the development of society to Paustovsky?"

"I don't know. What does it matter?"

"Of course it matters. I've noticed for a long time now that we don't really think problems through. We harrow one plot of the land, then abandon it for another, even before having sown seeds. We're incapable of deep, radical thought. Don't you see? All our romantic enthusiasm, our superficial ideals only lead us astray, to failure and disappointment. As for Paustovsky, you like him a lot, don't you?"

"Enormously."

"There was a time when Paustovsky was my favorite author. He was for everyone in our generation. I knew *The Gilded Rose, A Rainy Autumn, Natasha*, by heart. Even now, I just close my eyes, and I could describe the wooden boats on the edge of the Russian forests, the golden autumn on the Volga, the icy footpaths shrouded in fog, the Matisse and Lépine paintings on the walls of apartments filled with women in glamorous evening gowns, the air filled with their heady perfume. Paustovsky was a writer who excelled at evoking the sentimental feelings of high school students, all their flowery dreams. Good, easy feelings, miraculous opportunities that you could pluck as easily as the hazelnuts on the hills of Nha Nam in autumn. No, I can't stomach Paustovsky anymore. You are luckier than I am to still be able to admire him when you're thirty."

"How old are you?"

"You wouldn't believe me if I told you . . . Thirty-two."

"You're right, I wouldn't have believed you. That's amazing."

"Let me continue what I was saying. For a long time now, I've wanted to write an article on our habit of never getting to the bottom of an idea, or thinking rigorously. It's made us superficial, impulsive. Every people has its strengths and weaknesses. But only a people who can look its flaws in the face is a great people. Death begins when self-satisfaction sets in. Just like a writer is lost when he thinks his oeuvre has reached the summits of art. A people that only knows how to live by resting on its laurels is doomed. That's what I want to say to you. We intellectuals, it's not our mission to flatter the pride of our people, but to look deeply into its flaws, to spot them earlier than others."

Nguyen stopped, realizing he had said too much. Trong stared at him, mesmerized.

"My, what a strange fellow you are," Trong sighed. Nguyen had such noble, intelligent ideas, yet somehow he always acted the part of the dutiful employee. Trong found it even odder that Nguyen had accepted the shameful role of the cuckolded husband. Half the town knew that his wife, Linh, was the new, passionate love of the famous composer Tran Phuong.

5

"I LOVE YOU."

"Mmm."

"Happy?"

"Yes."

Linh gazed elsewhere as she replied. Tran Phuong didn't notice his lover's distant attitude. He was contented, and softly whistled the popular melody to the song "Paradise." Suddenly, inspired, he raised his voice: *"Welcome to paradise, receive our offerings, our fragrant peaches. This celestial love, this unique, crazy dream of a life."*

Linh listened, her heart drowning in shame. Their first embraces had brought her neither pleasure nor happiness. Here in this strange suburb, facing rows of corn as far as the eye could see, the sails on the boats bobbing on the river, she felt lonely, adrift. A sense of foreboding, like a premonition, seemed to hang in the air. Another feeling, of guilt, gnawed at her conscience. Tran Phuong's gaze, his lips, his breathing so close to hers, made her anxious, vigilant. Perhaps love must pass through stages slowly, not burn through time. Linh remembered the first moments of her married life with Nguyen. Moments of complete, perfect happiness for body and soul that were seared into her memory, as eternal as sunlight, or air, or the green of spring. Moments of complete, utter fulfillment. But at that moment, a dark malaise overcame her, as if she were being carried off by the muddy waves of a flood.

Tran Phuong was still singing, crooning seductively. His cheeks aflame, his eyes glistening with happiness, he was completely unaware. Why? He must be used to secrecy, she thought—the secrecy of extramarital affairs. He didn't even think about it anymore. No doubt she was just one of countless women who had fallen into his arms. There had certainly been others before her. And there would be after her, too. In a flash, her shame turned to jealousy. Anger surfaced, and she was powerless to hold it back.

"Tran Phuong . . ."

The composer had been dreamily contemplating the fields of green corn on the banks of the Red River. Startled, he shifted and turned to her. He could somehow sense the hostility in Linh's voice, and he moved toward her, gently taking her warm hand in his. "What's the matter, darling?"

"I was thinking . . . thinking that . . ."

Linh stuttered, consumed by jealousy. But pride held her back. Only after struggling for a long time did she finally find the words.

"You must be used to . . . with the others . . . the women before me . . . this kind of thing."

Tran Phuong laughed softly. He understood. He cocked his head, gave Linh a deep, kind look. "There have been a lot of women before you, that's true," he said sadly. "Let's not deny it; that would be cowardly, hypocritical. But those women came to *me*. Perhaps it's in poor taste, so forgive me, but there are a lot of very common women out there. I've been with some out of pity, some out of boredom, or even because I was disillusioned. But you are the only woman I've ever really loved, the first who I call by name, the one I've always been searching for. Never forget this, whatever happens. I'll just say one thing: You are the woman I love. You, and only you."

Linh sat motionless, staring into the distance. The composer suddenly understood the guilt that lurked behind those sad, brown eyes. The happiness he had so easily gained was the very pain that gnawed at her. He drew Linh to him and stroked her hair.

"Please don't be sad. A human being is bound by many chains, invisible most of the time. The hardest thing is to see beyond the masks. I love you, you love me. That's the most important reality, the only truth. Nothing else matters."

Linh sighed. Tran Phuong saw her shudder and close her eyes. She feels remorse, she's suffering. What a pity, he thought, overcome by compassion for her. At that moment, she seemed to him like a fragile child, like the bird with broken wings that had fallen into his orange grove as a child. He remembered how he had cared for it, how he had wept when he buried it a week later.

BY THE TIME he and Linh went their separate ways that afternoon, the sun was already setting. The leaves on the trees glowed in the golden light. Along the road back to town, from time to time, a boy would try to sell them fish skewered on a bamboo stick. Linh suddenly remembered that she had nothing to eat at home, so she made a detour to go to the market. Linh pedaled all the way to Hang Buom Street to buy medicine from a black market vendor.

"Just one drop, that's all you need. I guarantee you," the woman boasted, stuffing the money in her pocket.

A few yards away, a white-haired old man squinted at Linh. When she passed him, he whispered to her: "Don't put that stuff in your child's nostrils! She'll just get worse. But don't say anything. I don't want trouble from these black market people."

Linh stopped and scrutinized the label on the vial. The old man was right; it was covered with an illegible, handwritten scrawl. Exasperated, guilt-ridden, she promptly dumped the bottle on the sidewalk. If only she had gone to the pharmacy that morning, this wouldn't have happened. Unfortunately, Huong Ly was always catching colds. She imagined her daughter's eyes watching her, brimming with reproach. *Mama, why have you been gone so long? I want to be with you. I've lived with Grandpa and Grandma for too long. I miss you.*

A shadow of worry clouded Linh's mind. She entered a pastry shop and hastily bought all kinds of candy for her daughter. She pedaled back to the house, intending to pick up Huong Ly from her grandparents' house after putting the food in the refrigerator. But when she opened the door, Linh saw that the little girl was already there in Nguyen's arms. Seeing Linh, she shrieked: "Ah, Mama's back."

Her daughter's cries pierced Linh's heart like needles. She tried to reply calmly. "Oh it's you, my girl. Wait just a minute. I'm going to wash up, and come and hug you. Don't kiss me now, I'm sweaty."

Linh dropped the food onto the table and went into the bathroom to wash her face. It wasn't the sweat and the dust of the road, but rather the shame that made her feel as if she were covered with an invisible layer of glue. She felt miserable. In the bathtub, the rush of water drowned her sobs. After a long time, Linh regained her composure. She entered the room, her eyes red. Nguyen passed Huong Ly to her, avoiding her eyes.

"You play with her, I'll make dinner," he said calmly, as if everything were normal.

"No," Linh replied feebly, "I'll make it, in a moment."

In the kitchen, a pot of spareribs was simmering and the aroma spread through the room. A lock of hair fell over Nguyen's forehead. He pulled it back with his slow, familiar gesture. Linh gazed at her husband's smooth, elegant hands. Behind these hands she saw golden rice paddies in autumn, forest paths, a clear sky above the plain, mountain ranges as far as the eye could see, all the way to the clouds. He had been her universe, her entire life, her happiness. Why had he suddenly pushed her into this void, this yawning abyss?

Forgive him . . . Return to your tranquil, happy life with him . . . Forgive and forget.

But the jeering voices rose in her memory:

"Yes, he's a model of social mobility. And clever enough to know just how to please the authorities. A soul passionate enough to sing the praises of the powers-that-be, a real actor.

"Yes, Nguyen is talented. Why he's created an art form—the art of tolerating everything. Remember the Thac Ba Dam controversy? A single word from the editor-in-chief was enough to snuff out his indignation."

No, she could never forget. Unless she were to go crazy, or suffer amnesia. Unless she were to find some miraculous drug that would preserve the memory of the happy moments while effacing the horrible reality of their last few years together. But Linh knew these were fantasies. She would never forget, never be able to love Nguyen again. She couldn't force herself to become someone else.

BACK HOME, Tran Phuong found Ngoc Minh deep in conversation with his wife, Hoa. Heavily made-up as always, she wore a red blouse with a dragon embroidered in the middle, tight white velvet jeans, and white satin high heels. Seeing him, she shouted, "My dear Tran Phuong, we've been waiting for you for half an hour."

"Sorry, I had business," he replied.

The composer went into the bedroom to change and to shake off an uncomfortable mixture of embarrassment and irritation. Ngoc Minh had a reputation among Hanoi women for her affairs. She needed to be constantly accompanied and adulated by men, whether by aging professors or young greenhorns, the kind of men who didn't mind lining up day in and day out for a game of human Ping-Pong. Her love affairs followed no particular logic. She thought of herself as young, gorgeous, and talented. This extraordinary self-confidence titillated male curiosity. Like some giant algae floating in the middle of a river, she intrigued men; they felt compelled to go and take a peek at this exotic plant. Tran Phuong was not lacking in beautiful women who were in love with him. But unlike most men, he no longer felt any curiosity toward Ngoc Minh. He was anxious to keep her as his ally. Aside from her adoration, she had proved to be a militant advocate for his reinstatement to his old position.

Tran Phuong changed into his house pajamas and returned to the living room. Ngoc Minh looked up at him. "So, I've just discussed your situation with Hoa."

"Oh, really?" Tran Phuong commented. *So she's able to speak calmly with Hoa.*

"Everything's going just as smoothly as I predicted," said Ngoc Minh. "Maybe even better. But we missed you and your culinary talents today. You should have been here to serve us."

Hoa arched her neck proudly. "He left me with nothing but sticky rice and Chinese sausage to nibble on. Isn't that scandalous?"

Tran Phuong turned his head away so he didn't see his wife's smile. "How could I know you were going to come by?"

"My dear Tran Phuong," Ngoc Minh said. "I've seen to everything. Now, there's just one thing that requires your help: Can you see Luu early next week?"

"Luu who?" the composer scowled.

Luu was the private secretary of an old comrade-in-arms who had become a party leader. During the war, they had been in the same company, carried colts on their belts to accompany the artistic troupes to the front. At the time, Luu was just a puny guy who smelled bad and hung around the kitchens to salvage grilled manioc and burnt rice crusts. After an enemy raid killed his parents, Luu had become the adopted son of a soldier. But on the way to the front, this soldier had had to leave him with an ideological education division, where a widowed cook had looked after him.

This orphaned kid would later become personal secretary to a party leader and former colleague of Tran Phuong's. Now, the man was ready to help Tran Phuong but wanted the famous composer to be the one to seek him out.

Tran Phuong was speechless with anger. *He should receive me personally, not some guy who was an illiterate kid when we left for the battlefields.*

Furious, Tran Phuong sulked and mouthed a "thank you."

Ngoc Minh stared at him, insistent. "So?"

"I thank you."

"You will see him, won't you?"

"I've got a business trip scheduled for the southern provinces."

"You can go South whenever you like," his wife interrupted. "You're just undermining all Miss Ngoc Minh's hard work. She went to so much trouble for you."

"Excuse me, I'm busy," Tran Phuong snapped icily.

He stood up and poured himself a glass of cold water. The two women glanced at each other. Ngoc Minh fumbled in her handbag, pulled out a bag of watermelon seeds, and cracked them between her teeth. Hoa went to the kitchen cabinet, took out a pair of chopsticks, and plucked apricots, one by one, from a jar of brandy, to transfer them to another jar, a task she had dutifully performed for the last six or seven years. Emptying his glass, the composer sat back down at the table. The journalist stared at him, mesmerized.

"Go see Luu," she pleaded. "Just for a morning. Everything

will be fine, I promise. In life, you have to know how to stoop once in awhile. I thought you were a veteran when it came to this kind of thing."

His wife turned to him, adding, "You can't choose your colleagues. That only happens with a spouse, and even then . . ."

Tran Phuong bowed his head. An idea flashed through his mind. *It's you, you're the most unbearable choice that destiny planted in my head. You are the worst error of my life.*

Hoa continued to try to convince him: "You lack patience. Without it, you'll never be able to accomplish anything. Listen to Ngoc Minh, just go see him."

The journalist raised her hand. "Don't miss this opportunity. All you need is a bit of flexibility, and you win."

"Thanks, but I am busy," Tran Phuong replied coldly.

Ngoc Minh stayed a little while longer, but remained silent. Then she excused herself. Tran Phuong stood up and accompanied her to the staircase. As the stairs creaked, he felt a pang of regret at the thought of letting an opportunity slip through his fingers. A breeze rose from the floor, making him shiver as he remembered the icy, northern winds during the war. Had he grown too old? Wild regret and envy suddenly reared up in him. He couldn't bear the idea of slipping into obscurity, resignation, oblivion. And then he saw it again: the white Moscovic rolling up in front of his eyes, the chauffeur obsequiously opening the door, waiting.

Just as Ngoc Minh reached the bottom of the staircase, she felt the composer's hand on her shoulder. "Tell Luu I'll be there next Tuesday."

Ngoc Minh turned and looked at him, perplexed. Then, she took his hands and shook them furiously. "*Now* you're being reasonable. You were going to dash all my efforts."

Tran Phuong laughed, said softly, "You mean a lot to me, Ngoc Minh."

He stood there, waiting until Ngoc Minh had pushed her Honda 50 across the courtyard and revved the motor. The motorcycle traced a half-circle, then lurched into the street. In the blink of an eye, she was lost in the dense whirl of traffic. It was Sunday night. Tran Phuong let his mind wander. But his scattered thoughts couldn't dispel the feeling of self-loathing that had just welled up in his heart. *What am I doing? What nonsense. That guy Luu is just a stone in my path.*

MISS TONG was the most powerful person in Nguyen and Linh's building. Yet no one seemed to know where she had come from. According to the older tenants, she had moved in just a few weeks after they did. When Hanoi was liberated, the rooms of the abandoned building had been divided up among the cadres who had seized control of the city government. Right from the start, Miss Tong had laid claim to the first room on the corridor. She was thirty-one years old, five feet two, and weighed one hundred and sixty pounds. At the time, her size and her weight made her seem like a monster to the young people. Even the most arrogant young men and the boldest middle-aged men were terrified of her, avoided her like the plague. Miss Tong knew this. She did not waste time fussing over her appearance, or flirting.

The years had gone by. Miss Tong was still vigorous, but her gaze had become vapid, dull. She ran a small business selling pickled eggplant, chili paste, vinegar, and soy sauce. In the evenings, she invited the neighborhood kids to come play cards with her. If she lost, she gave them roasted kernels of corn; if she won, she made them keep on playing. Yet, when this ox-like woman slowly mounted the stairs hauling two buckets of water, you couldn't help but sense something of the sad fragility of a lost animal. Professor Le had been the first to notice. He discussed her with the cadres in the neighborhood, suggesting to the other tenants that they make her deputy chief of a committee in charge of hygiene and security. Everyone agreed. From then on, Miss Tong had become an all-powerful person in the building, supervising the electricity and water supplies and organizing security. She was the one who made the rounds, collected money to repair the communal toilets. With time, everyone came to respect this loyal "servant of the people." But little by little she began to bully everyone, even Professor Le. No one dared to stand up to her, or to keep her waiting. People trembled when they forgot their turn at security guard duty and this giant woman appeared at the door wielding her clipboard: "Today it's your turn to clean the common rooms!"

Huong Ly was the only one who spoke kindly to this lonely soul, who stroked her fat, wrinkled cheeks with her little hands. Nguyen and Linh would often drop Huong Ly off with Miss Tong before leaving for work. They had both tried to cultivate friendly, harmonious relations with the other families in the building. A refreshing light filtered through the blue curtain on their window, and pleasant music always seemed to drift from their home. Though estranged, the couple tried to speak softly, respectfully, to each other.

That night, at about eleven o'clock, Miss Tong hung the mosquito net over her bed to sleep. As usual, she fumbled under her pillow to make sure she had her two sets of keys and her lighter. She always kept them there, at hand, in case of need. Suddenly she recalled having given one set of keys to Huong Ly. The little one must have put them in her pants pocket and forgotten to return them when she left with her father. Miss Tong ran to knock at the door of Nguyen's room.

"Open up, it's me."

Nguyen and Linh both sat up.

"Coming, coming."

Linh had been asleep on the mat, right next to the door. She rushed to open it. Entering, Miss Tong grumbled: "Give me back that set of keys. Huong Ly must have them in her pocket."

"Yes, wait a minute," Linh said. "Nguyen, where did you put Huong Ly's clothes?"

"I think I put them in the washbasin," said Nguyen, still under the covers.

With her ferret-like gaze, Miss Tong had taken it all in. She shot a look at Nguyen. "My, my, now that's a big bed. Why not share it with your wife and daughter?"

"Uh . . . uh," Nguyen stammered.

"Kids are too fragile," Miss Tong warned. "Your daughter's going to catch pneumonia sleeping on the floor like that. That's expensive to treat, I can tell you."

Just then Linh returned with the set of keys. "We like to sleep apart. We breathe better," she said, replying for her husband.

Miss Tong shot her a suspicious look. "Hmm. Odd habit! Spending all that money on a bed. Well, I must be going."

She took the set of keys from Linh and left. Only after the thud of her footsteps had faded, then was lost down the corridor, did Linh and Nguyen dare to go back to their separate places on the bed and the mat. Neither of them could sleep. Though they each chased their own frantic thoughts, they both knew that from then on everything would be different.

The next morning, Miss Tong virtually interrogated Huong Ly. "Why don't you sleep in the bed with your parents?"

"Mama won't let me."

"Why?"

"I don't know."

"What does she say? Try to remember, I'll give you lots of corn kernels."

"She says, 'If you want to sleep with Mama, sleep here, on the mat.' "

"And then?"

"Then she cries."

"She cries?"

There must be a problem. They are really discreet. But even the needle at the bottom of the haystack always emerges. Miss Tong was suddenly animated by a sinister excitement. Motivated by her old petty, malicious zeal, she decided to bring the mystery to light.

Household troubles are always the woman's fault. Try to dig up something at her high school; perhaps that's where we'll find the dragonfly's nest.

The next morning, Miss Tong put on her best clothes—black satin slacks, and a blouse with covered buttons and a ruffled collar. The loose slacks and silky fabric made her look more feminine, masking her chunky, masculine thighs. Miss Tong carefully put her hair up in a chignon and, exceptionally, decided to wear the spectacles she normally only used to go over accounts for the building. She hailed a cyclo and climbed into it with an air of self-importance.

"Where is she going all dressed up like that?" the neighbors muttered, perplexed. No one knew that the cyclo was headed straight for the high school where Linh taught. The teachers and the students were lined up in the courtyard to salute the flag and hear the principal read the previous week's results and goals for the upcoming week. The cyclo stopped in front of the high school gate. Miss Tong strode toward the administrative offices.

"I'd like to see the principal, comrade," Miss Tong intoned to the old school guard. A sweet, gentle man, the guard had spent his life tending trees and plants for the city's public gardens. Recently retired, he had just started this job on a contract basis. This tall, imposing woman and her harsh voice intimidated him. He guessed that something important must be happening, that this woman had been sent by the authorities on a mission to investigate something. He scurried to oblige her.

"Please have a seat. I'll call the principal."

Miss Tong sat down and crossed her legs. She already took

herself for an important person in charge of handling an affair, the scope of which she had not yet been able to assess. The old guard was edgy: It was almost time to salute the flag and he didn't dare interrupt the principal. He rinsed the teapot and began to prepare tea in an effort to stall for time.

Miss Tong was pleased. "Have some tea," said the old man, serving her a cup with both hands, then carefully placing it on the table in front of her. No one had ever served her tea so respectfully. The old man nervously scratched the back of his ear. "Yes, yes, if you'll just wait a few minutes . . . they are saluting the flag. The principal is busy."

"Fine, I'll wait."

"Please understand, madame."

"Yes, I understand."

Miss. Tong lifted her cup of tea and sipped it, nodding her head. Then she relaxed, leaned back into the chair, and waited. The old man paced, glancing anxiously at the clock on the wall. "There, the ceremony is over. Please wait just one more minute; I have to beat the drum, then I'll go look for her." He dashed off. A drum sounded. A moment later, he reappeared, smiling, and announced: "If you'll just come this way, the principal is waiting for you in her office."

Miss Tong stood and followed him across a courtyard where students were playing, screaming like demons. The guard showed her to the staircase. "It's the first door on the second floor," he said, then disappeared.

Miss Tong hesitated for a moment, then strode confidently up the stairs. The door was wide open. A shaft of sunlight illuminated the office. A woman stood up from behind her desk and smiled modestly: "Hello, madame."

"Hello, miss," Miss Tong replied briskly. Without further invitation, she sat down. "I work for the state," she announced. "I'm here to discuss Linh's family situation."

Confusion flashed across the principal's face. Miss Tong immediately noticed it. "Linh is having an affair. They want to cover it up," she said, her eyes twinkling maliciously. "I know you share our concern. It's our duty to defend the morality of revolutionary cadres."

"Uh, yes," the principal replied mechanically.

Miss Tong stared at her, then added: "Miss Linh's family situation is causing symptoms of great concern to the authorities. I'd like your assessment of the situation?"

Miss Tong's imperious manner made the principal jittery. She had met many women of this ilk—the type with their hair piled up with glittering combs who lectured you about politics and morality every time they opened their mouths, who always wanted to preach, to reform others. From experience, she knew that, while lacking in education, these women were unrivaled in their thirst for power. When they wanted something, they went for the jugular vein. Trying to oppose them was like deliberately smashing your head against a rock.

The principal, Kim Anh, liked Linh. She was sincere, genuine in both her strengths and her weaknesses. None of her colleagues could bring themselves to dislike her. Her reputation as a superb literature teacher was well established. Many of her students had won national competitions. Everyone knew about her marital problems, and her liaison with the famous composer. Some of them had tried to discreetly offer advice; others prudently kept silent. No one had the heart to gossip about her. While few could understand how or why Linh had gotten herself into this situation, everyone instinctively trusted her, knew that she was never driven by pettiness or self-interest.

Nevertheless, this stranger's harsh words unsettled her: "Excuse me, what exactly are you asking of me?"

"That you and your comrades try to get to the bottom of this matter, for Linh's sake."

Kim Anh fiddled with her pen. *Who is she? What's her position anyway? And why should I do her bidding?*

But Miss Tong's threatening look stopped those thoughts. After a moment's reflection, Kim Anh replied, "We know that the couple has problems, but we don't know why. And right now we aren't in a position to judge. In my opinion, we'll need time to know more." This was the wisest reply, she told herself. Then, weighing each word, she added, "Given our position, and what we know, that's all I can tell you."

Miss Tong stiffened in her chair, watched the principal in silence for a few more moments, then stood up. "We'll see," she said, turned, and left without saying good-bye.

That evening, after dinner, she knocked on Nguyen's door. "Open up, it's me."

Nguyen and Linh had just finished dinner. They hadn't had time to clear the table, but they let Miss Tong in and began to hurriedly put away the dishes and prepare tea.

"Where's the little girl?" Miss Tong asked.

"She's with her grandparents," Nguyen replied.

"Oh, where do they live? I've been meaning to ask for some time now."

"Huong Ly's maternal grandparents died a long time ago. Her great-uncle and her great-aunt live in Chen village."

"Ah."

Miss Tong nodded her head and placed her hands on the table. After a few moments of silence, she said, "Dear Nguyen, dear Linh, we have something to discuss with you."

Nguyen was pouring tea; Linh was washing her hands in the bathroom. The neighbor's cagey voice unnerved them, so they moved to sit back down at the table.

"There is a problem with your marriage. As you know, we are a model housing unit for this neighborhood. The town's party committee even gave us the Modern Socialist Culture Family award, and of course the flag for meritorious service. Now, your problems do have consequences for the community's reputation. So I want both of you to struggle, rigorously and energetically, against your errors to . . ."

Since Miss Tong had begun speaking, Nguyen had been carefully watching the stony mask of her face. The closer she came to making her point, the more enraged he became. Incapable of keeping his usual calm, he stood up and cut the woman off: "There are no problems with our marriage. No one has the right to question us about anything."

Miss Tong didn't know what to say or how to react. Her nose twitched. Wounded, this woman whose ego had long been flattered was now forced to confront her powerlessness; she was frantic, sensing something indomitable.

"I . . . I am saying this for the common good . . ." she stuttered after a moment of confusion. She stood up. Nguyen did the same, as if waiting for her to leave, and stared icily. Miss Tong left the room; her footsteps thudded down the corridor, faded out, then disappeared behind the slam of a door.

The room fell back into silence. Nguyen wheeled around, the muscles in his cheeks twitching. "So, are you satisfied?"

Linh looked at her husband without replying.

"Well?" Nguyen repeated, clenching his jaw.

He stared at his wife, crushed by shame and pity. But beyond all these feelings, hope stirred in him. "Come back. I forgive you for everything; I'm waiting for you. For your own good, put an end to this affair, come back to our home."

But Linh just glared back, unflinching, defiant, without the slightest sign of guilt or shame. Nguyen watched those beautiful, accusatory eyes, transfixed. He contemplated her soft white cheeks with their tiny freckles, the curl of hair under her left ear, the beauty mark at the nape of her neck—these familiar images kindled the repressed, thwarted love that continued to obsess him. It was at once the love of a twenty-year-old and that of a patient, mature man, hardened by life. After days and months of solitude, after long sleepless nights of waiting and hoping, this many-faceted love screamed inside him.

"I hate you," he rasped. Then, bending down, he whispered in her ear, "If only I had married another woman, I could have been happy."

At that moment, he remembered the boatwoman in Bac Giang, the gentle, lapping cadence of her oar on the water, her humility.

Nguyen repeated his words, his voice choked. "If only I had married someone else . . . What do you want, Linh? Haven't I been faithful? Haven't I always provided for you and Huong Ly? You know I try to live honestly, treat people well. What more do you want from me?"

Linh brushed back the hair that had fallen in her face. She pushed Nguyen away, replying in a no less brutal voice. "You're a liar. Marry anyone you want, whenever you like. I won't stop you."

Linh opened a drawer and pulled out pen and paper. "It had to end like this. I have never lied to you. I've told you for a long time that I don't love you anymore, that I don't want to live here anymore. *You're* the one who begged me to stay."

She scrawled hastily: "Request for Divorce."

Nguyen stood motionless, stricken. His rage had subsided, but his heart had frozen. As if paralyzed, he watched her slanting handwriting cover the paper. Suddenly he felt abandoned, alone in this big, cold room where everything reminded him of Linh: her pants against the blue and white floor tiles; her favorite hat hanging on the wall; her coat with the wide belt draped on the back of a chair; her violet blouse with the white buttons that glinted like pearls. Alone with his sad, hasty little meals. And the long, empty Sundays that dragged on. A life emptied of meaning. What was the use of struggling alone, every day, to survive? The articles, the interminable, boring meetings, the mind-numbing ceremonies. Without her, when he returned from his long trips abroad, the blue light filtering through the window would have no meaning. Without her, without the hope of winning her back, nothing would sustain him in his moments of weariness, hold him back from sliding into despair. Despite everything, Linh was still the best he could imagine, the best a man could hope for. He, more than anyone, understood what mettle her heart was made of; he knew the passion that had driven her to Tran Phuong.

But you are going to be disappointed, my naive, ruthless darling. If only you had heard what Lan told me about him. If only you . . .

Linh wrote methodically, covering the page, line by line. She was almost finished. Her hand didn't even shake. The pen scraped the paper like a rake sweeping away dead grass in a garden. At the end of the page, she suddenly raised her head. Nguyen saw that her eyes were moist. Pain wrenched at his heart again, like a blade stuck in his throat, twisted his gut. Tears fell from his eyes.

"Stop," he said, grabbing Linh's hand.

Linh threw aside the pen and collapsed on the table in sobs. Nguyen sat down at his wife's side, silent. Salty tears trickled into the corner of his mouth. Street sounds filled the room: children laughing and playing; vendors clicking their bamboo sticks; the rustle of trees in the wind. Gentle sounds that called for forgiveness, that reminded them of their past moments of happiness, that seemed to whisper of tender, youthful love. Nguyen burrowed his head in the hollow of Linh's shoulder. His tears seeped through her blouse. "Stay with me."

Linh sobbed. After a long moment, she stood up, wiped her eyes with her handkerchief. "I have to leave."

"No."

"I have to, there's no other way."

Nguyen took his wife's hand. She looked him straight in the

eye. This was the first time that she had looked at him like this, with an odd indifference—no resentment, no hatred, no contempt. Only an immense sadness.

"Let me go," she repeated, gently withdrawing her hand from Nguyen's.

"Who cares what people say? Stay with us."

"I love Huong Ly, but I can't continue to live with this lie."

A silence. Nguyen said nothing. Linh repeated: "Sign it. Please."

"No!" Nguyen shouted. His face was contorted, "I am not the kind of man who gambles with love. I can't lose you!"

"But I can't love a man I no longer respect."

Nguyen lifted his head. "What do you find so respectable about your composer, the fact that he's twenty-four years older?"

Linh frowned. "You have no right to talk about this. He's not the kind of man who sells his soul to earn his daily rice—not like you and your colleagues."

Nguyen snickered. "That's it, nobody can compare to the saint, to your hero. That's it, isn't it?" he said theatrically.

Linh glared at him, almost screaming. "Envy and jealousy are the basest human sentiments."

Nguyen saw his wife was furious. *She still has the fanatical zeal of a sixteen-year-old. And all her beauty too.* He lowered his voice. "Linh, please, don't have any illusions, about anybody. I'm a man, I know the darkness of men's hearts."

His words had no effect; they only sharpened Linh's contempt. She smiled, pursing her lips contemptuously. "You're just a coward."

Nguyen took the blow, then attempted to have the last word: "So who is the real man behind your famous composer?"

"He's a true artist, a renaissance man of our time."

"Ha, ha." Nguyen burst out laughing. Suddenly realizing that this sudden outburst might intrigue the neighbors, he put his hand to his mouth. His face fell, went dark, but an inconsolable pain still flashed from his eyes.

Once, Linh might have been intrigued by this laugh, by such behavior from a man who was usually so self-controlled. But she was in love, and madly enough to be unfair to Nguyen.

"You're crazy," she said. Then she packed up the last of the clothes into the old suitcase and left. It was eleven-thirty.

Nguyen heard the echo of Linh's footsteps on the staircase slowly fade away. This familiar sound had been engraved in his memory for years; it was a mere detail, though one of many that had made up their life together. He lit a cigarette. It tasted bitter. He paced around the room, then sat back down on the chair where she had been seated. It was still warm. Tears spilled from his eyes, down his cheeks, crawling toward his chin. Why was Linh so cruel to him? Fanatics were always cruel, ruthless. The most barbarous wars in human history have been between the followers of opposing gods. Linh had transformed Nguyen into a god once too, and adored him. When they were first in love, she even wore a silk shirt with a collar in the form of a lotus flower. Then, when she discovered his weaknesses, when the idol had been dashed into smithereens on the cement floor, she had walked away without a second thought.

It's a curse to love a woman like her. She isn't capable of making an ordinary man happy. Today's separation was inevitable.

But then he remembered her eyes. Linh had none of the flaws so common in other women. She had never used her beauty. She didn't know how to lie or dissimulate. She didn't know how to hide her shortcomings, or how to act to get what she wanted. And the worst thing was that he still loved her.

Nguyen pressed his chin on his raised fist. He pitied himself. As a boy, when he lived with his two elder brothers and two little sisters, he had been shy and fearful. He wasn't the eldest, in whom parents invest all their confidence and respect.

He wasn't the youngest, the one spoiled by the whole family. He was the middle child in this little community, the last to get anything—a ball of grilled rice, a few melted candies, a handful of boiled peanuts. His two brothers, their fists raised, had always forced him to share the loot. Or, when his little sister cried to get some, his mother, overworked, would shout: "Give some to your sister; you're older than she is."

This feeling of always being deprived of his share had haunted Nguyen since childhood, that distant time long before he could even form the thought. When he became a young man, he learned to triumph through sheer willpower. His successes, the reputation that he had earned early on, had finally overcome the memory of the five-year-old boy sobbing at the foot of an old guava tree. Childhood tears were the bitterest, and they had left painful scars in his memory. Nguyen suddenly found himself a boy again, his piece of cake grabbed from him, abandoned. A wild yearning rose in him: to be a baby again, crawling the length of his mother's bed. She would love him, give him back everything that had been taken from him. Instead of scolding, she would sing him a lullaby, caress him, kiss his cheeks, massage his legs each time he fell. She would take him in her arms, rock him until his eyelids drooped heavy with sleep. He felt overcome by an intense, sweet sensation. He rose, took his bicycle out into the corridor, locked the door, and pedaled toward his parents' house in the suburbs.

When Nguyen arrived, an hour later, his parents were still asleep. They suddenly got up, turned on the lights, and put on the kettle for tea. They had had five children. And yet, in their old age, they lived alone. Their children, all married, lived hundreds of miles away from one another. In fact, only Nguyen had stayed in Hanoi, so Huong Ly was their closest granddaughter.

"The little one has been sleeping soundly for a while. Have

you eaten?" his mother asked, noticing her son's swollen eye-lids.

"Yes, Mother," Nguyen answered, his voice hoarse.

Pedaling toward the house, he had yearned to throw him-self into her arms, bury his face in her shoulder, tell her every-thing—all he had lost, all that weighed on his heart. Now, he realized he couldn't. An invisible force held him back, the ir-rational force of habit.

"Come on in, my child. I've got some persimmons for you. Why are you so thin these days?" his mother asked.

Nguyen stood motionless and haggard as his mother bus-tled about preparing tea and peeling persimmons. Only then did he understand this painful regret. Like love, a human be-ing's childhood was a glass castle that, once broken, could never be rebuilt.

6

THE SUN, a silvery ball, glided above the blue line of the mountains. In this season, the clouds were pure white, magnificent, floating slowly through the sky. Birds traced mysterious curves with their wings. A man could lose himself in the vast, inviting emptiness of this space. The wind felt heavy, damp with the muddy smell of Red River silt. Tran Phuong contemplated this familiar landscape; he was happy, his mind empty, his heart lulled by this vision of softness. He took Linh's hand, sighed. "My marriage is hell. It's only with you that I lead a human life."

Linh said nothing.

He stroked her hands. Her nails were not meticulously clipped and filed, or shaped like almonds or peaches, or varnished pink or red, or purple like lotus seeds. Linh wasn't like other women. She was totally unconscious of the power of her femininity. Her beauty was utterly natural. To him, she was like a pure, peaceful wind untainted by hatred, despair, or bitterness.

"I'd like to write a song for you."

"No, no," Linh said, blushing.

How could she be so modest? The other women in Tran Phuong's life had been no more than a ravenous, clamoring horde, each out for her piece of his fame. "Write me a song, oh please, a beautiful song." And he had promised, had written horrible songs that he'd wanted to toss in the garbage. Linh was different. Her pure soul moved him. She was like the dawn, the moment each day when he forgot life's bitterness, opened his window to admire the whiteness of rose apple blossoms against the azure blue of the sky, when he too shared the refreshing chill of the dew, when life's myriad sounds resonated like birdsong from some faraway mountain gorge. Wave after wave, life's echo would quiver through his body like a tide. He would gasp under its weight. His gaze would blur as a surge of sound spread through his soul, as a dazzling cloud of birds emerged from the fog, their wings silhouetted in the breaking dawn. This melody was distilled in him, and suddenly he had to free himself of its mysterious weight.

Linh saw Tran Phuong sit up. Surprised, she asked him, "What's the matter?"

Tran Phuong gently kissed her forehead. "I'd like to give you a gift."

"No, please," said Linh, "I just want to give you back some of what life has taken from you."

Moved, the composer gazed at her and said, "You're so generous. Since my mother and grandmother died, you're the only one who has loved me like this. You alone."

His eyes clouded over, his face shrouded in sadness.

Time flew by in their silence. A breeze wafted through the window, moist with the earthy scent of the Red River, the cornfields, the mist off the water. A small sailboat bobbed slowly on the dark green current.

"All we have left is a half hour of happiness," Tran Phuong said. "Wait, just a minute. I want us to have a beautiful memento of this day."

He went over to a small table, sat down, and began to write. Note after note fell onto the wavy lines of the musical score. After fifteen minutes, he stood up. "Let's go back. I want to listen to this on the piano," he announced, pale with emotion.

They returned to the city together, forgetting, in their giddy state—he, lost in the intoxication of art, she, proud to love and be loved—that they were adulterous lovers.

They reached Hanoi just as the city lights were flickering out. The courtyard of the Musicians' Union headquarters was scattered with dead leaves. The old guard was eating dinner. Hearing footsteps, he hastily set down his bowl on the tray and got up to open the door to the concert hall. The composer hurried inside, forgetting to thank the man. He sat down at the piano and began to play. The music echoed clearly through space. This was unquestionably the most beautiful song he had written in ten years. The final harmony resonated, then slowly faded. Tran Phuong sat motionless for a long time afterward, then he turned to Linh.

"You are my muse. Thanks to you, I've composed this song."

Linh kept silent.

Tran Phuong approached, dropped to his knees, kissed her feet, her round, tender, child's knees. He closed his eyes, drunk on this marvelous moment. The door opened abruptly, and the old guard entered, bearing tea and two small cups.

"Please have some tea, boss."

Tran Phuong immediately jumped up. "Just leave that, thank you," he snapped, waving his hand imperiously.

Turning back to Linh, his voice suddenly patronizing, he asked, "There. Have you grasped the spirit of the piece?"

Linh stiffened. She had never imagined that he could behave like this with her. She stuttered something inaudible. The composer strode across the room, his head high. "Now remember the spirit of this piece," he said, enunciating each word. "When it comes to art, I can't stand imprecision, or lack of appreciation."

Linh was speechless. Then, Tran Phuong repeated: "Well? Do I need to explain it to you again?"

Linh finally understood that he was acting for the sake of the guard, and replied, "Yes, I understand. I'll remember."

The guard appeared oblivious to what was happening. He continued to methodically wipe the table with a rag that he had taken down from the wall. Then he set a teapot and two cups on the table, poured tea, and shuffled off. When he was out of sight, Tran Phuong moved closer to Linh, put his arm around her shoulder. "Forgive me. That's just the way life is sometimes."

Linh felt a pang of sadness. How could he act so well? There hadn't been a moment of confusion. When he frowned, furrowing those bushy eyebrows, he looked so cruel. A man has many masks; Tran Phuong seemed to wear several at the same time.

"My God, it's already seven forty-five," exclaimed the composer, looking at his watch. They were supposed to go their separate ways at six-thirty. Linh felt anger rise in her. "Go then, just go home."

The composer looked at her, conciliatory. "Don't be angry, I'm worried about you. As for me . . ." He shrugged. "What do I have to lose? I'm already a victim of history."

Linh looked at Tran Phuong with her deep eyes. Once again, she was overcome by compassion. She forgave him in a flash. Whatever had been, he was still the one, the man most worthy of her love and admiration.

AT NINE O'CLOCK the next morning, in the café where Lan had taken Linh, there was only one customer, the man with the old satchel. He was seated, swaying slightly. Lien, the plump little waitress, served him a plate of sausage and a pack of Samit cigarettes.

"Anything more, sir?"

"Thanks, that'll be all."

The man pulled a leather-bound book out of his bag and began to read. He had barely finished two pages when the owner returned, tapping his boots together to shake off the dust from the staircase. The man set down his book and greeted him.

"My God, you're still here?" the owner exclaimed, incredulous.

"Of course, and if I remember correctly, I owe you money."

"No, no, that's not what I mean. I thought you'd left for Canada. They told me your aunt was set on taking you with her, on paying your way."

"That's true."

"And you refused?"

"Of course. If not, would I be here talking with you, in old backwater Hanoi? Come on, friend, how much do I owe you? Get out the accounts."

"Not necessary. My memory is more accurate. Before you left for Saigon, you owed me 3,785 *dong*."

"It's a pleasure to have you as a friend. Without you, folks like me would die for lack of caffeine and nicotine," the man said, taking a wad of bills out of his wallet and tossing it on the table.

The owner took the wad of bills and smiled mischievously. "Why give me so much? There's five thousand *dong* here. Okay, let's say you've got credit. You must have sold a lot of paintings."

"Not at all," the man laughed. "All I did was eat, drink, and gaze at the Dalat countryside. I'll go back in the dry season to do some oil paintings. This is a little salary my aunt gives me."

"She pays you? To do what?"

"Oh, to party to my heart's content before going with her to Canada. She doesn't have kids. My father's the eldest in his family and I'm an only son. So, I'm both chief and the continuation of our entire lineage."

"My, my," the owner said, fingering his mustache. "Now that's a stroke of bad luck to have you as the family headman."

The man laughed too. "Yeah, really bad luck. Do you know how the family in Saigon greeted me, a forty-year-old man, filthy as a toad? I ring the bell. Their old maid opened the door. As soon as she saw me she shouts back to my family assembled in the courtyard, 'Namo Sakyamuni Buddha, come in, come in quickly!' Then, my aunt screams from the fourth floor. My cousins all come running out of their rooms, rush to boil water to wash my face and hands. Then they whip up soup with rice noodles, which they insist I eat with fresh bread. They practically tear off my ragged clothes and shove me into the bath. Hot water, cold water, scented soap—luxuries I hadn't touched for years in the North—are just waiting for me. When I finally emerge from the bathroom, I'm wearing all these fancy clothes they had ready for me. The entire family is ecstatic, as if I had brought them buried treasure, or narrowly escaped death. Then, we sit down to a feast in my honor where my aunt and female cousins stuff me like a goose being fatted for the Dong Xuan Market. They gaze at me tenderly as if I had just been released from prison after years of deprivation. 'Come on, another bite. It's really nourishing. Come on, just a bit more. You have to get your strength back, big brother, then we'll be able to breathe easier.' "

The owner burst out laughing, baring teeth blackened by tobacco. The painter watched him, his eyes twinkling, and continued.

"They made me dress up to go meet the family. As if I were

some rich, affected playboy. But after all their fussing, look at me now."

He stood up, turned around, and modeled himself from all angles. His expensive velvet pants were stained with oil and mud. The white silky shirt looked as if it had been dipped in pale brown dye. He showed his hands—handsome fingers, but yellowed by cigarettes, nails black with dirt. The owner almost choked laughing, tears in his eyes. The painter laughed, stretched out his hand, took a piece of salami, and munched it noisily. He was handsome, or rather, his face was honest, intelligent. But his shaggy hair, tousled beard, and rumpled clothes gave him an eccentric look. After he had recovered from his fit of laughter, the owner glanced at the man's plate of cheap salami and asked, "Why not treat yourself to some pastry? Why eat this teenage junk food?"

"I like it," the painter said, closed his eyes and took a long, hungry drag on his cigarette.

Then, the owner sat down at his side. "Tell me . . . I still don't understand."

"What's that?"

"I was baffled by your refusal to go live in Saigon. Now you refuse to go live in Canada. That's totally incomprehensible. People who can't get permission to go because no one will sponsor them risk their lives on small boats to leave this country. But you act as if it were nothing. The other day, I overheard some psychiatrist and a writer say you painters are often mentally ill."

"Ha, ha, oh the artist isn't far from being crazy. It's possible that I'll go crazy like Van Gogh. But tell me, do you find me crazy?"

"Not yet," the owner replied warmly. The painter's mocking, inquisitive stare made him uncomfortable. His head cocked to the side, the painter puffed on his cigarette and gazed dreamily out at the street. The cedar trees by the window silhouetted his sweet, childlike face. After a moment of silence he turned to the owner and said, "I like you a lot. You know how to treat people right. An ordinary café owner would have gone berserk if he found out I was emigrating, he would have rushed over to the Painters' Union to file a complaint. But you," said the painter, slapping the owner's shoulder, "you're great. You care about values more precious than money. You knew I wasn't the type to forget a debt, right?"

"Yes. My wife made a scene, wanted me to write to Saigon, but I told her to keep quiet. I thought you'd left. For a trip like that, you've got a thousand things to do, and it's easy to forget a small debt."

"Because you trusted me, I'm going to tell you what I think. I wouldn't waste my time talking to anyone else. You know me, I don't care what people think, whether they call me a genius or a bum. I live my life. Drink coffee. Paint. Like the sun rises every morning." He stopped a moment, tossed his cigarette butt into the ashtray, then continued: "Do you know how I've been living the last eighteen years? In a nine-and-a-half-meter garret apartment, with a leaky floor, eaten away by green and white fungus. I eat there, drink there, paint there, bring my models there. That's where I bathe too, where I stay when I'm sick . . . My boss at the Painters' Union is an illiterate jerk. He flunked the qualifying exam for three years straight before he got the degree. In professional terms, he's barely got the talent of a street portraitist or a provincial poster designer. But he was the first painter in our class to become a party member, so he's their man, the one they trust, the one with the power. He knows better than anybody that our icy silences and sarcastic looks mask our contempt. He retaliates with intrigues and investigations, nasty bureaucratic procedures. He can allocate an apartment in no time to some low-level employee. But the best painting teachers have to fawn and flatter and fight each other to get a roof over their heads. He's crushed countless artists, tortured them by reducing them to a constant, exhausting search for housing. In the end, he breaks them, enslaves them. Many just snap, surrender, grovel. Others tire themselves out banging at his door, griping until they get some tiny room, a trip abroad, a corner in some exhibition hall. You remember Huynh?"

"Yeah, the big guy who ordered cold milk because he said he didn't like coffee?"

"He has high blood pressure. He can't have stimulants."

"He hasn't been here recently."

"How could he? He had a cerebral hemorrhage after a run-in with the boss."

"And you? What conflict do you have with the boss? Same as your colleagues?"

"No, I've never cared. I live alone. I don't need things; nothing is worth the struggle. But I can't stand it when others who do struggle are persecuted. I jumped into the fight precisely because of Huynh. The boss penalized me for it. No housing. No trips abroad. Who cares? Once, I was invited abroad, to get some international prize. My boss handed me an invitation five days late. I made a scene. Nothing happens if you don't open your mouth. Tons of people rallied to my cause. He was forced to meet with me, to make a settlement. The bait was an apartment in a new building and a training session in Europe. I refused."

"I remember," said the owner, nodding. "At that time, you and your friends used to come all the time with that toothless old Dao Hung. They say he's chasing some pale young thing named Kim Cuc."

"That's right," the painter said, and continued. "That's when we learned that Saigon had been liberated. Everyone thought it was certain that I would go and settle there. First, I couldn't stand our idiot boss. But also because I wouldn't have money problems. A three-story villa, fourteen rooms all to myself; you can't even dream about that here. But I refused. They called me crazy. In fact I did have other reasons, and they were crazy ones. Now, they ask me: Why not leave for Canada, why waste this godsend? Why, why? Life is full of whys. As many whys as there are human beings. As for me, ninety percent adventurer at heart, why would I refuse a trip to the West, to the other side of the planet? But life is like that, full of contradictions. I've gazed at the clouds on the Truong Son mountain range. I've drunk snake liqueur, eaten grilled cobra with the old men on the Cambodian border. I've fished off Koto Island with the islanders, eaten sticky rice in Laos. Why shouldn't I want to travel abroad? But for twenty years I have been the only painter in the Union who's never filled out a passport form, even for a weeklong conference. The urge to explore, to understand is natural, especially for artists. But for me it's got nothing to do with this lust for material things, for imported foreign goods, for black marketeering or bargaining . . ." He fell silent, glanced distractedly out at the street.

The owner stood up and brought out a small teapot kept warm in a padded tea cozy and two gold-rimmed cups. "Let's have some of this lotus tea I made."

The painter nodded. He emptied his teacup and continued. "If today a politician said to me, 'The state authorizes you to travel, but you'll have just enough for daily meals, and you'll be forbidden to bring back foreign goods,' I'd sign on the dotted line. Money is not as important as people think. Do you know how much I spent in Dalat when my aunt invited me? Forty-five thousand *dong*. That's more than twenty ounces of gold. But the next week, I may be drinking coffee on credit, or eating a five-*dong* bowl of corn from a street stall. Life is a river; it brings riches and poverty, fame and misery. But it's a reality that an artist always carries with him, because every morning, he has to look himself in a mirror, whether it's made of crystal or just a muddy puddle of water. The most important thing, when he sees his face, is being able to answer the question: Who am I? If I left for Canada, I would see this bearded face in some mirror and I would ask that question. What could I reply? Surely, 'You're an employee, a man earning his keep abroad.' Well, if that's it, then why not repair shoes or shovel snow, or even be a secretary or a maid? But not an artist. Why leave the poplars of West Lake and Bac Ninh countryside to paint pine trees in Montreal or Quebec? How could I paint a pine tree when from childhood I've only known banana trees and bamboo groves? No, I couldn't do it, not even out of wanderlust. I could never swap my life for a life outside myself. Why?"

He suddenly clenched his fist and struck the table, making the plates and cups jump. "But why the hell do I have to run off to Canada to avoid that bastard? The country doesn't just belong to those bastards. It belongs to us, all of us."

He stopped speaking, his eyes brimming with tears of rage.

The owner served more tea. "Have another cup." He turned toward the room behind him, and called out, "Lien, bring us some coconut cakes."

"Right away."

"These just arrived," said the owner. "I'm going to treat you to a few before I put them on sale."

The plump young waitress brought out a white porcelain plate piled with little white cakes, as round as the spider's egg–shaped cakes they used to make, dusted with golden coconut shavings and powdered sugar. As the owner and the painter ate in silence, Tran Phuong arrived with Linh. The owner looked up and greeted them.

The composer smiled and nodded back as he led Linh to a table near the window. The painter watched the young woman. His eyes clouded over. He picked up his satchel.

"I've got to be going."

———

LINH HAD TOLD Tran Phuong many times that she didn't want to hide her love.

"I don't want to become some half person. If you still love your wife, you certainly can't love me. Why do we have to hide from the world, like rats in daylight?"

The composer smiled. "You're so innocent. The secrecy of the night has its own charm, its own magic." His eyes closed, masking their black flames. Linh could only dimly sense the disillusionment that lay behind them.

"I can't enjoy stolen pleasure," she cried.

Seeing her anger, Tran Phuong rapidly retreated. "Stay calm, my girl. What can I do? I'm between a rock and a hard place. On the one hand, there is my love for you; on the other, I do feel compassion for my wife. I yearn for the day when we can love each other openly. You're young, you're beautiful, you've got your entire life ahead of you. But what do I have left? I've been cast out of my native territory, had my shirt thrown in the fire. Everything I've tried to build—my youth, the patient effort of an entire life—has evaporated like soap bubbles. I've been robbed. I walk through life with empty hands."

As he murmured these last words, he stretched out his palms. Linh looked at his hands, the long, slender fingers with their complicated wrinkles. She suddenly pitied him, and put her hand in his. Tran Phuong pulled a lock of hair back from his face.

"For many years now, nothing has linked me to that witch. She's an ugly, cunning woman, a spoiled child. But if I divorce her, she's capable of committing suicide. How could you and I live together then, with the pressure of public opinion? A criminal released from prison can go back to normal life. But for us, once we stand before the court of public opinion, we'll never be free."

He paused, rested his chin in the palm of his hand, sullen.

Suddenly Linh felt she was to blame, that she had brought more unhappiness into this man's already sad life, had pushed him into another moral impasse. She should never have demanded that he marry her: Hers was the normal yearning of a normal woman.

But would she always have to resign herself to this secrecy? Humiliating memories haunted her.

They both stayed silent for a long time. Then, Linh asked, "Are we always going to live like this?"

Tran Phuong knelt down, laid his head on her knees. They were in a little room in the suburbs of Hanoi. Outside the window, green dikes stretched in long rows. Sailboats floated by on the Red River, just beyond banks covered with cornfields.

"I'm grateful to you. I know that loving me entails suffering and sacrifice that no woman would freely choose. I've tried to let go, to free you to find a lover worthy of your youth, your beauty, your soul. But I don't have the courage. Forgive me."

In truth, he had never even contemplated a separation. But, as he said this, he was gripped by the fear of losing her. His cheeks burned, his eyes glistened with desire. In their lovemaking, he seemed possessed by a desperate passion. Linh felt herself swept away by this tidal wave, this terrifying love in which Tran Phuong was drowning. She saw herself for what she was, an ordinary schoolteacher among tens of thousands of ordinary schoolteachers; and yet, this talented, famous man loved *her*. She felt proud to be loved. And yet she was ashamed of her pain, the impatience that had pushed her to demand marriage like all the others. She felt petty, cowardly. She embraced Tran Phuong. "Forgive me. I'm just an ordinary woman," she wept.

"No, don't say that."

Tran Phuong clasped Linh in his arms, caressing and consoling her. A wicked flame flickered in the depths of his eyes: *You're mine again, all mine.*

Linh was sincere. She was not looking for an affair with a famous composer, like the other women he had known. She wanted to live a full love, and aspired to a wholesome, happy life. She didn't want to play hide-and-seek in the shadows like other women had, savoring the nervous exhilaration of waiting for him in cafés, in front of an empty restaurant, at an intersection. For these women, it had been the thrill of an affair, the exciting rush of fear mingled with desire.

Tran Phuong hid his smile in Linh's fragrant hair. "I'll always be grateful to you, always." Then, in a soft voice, he continued: "We have to wait. I'm not a brute. As you know, Hoa is sick, mentally and physically. Death will carry her away one day, naturally. Time is a man's best friend. Know that expression?"

Months later, Linh would think of these words. *Horrible. To have to wait for his wife's death. Happiness that depends on someone's death. There is something barbaric in this plan.*

"But there's no other solution with a woman like this, so lacking in dignity."

Finally, her heart imposed its logic; Linh began to believe in her sacrifices, like a pilgrim preparing for the long journey to the Holy Land.

LINH HAD MOVED three times since she packed her bags and left Nguyen. The first night, she had taken a train to the suburbs to stay with another aunt who Huong Ly liked to call "grandmother." The house had three rooms spread over one hundred and five square feet, surrounded by a small garden of about sixty-six square feet filled with basil, licorice mint, and coriander. Her aunt's six children were all married, but only two of them had been able to find housing. The others had stayed with their husbands, wives, and children under the same roof. The little families set up on beds, building separate kingdoms divided by curtains. A slight breeze could lift a curtain, and the couples could only laugh to excuse themselves. In the winter, all you had to do was step from one kingdom to another to play chess or cards. When one of the women grilled corn, you merely had to stretch out an arm from under the curtain and serve yourself from the same basket. This was fun in the winter, but when summer arrived, the heat was unbearable. Linh's cousins all loved her, and understood her unhappiness. But after three days there, Linh had to pack her bags and leave. Then, for a time, she had stayed with a former college friend who had never finished her studies. Instead, the woman had done an intensive secretarial typing course, and after completing it, her uncle found her a job in a scientific research institute. There, a good, gentle doctor fell in love with her, and they were soon married. Two years later, the man left on a research trip abroad. Ever since, he had never stopped traveling, dragging his suitcase around the airports of the world, supervising a friendship delegation or assisting some high-ranking cadre sign a cooperation treaty. The man would jet off without a second thought, leaving his young wife behind to care for their son.

After Linh had stayed with this friend for two days, she realized that she had been fooled; the friend wasn't lonely at all, as she had claimed. On the contrary, she had more than enough trysts to compensate for the emptiness of her marriage. Linh realized, too, that she had been naive, that her happy, comfortable life with Nguyen had sheltered her in a soft cocoon. Now, she saw life's darker, seamier side. She packed her bags and returned to the high school. Kim Anh had told Linh she could stay in the dormitory room of a librarian who was on sick leave, in hospital being treated for cancer of the uterus. Her room was just seven square feet, dark, humid, lit only by the pallid winter light. Linh spent two whole days cleaning and decorating the room. She scrubbed the doors and windows and covered the cement floor with a new reed mat. She bought a pink glass vase for some flowers. The librarian had left behind an electric stove, but Linh had replaced it with a frugal old gas range.

That evening, after the teachers' meeting, the principal paid her a visit. She found the room transformed. A beautiful coverlet was spread over a single bed.

"It looks wonderful!" she said, sitting down on the bed.

Linh had just washed up and was combing her hair. She turned and smiled, her face radiant. Kim Anh studied her attentively. "So, how are things?"

"Fine, is there a problem?" replied Linh, glancing hesitantly at the principal.

Kim Anh shot a look at the shiny pots arranged on the gas stove, the bowls and chopsticks, the pocket mirror, the tiny vase set on the windowsill. These could have been the meager possessions of a young college student. Once a woman married, the pots and pans got bigger, the bowls and plates prettier; there was all the cutlery, hand towels, and utensils needed to cook for a family—the potato peelers, papaya graters, mortars for pounding crabs, the stewing pots and sticky rice steamers. Not to mention the glassware and all the appliances, the electric food processors and ovens that housewives dreamed of. Kim Anh knew that Linh had had all this, that people had envied both her happiness and her material comfort. Now Linh had reverted to the lifestyle of a college student, with a cheap portable stove and crude utensils. Kim Anh was moved.

"Is there a problem?" Linh repeated. She sat down beside the principal. Kim Anh said nothing, just gazed at the fresh flowers.

"My, they're lovely. You like buttercups?"

"Once, no. Now I like them a lot."

She couldn't tell Kim Anh that in Tran Phuong's favorite café, there was always a vase filled with these flowers.

Suddenly Kim Anh sighed. After a long silence, she asked, "Are you happy?"

Linh looked at her, said nothing. How could she answer such a question? She was at once both happy and miserable. Each of her joys masked a feeling of sadness, anger, or humiliation. She would never again know the carefree times of the past, the days when she and Nguyen had been happy.

"You know," said the principal, measuring her words, "if we had applied the rules, the collective should have condemned you a long time ago."

"I know."

"No one has the heart to do it. Not me, none of the people close to you. But we don't understand what has happened."

Linh said nothing.

"Were you swept off your feet by the composer?"

"It was over between Nguyen and me, physically, before I met him."

"So it's Nguyen's fault?"

"I don't know."

"I don't think Nguyen betrayed you. He loves you, he's serious."

"Yes, that's true."

"Why, then? I remember many times you could have fallen for handsome, younger men who were in love with you. Compared to them, Tran Phuong is an old man. Talented he may be, but he's a generation older than you."

"That's not it."

"So, how did you get here? You should at least tell me the truth."

"I thought Nguyen was a man with a noble soul, with self-respect, who lived for his ideals. But little by little, I uncovered horrible lies. I realized I had made a mistake."

"And you hate him?"

"No, not hate. But I don't respect him anymore, and I can't love someone I don't respect."

"Does Nguyen know this?"

"Yes."

"He says nothing?"

"He wants me to stay, for Huong Ly, but I can't."

"I understand. But Tran Phuong, what kind of man is he, really?"

"He's an artist, a talented man who's been unfairly persecuted. I'm prepared to sacrifice a lot to share the unhappiness he has to bear."

Kim Anh remained seated, silent, for a long time. Then she rose, opened the corner of an aluminum box sitting in the corner of the room.

"You still haven't bought rice?"

"No, I'll get some bread tonight. Will you join me?"

Kim Anh shook her head, and pulled an envelope out of her pocket. "Here, this is a bonus I just got. You probably don't have any money left. Please use it for the groceries." She looked once more over the room. "I've got to be going." She walked out into the school courtyard, awash in eerie, flickering shadows.

If I suddenly discovered some baseness in my husband—lies, cowardice, infidelity—and I could no longer live with him, everything would crumble. I would have to start over, from nothing. Kim Anh shuddered thinking of the crystal glasses from Germany, the living room, the tea service she had just bought, the porcelain sugar bowl with its top in the shape of a grapevine, the electric food processor. All these objects would disappear and with them not only their material value, but also the peaceful, happy family life she had built, the foundations of her happiness.

And what if I had irrefutable proof that my husband were a bastard, would I have the stomach to continue to live with him? No,

*certainly not. Luxury goods would have no meaning. I'd have to find
a hole like this to take refuge, cooking off a cheap, tin range. Without
love, it's better to abandon kingdom and castle for the simple life of
the poor. History is filled with such stories. But these are legends.
People today are too pragmatic; we calculate and weigh love according
to life's circumstances.*

These thoughts raced through Kim Anh's mind. When she
stopped in front of the familiar door to her house, she heard
her son call out: "Papa, Mama's back. Quick, we can eat now."

The woman dropped her thoughts. Her husband came out
of their house and helped her put away her bicycle.

"What happened to you, we've been waiting for you for a
long time," he asked, an affectionate smile lighting his face.

No, he's no womanizer. She composed herself like someone
who had just set foot on terra firma after a rocky boat ride. Joy
overcame her, sweeping aside her anxiety. She hugged her husband to her.

"What happened?" her husband asked again, worried.

"I was almost run over by a car," Kim Anh said hastily, as
naturally as if she had really just avoided an accident. The husband squeezed his wife's hand. They gazed at each other
fondly, as if lucky to have escaped disaster. All they had to do
was imagine losing each other to feel their bones go cold.

AFTER KIM ANH'S DEPARTURE, Linh nibbled a bit of bread
with salt, drank a glass of sugar water, and crawled into bed.
She couldn't sleep. At first she thought it was because she
wasn't used to this new room. She had never lived alone. Even
though it was small, the room seemed empty and desolate.
Linh began to feel the immensity of her solitude. She didn't
have to worry about anyone and no one was worrying about
her. There were only objects here. Even the flowers on the
windowsill seemed cold and unfeeling. Roaches from the library crawled slowly up the walls. A small black lizard chased

mosquitoes around a bare lightbulb, the dry click-click of its tongue echoing through the room. Linh picked up a copy of Victor Hugo's *The Hunchback of Notre Dame*, opened it, and began to read. But the letters swam in front of her eyes. Mechanically, she reached out her arm, but it fell onto the mat; Huong Ly wasn't there. She dropped the novel down on the table, pulled the covers up over her arms. But this didn't stem the tide of homesickness that washed over her. The reed mat on the bed felt cold and rough to the touch. She remembered Huong Ly's warmth, her sweet smell, the familiar joy of living that had soothed her soul, day in and day out. The little girl liked to sleep with her legs wrapped around her mother's stomach, her head burrowed in Linh's armpit.

Now, nothing. No chattering, no silly questions, not even the naughty words that Huong Ly had learned that day. While Linh searched for an apartment, all the worries and calculations needed to get by had exhausted her, numbed her pain. But now, just when she had finally created a small space for herself, the homesickness flooded back, tearing at her mother's heart. Linh lay motionless, silent. Tears trickled down her temples. The pain was unbearable; she sat up and hugged her knees to her chest. She felt exposed, bathed in the harsh, tawdry light of the room.

What is my little girl doing now?

Linh imagined the old room where, between four walls, her happiness had dissolved like smoke. Huong Ly was living there with Nguyen. He had probably just bathed her and changed her clothes. The two were probably sitting down to dinner. Or had he taken her to a restaurant for a *pho*? Or were they chatting on the bed? Maybe Nguyen was translating documents. These were the images that formed in her lonely mind. Naturally, Huong Ly loved her father. Nguyen had always been an affectionate, loving father. But he was a man; he couldn't provide the warm tenderness that a mother could. In the end, it was their little girl who was suffering for this. When she missed her mother, she couldn't light a cigarette or drink a few glasses of alcohol to dull the pain. All she could do was watch other children and silently envy them. Or call out to her mother in her sleep. Linh choked back sobs at the thought. But the tears streamed down her cheeks and trickled hot and salty over her lips. She got up, washed her face, threw on a coat, and, without really thinking, went outside and mounted her bicycle. Some instinct pushed her to flee the chill sadness of this room.

The streets were deserted. Here and there, in the shadows of the trees, Linh saw couples embracing. Her forehead burned, yet her cheeks felt icy. A vague, floating sensation came over her, as if she were walking a plank suspended above a chasm on a windy night. At the other end, she could see a tiny halo of warm, tender light, a child's face.

The clock at Miss Tong's chimed ten times as Linh mounted the stairs. She stopped in front of the door to their apartment. A pale blue light filtered through, the light that Nguyen read by at night. Huong Ly must have been asleep. Linh suddenly realized the humiliating situation she was in. *Just to hold her in my arms. If I could just see her, take her with me.* But she didn't dare ask Nguyen. He was lonelier and more unhappy than she was; he was the one raising their daughter alone. He was the one who waited in silence, gritting his teeth in pain, clinging to the dimmest of hopes that her affair would end. In her heart, Linh knew that he was the loser.

Linh inadvertently bumped into the door with a thud. She jumped back, her heart beating fast. Inside, Nguyen looked up from his reading and walked slowly toward the door.

"Who is it?" he asked softly, surprised by such a late visit. He stopped abruptly when he saw Linh's face.

"Is Huong Ly . . . ?" Linh stammered.

Nguyen opened the door wide. With a nudge of his shoulder, he pushed Linh into the room. He closed the door, his back to her, as if he wanted to lock her in that room forever. Linh rushed to the bed, losing all control of herself. "Huong Ly, sweetheart, my little girl, my darling."

Like a madwoman she covered the child's face with kisses, holding Huong Ly so tightly that she woke up. Neither sleepy nor surprised, the little girl sat up and broke into a smile. "Oh, Mama, it's you, where did you go for so long? Give me your cheek. It's my turn to give a kiss. You're all wet. Did you just wash your face? Grandma told me you should never take a bath at night. Come sleep with me. Tomorrow I've got to get up early to go to school."

Linh couldn't speak. She was beside herself. She hugged the little girl to her passionately. "I'll take you with me, whatever happens, I'll take you with me," she cried, as if in a dream.

Nguyen, still standing by the door, moved slowly toward her. He put a hand on her shoulder. "Quiet, Linh, it's late."

Linh suddenly composed herself. She looked at him, her eyes brimming with tears: "I can't live without her, I have to take her with me."

Huong Ly sat up and looked at her two parents with her intelligent eyes. She murmured, "Papa, can I go for a walk with Mama? I'll bring her back to the house next Sunday."

Nguyen tucked his daughter back under the covers. "Sleep, my girl."

Then he sat down on the edge of the bed next to Linh. A lizard, somewhere in the branches of the tree by the window, clucked its tongue. Never had this sound echoed as loudly, as sadly for him. Nguyen turned, gazed intensely at his wife for a moment, then said, "Okay, take her with you."

7

LAN WAS THE FIRST to detect the unhappiness in Nguyen's family. From the moment she had introduced her niece to Tran Phuong, she could predict, in the shadowy, bewitching gaze of her former lover, the events that would follow. She had once warned Nguyen of the dangers that lurked for every couple. He had understood, but he had never anticipated the speed at which this man would win Linh's heart. A love can die slowly, painfully, or, when another love presents itself, be ruthlessly and rapidly snuffed out. Lan knew this from experience. She understood her niece. She also felt remorse as she was partly responsible for their first meeting.

One morning, Lan went to find Tran Phuong. "I'm inviting you for coffee, okay?"

Tran Phuong replied with a gentle, silent smile. They entered a small bar near the intersection. Ngoc Minh was chatting with an old man with legs as thin as copper piping. Her square face was covered with thick orange base makeup, her eyebrows traced with black pencil. Seeing Tran Phuong enter, Ngoc Minh and her companion turned around and noisily greeted the famous man. The vulgar, affected familiarity of their behavior made Lan smile.

"You'd better hide in a corner, otherwise that pretty journalist is going to turn you into a clown for everyone to gape at."

The composer squeezed into a secluded corner, behind a clove tree. In a hesitant voice, he tried to explain himself, "Please understand, Lan, I didn't go looking for this."

Lan said nothing, then ordered two coffees and offered him a cigarette. Tran Phuong remained silent, so she started to reminisce: "I remember how you used to wear a brown leather cap. In the summer, it was white shirts. I knit you a gray wool sweater, with a boat-neck collar, remember?"

"Uh, sorry, Lan," Tran Phuong stammered. "I, I gave it to a friend and they stole his suitcase."

Lan chuckled. "That was no friend. It was your wife's little brother, Tu, the gardener. He requested early retirement to go into the nursery business, in Buoi village. Well, I've been there a few times to buy plants and I recognized the sweater on him." She squinted mischievously.

Tran Phuong puffed away furiously at his cigarette, feigning indifference. Lan looked him right in the eye and hardened her tone: "Spare Linh, will you?"

The man looked up. "What do you mean?"

"Leave my niece alone," she said, her voice cracking. She slapped Tran Phuong's hand, a vulgar gesture that clashed with her elegant, dignified bearing.

"Stop acting. My niece is still a girl. She lost her father early on. Leave her alone. Or do I have to beg you?"

"Oh, you exaggerate, Lan," Tran Phuong chuckled, softly, naturally. "Linh is no Young Pioneer with a red scarf anymore, she's a young woman."

"No one rivals you when it comes to seducing women," said Lan bitterly.

Tran Phuong shrugged and sighed. "Is that my fault?"

Lan glared at him. "Your vows are as numerous as seashells, as light as the wind."

The composer shrugged his shoulders again, saying nothing. His sweet, innocent act exasperated Lan.

"Don't force me to say too much. Linh is as naive as her parents. She has always led a happy, peaceful life. Let her go."

Tran Phuong closed his eyes, and said in a slow voice: "Don't be angry. I am always grateful to the women who have loved me, even if it didn't last . . . I remember"—he lowered his voice—"the sweet days of tenderness you gave me, Lan. The years go by but I still shiver at the memory of what we once shared . . ."

Lan stared at him, furious. *You bastard.* The cry went through her mind, but she couldn't utter it. Tran Phuong placed a hand on the shoulder of his old mistress.

"Let's go home, Lan. I'd like to play something for you, some of the music you used to like."

"No, no," Lan refused weakly. Tran Phuong settled the bill and got up to leave.

Why listen to him? He's so clever, so calculating.

But she followed him like a zombie. They passed an old tree and Lan tripped over a root. "Careful, Lan," Tran Phuong cried out. She didn't reply, straining to contain some long pent emotion that threatened to surge forth. They crossed the octagonal courtyard of the Musicians' Union, mounted the stone staircase, and started down the corridor that led to the second floor. In the narrow stairwell, Lan could hear Tran Phuong's breathing; she saw the wrinkles at the corners of his eyes. Her emotions swirled inside her as she climbed the steps. Tran Phuong stopped in front of the door to the concert hall.

"Watch the steps. Give me your hand, a lot of people have

fallen here." He squeezed Lan's hand and pushed open a bi ken door held together with a few planks of wood. This thoughtful gesture stirred the memory of an entire world for her, a previous life of passion and romance.

Two secretaries poring over accounts quickly piled up eir documents and carried them hastily outside, making way for the composer. With an affectionate wave, Tran Phuong invited Lan to sit next to him on the piano bench. He started to play a sonata by Enrico Tosselli. It had been Lan's favorite piece when they were young and in love.

Lan left for home at three o'clock that afternoon. She reentered her life, her reality, when she plunged back into the bustling streets of Hanoi. Near the door to her house, under a canopy of linden trees, a young girl, about fifteen years old, was singing to herself. Entering the courtyard, Lan saw her husband pulling out on his Mobylette.

"Hi Lan, there's a letter for you under the flower vase." He nodded and drove off. They had lived together for seventeen years after her affair with Tran Phuong, but he had never forgiven her. He was brought up in an upper-class family and considered fidelity a sacred virtue. But he didn't want a divorce; he felt sorry for the children and was afraid of what people might say. He both loved and hated her.

Lan picked up the letter and opened it. It was from a friend in Saigon. A few polite inquiries about her health, the mundane details of daily life. *Boring.* Lan tossed the letter in a wastebasket in the corner of the room and collapsed on the bed. *Another wasted day. He charmed me again. And I fell for it.*

But the memory of Tran Phuong's face, the clear, rapturous notes of the piano, no longer worked their magic. Now she only felt rage.

IT HAD BEEN RAINING from dawn to dusk. A grimy, monotonous drizzle, the worst they had had in years. Gutters overflowed with dead leaves and garbage. Street sweepers, wrapped in their raincoats, their conical bamboo hats perched low on their heads, swept in silence, piling trash into wheelbarrows. They toiled for hours like that in the rain. From time to time, a rosy-cheeked teenager pedaled proudly down the sidewalk, oblivious, her hair matted to her face, wet clothes clinging to her lithesome body.

Four customers huddled under the drink stand where Nguyen had taken refuge from the rain. Nguyen, another man, an older couple, lovers. The man looked about forty; the woman was the same age. They sat across from each other at a small table. Two servings of rice pudding that had gone cold sat next to a plate of sweet bean paste candies. The couple stared at each other adoringly, oblivious to Nguyen's presence. The old woman who owned the stand was pounding lime in a copper mortar to mix with her betel nut.

"The rain. So sad," she said. Nguyen realized she felt like chatting with him.

"Yes it is," he replied. "This year the spring rain is dragging on."

"When I was little," the old woman mused, "in weather like this, the young girls would grill green paddy rice and fry sweet potato fritters."

She popped a roll of betel in her mouth and stared out at the street, lost in thoughts of her childhood. Nguyen had stopped listening to her, captivated by the conversation between the older couple.

"That's what he told me," said the woman, after whispering in the man's ear. She furtively wiped back her tears. Blue veins pulsed on her thin neck. The man stared at these veins. The woman turned away, her eyes red, shameful.

"Are you still taking those antibiotics?" the man asked gently.

"Yes, but it's getting harder and harder to find them."

They remained silent for a long time, their eyes anchored to each other like the roots of plants in salty earth. Their eyes still burned with the turbulent passion of youth, and even more, with the pain of some tragedy. The woman was not beautiful—average body, ordinary face, no particularly attractive features. And yet there was something poignant and genuine about her that inspired sympathy. She was dressed simply, her weary face only lightly made-up. Her eyes were darting, fearful, her gestures hesitant and humble. She wore an old wristwatch with a worn leather band, a blouse with a threadbare collar, and an old-fashioned, worn-out pair of slacks.

"Did you finish that packet of ginseng I brought you the other day?"

"Not yet."

"I go to Haiphong this Friday, I'll ask sister Hau to buy you some antibiotics."

"No, please don't go to the trouble." The woman fell silent and lowered her head. "If only I had . . . that day . . ."

The man interrupted her: "Don't say anything more. It was my fault. One day, it's certain, you and I, we'll . . ."

They looked at each other, and in an instant, their eyes spoke what words could never express. Regret, remorse, a love that rose from the ashes of the past, promises of a future salvaged from a marsh of lost opportunities. Nguyen once thought that love's tragedies were reserved for an elite, people with complicated feelings, lofty ambitions. Now, he knew that he was wrong. Love's misery haunted everyone. People always seemed to be chasing after their other half. They fell in love, succumbed, woke up, made a mistake, stopped to analyze their errors, then fell in love all over again. What mysterious, invisible hand had shuffled the cards of love before dealing them? So that's how the games went, like Chinese chess—the red chariot was linked to the black elephant, the red pawn to the black mandarin. An elephant would always spurn a chariot, a mandarin would always turn his back to a pawn.

The lovers got up and put on their raincoats. As they left the stand, the rain fell, slanting, on their shoulders. He wore an old army-issue slicker, she a gray raincoat. These people were not privileged. A pawn simply in search of another pawn. And yet this was the real path of love. Their shadows faded in the distance, vanishing at the intersection.

Nguyen recalled the images from the science fiction film he had just seen. On a desolate, destroyed planet, blind men wandered in a thick, greenish fog, groping for their way. Maybe this was how it was for people in search of love? Perhaps Linh was like them. She would stumble, fall, suffer. And maybe, one day, she would agree to a date with him at a soda stand, just like old times. Would he look at her the way the man who had just left gazed at his old sweetheart?

Whatever happens, I still love her.

A few minutes later, Nguyen was calmer. He must be crazy; he and Linh had nothing in common with those lovers. A facile comparison, unfounded. But he missed Linh desperately; he could almost whiff the delicate fragrance of her hair. He remembered her firm thighs, her full hips under her canary yellow pants. Nguyen suddenly remembered every detail clearly. He couldn't control himself: He had to see her. He threw on his raincoat and hat, paid, and took his bicycle and pedaled toward the high school. On the way, he told himself that he'd get down on his knees, beg her to come back, and explain that there were certain situations in which a man wasn't free. She would understand, forgive him, love him again. No, nothing was as precious to a man as real happiness. He had held it in the palm of his hand, and had let it slip away. Now he had to find it again, even if he had to dive deep.

Nguyen found the gate to the library padlocked. Linh had gone out. He stood there for a long time, staring at the gate, disoriented, the rain pouring down the windowpanes. Slowly, he turned and left, pushing the bicycle ahead of him.

THEY WERE JUST A FEW YARDS AWAY from the Chu Dong Tu Temple, but Hoa ordered the driver to stop. "The countryside is magnificent. I've never seen such gorgeous hibiscus. Just look at that hedge."

She was awed by the beauty of the countryside. The car stopped right in the middle of the street leading to the village. On both sides, within hand's reach, were rows of hibiscus and chrysanthemums. The driver, accustomed to the woman's whims, left the car, leaned back into a bush of chrysanthemums, and lit a cigarette. Seated in the car, exasperated, Tran Phuong watched his wife. She tiptoed between the flowered hedges, followed by a gaggle of village kids. Curious, the kids gaped at the visitor from Hanoi, a fifty-something woman in jeans, a white sweater, and a wig of shoulder-length curls. Two strokes of brown pencil extended the arch of her eyebrows to her temples. Eye shadow as fluorescent as a firefly's wings was spread over her lids.

"My god, she has green eyes, like a cat's."

"That's beauty, silly."

"Maybe, but it's scary to look at."

The children commented brazenly.

"Hoa," said her husband. She turned around, hands on her hips. She cast one last look at the countryside.

"It's really romantic here."

Tran Phuong said nothing. He grimaced and called the driver. The man looked at the composer's tanned face and silently slid back into his seat. He had been their chauffeur for seven years. When Tran Phuong still had a high-ranking post, he had driven the white Moscovic reserved for the composer, not this old blue Lada. He knew the couple's behavior, their way of repressing anger to avoid fighting in front of others.

"The countryside here reminds me of the poetry of Nguyen Binh."

"Mmm."

"Remember the poems you used to recite to me around the time we were married? What was that poem called? *'Flowers bloom in the lemon tree grove; we are with our ancestors, the country folk.'* And then how does it go, sweetheart?"

"Mmm."

Hoa turned and looked at her husband. He seemed lost in his thoughts; his gaze floated, wandering toward another land. She cried out, "What are you thinking about?"

"Mmm."

The car stopped. They all got out onto the brick road and walked toward the three buildings that composed the temple. The chauffeur, sensing a storm coming, disappeared into the vast buildings that welcomed tourists from all over. Hoa grabbed Tran Phuong's shirt. "Stop. Answer me first. What were you thinking about so intently that you don't even hear what I say?"

Tran Phuong suddenly came to his senses. He lowered his head and looked at his wife's hand gripping his shirt, her eyes flashing under the artificial curve of her eyebrows. He felt he could strangle her, push her in the river that flowed past the temple and then flee into hell to end this disastrous marriage. Unable to contain himself, he raised his tone. "You think you can control my thoughts?"

"I'm your wife," she snapped back. "Husband and wife belong totally to each other. I have the *right* to know your thoughts."

She screamed out of habit. Instantly, he became accommodating; he explained, consoled, restored her self-confidence. At the end of these quarrels, he would always tell her that he loved her, that nothing was more important than fidelity, constancy. But this time, Tran Phuong looked at her with indifference.

"And what if I was thinking about another woman? What would you do?"

Hoa was totally unprepared for such a strange reply. She stopped in her tracks, stunned. Tran Phuong continued calmly: "What if I was thinking about a beautiful young woman?"

Hoa kicked the brick road violently with her foot. "You have no right . . . you have no right."

Tran Phuong continued in a cold, detached voice: "Don't forget. A man's love for a woman isn't protected by law. There's only one rule: Seduction maintains love. As long as one remains capable of seducing, one will be loved."

Hoa was dumbfounded. In the past, her husband had always yielded to her tantrums, appeased her. He had never been so cruel. Satisfied, Tran Phuong noted the terror in his wife's eyes, her contorted face. The fake brown lines that replaced her eyebrows were repulsive, glistening with sweat. Tran Phuong felt the urge to torture her well up inside him.

"What do you have left to seduce me with? Your beauty? Your virtue? Buddha himself would go crazy living with you, let alone a mere mortal."

Hoa stepped back, seeing the disgust in her husband's gaze. She realized that she was nothing to him but a rusty old Tu Duc coin, a worthless currency. For all her expensive clothes and jewelry, she was nothing but a beautified corpse. For a long time she had believed that, aside from her political connections, her fierce loyalty and fancy clothes would work their charm on Tran Phuong, would make him love her.

Tran Phuong looked at his wife's dull eyes. He yearned to humiliate her, to crush her underfoot. In the interminable charade of their life together, he had been trained to feign submission. But his submission had always been that of an animal hunted down and cornered, forced to heel, to wait, to lurk. Now, the beast had reared up and put out its claws, snarling.

"So, you've shut up? Normally you speak like a machine gun. Say it, what are you counting on to conquer my love?"

Tran Phuong grinned, revealing his white teeth. Hoa choked, unable to speak. She stood motionless, stunned by the amazing youth of those teeth that had forced her into the mud. For twenty years, she had loved him. Now she saw that she had been no more than his slave. She had suspected affairs, but Tran Phuong's cajoling words and her own pride had prevented her from admitting the truth. She had put on makeup, had done everything to appear intelligent and cultured, to keep him. Every time she threw a tantrum, he would come up with explanations, tell her she was the only woman who had his respect, his trust, his love. She looked at him, desperate, scrambling for reasons that would make him change his mind.

"If only I had known, I wouldn't have . . ." She was seized by regret. That morning, Tran Phuong had urged her to go see a friend of her father, a war hero who had died heroically, to seek his help in reinstating the composer to his former position. Tran Phuong had paid Luu a visit the previous week. Everything had gone well. All that was left was this one last visit. But, before going, she wanted to show him she knew how to appreciate cultural monuments, the beauty of nature, and she had forced him to come here.

"If I had known . . ."

She had fooled herself. Her eyes swam with tears; they spilled onto her powdered face and spread in blotchy patches. She looked at her husband with red, lost eyes. Once a fearless traveling saleswoman who went from jungle village to village, she didn't know how to defend herself against this kind of danger. She sobbed like a child. Tran Phuong looked again at his wife and his hatred subsided. Suddenly, he pitied her. He tried to lower the tone. "Don't cry. You're going to be the laughingstock of these people. Calm down."

His cajoling voice only hurt her more, and she wept violently. Half amused, half irritated, Tran Phuong put his hand on her shoulder and said in a soft voice: "You're so silly, why do you humiliate yourself for no reason? We're not twenty years old anymore, we're too old to be dreaming about love. As for me, I'm sick with worries."

He hit the target. Hoa stopped sniffling. Tran Phuong knew her superficial, capricious nature. He continued in a sterner voice: "You should support me. Stop persecuting me."

Repentant, she looked at her husband in silence. She realized she was entirely to blame; she had provoked his anger for no reason, failed in her wifely duty to share his burden. She took his hand timidly. "Forgive me, please forgive me."

Tran Phuong said nothing. His eyes froze like two shards of glass. Hoa moved behind her husband's back, toward the nearest house, to ask for a bit of well water to wash her face. She then sat down under a hedge to freshen her makeup. Fifteen minutes later, they entered the temple. Hoa began babbling away on a hodgepodge of subjects: politics, poetry, proverbs, events in several African countries, everything that her dull, chaotic mind had been able to pick up. Tran Phuong kept silent. He glanced at his watch and reminded her: "We only have a half hour left."

They returned to Hanoi before nightfall, then went out to eat. On the road home, as the streetlights blinked on, Hoa asked the chauffeur to drop her off; she wanted to visit her "uncle," a friend of her father's who had always adored her. Who would not cherish the daughter of a friend who had shared dark years of prison and torture? The man had even reportedly told his wife and four children: "I love you as my children, but Hoa has my deepest affection." His family was secretly jealous of the favors he lavished on her, but no one dared complain.

"Take your scarf, it'll be cold on the way back," Tran Phuong said to his wife, as they dropped her off. If, at that moment, she had turned around, she would have seen in his eyes an indescribable flame. But she was busy fussing with a button on her shirt. "I have it in my bag," she replied curtly.

The car door slammed shut. The Lada rolled toward the gate. In just a few minutes they arrived at Tran Phuong's apartment. The composer climbed the stairs and opened the door. Through the open windows, he saw tiny stars mixed with the city lights. The shivering black silhouette of the trees, the scent of hyacinths wafting in the mounting wind. A peaceful atmosphere. But his head spun with contradictory thoughts, like cars racing each other in the chaotic crisscross of headlights. He touched his forehead; it was as hot as if he had a fever. He drank a glass of cold water to try to calm himself. Troubled thoughts swirled in his mind.

How could I have fallen so low? There is nothing to be so upset about.

He paced about the room, cursing himself under his breath.

Fame is the biggest of all life's illusions. It's not the gold at the bottom of the deepest mine, or the salt in the sea, or the rice on the plains . . . Now where did I read that? In some Latin American novel, no doubt.

But entirely different thoughts competed with these in the composer's brain. *Success, failure, success, failure. Once, I used to try to predict a love like this, counting off the petals of daisies. Now I divine fame by counting my footsteps. Twenty, twenty-two, twenty-four, that's success. Twenty-five, twenty-seven, that's failure.*

His heart pounded. He poured himself another glass of water, emptied it in one gulp and strode quickly toward the piano.

La, si, do. His fingers fluttered up a scale in *la* major. The notes poured forth like pebbles from a bag, rolling as if down a steep hill.

This do sharp is a bit soft. I'll have to ask Hoang to come tighten the strings.

Tran Phuong tried to concentrate on the music. But his body went limp. He gasped for air, his head heavy, weighing on his neck and weary shoulders. He lay down on his bed and drifted off immediately. At about nine o'clock, he woke up, washed his face, and sat down again at the piano. This time, sounds pulled him out of his obsession with success or failure. He opened his notebook to the piece he had just composed for Linh.

That girl has saved me.

Linh's sweet face surfaced in his memory, as if from a valley drenched in fog. He pounded each note. The sounds opened the door to that intimate, golden space where he and Linh were happy. Notes followed and linked up with each other. A tide of tender memories transported the composer, his soul rising pure and free.

Just then, Hoa returned. "I knew it, my uncle really adores us. He said you have nothing to worry about."

Tran Phuong sat motionless, silent: the final flower petal of his fate had just fallen. He had won. The white Moscovic slid through the courtyard, carrying away the bitterness that had tortured him, haunted him for all those years. He turned to her. "Thank you, darling."

Hoa laughed, happy. "My uncle told me to stay and have a chat with him, but I didn't want to keep you waiting."

She glanced at Tran Phuong's score. "What are you playing?"

"I just composed a new piece . . ." Tran Phuong replied; then, an idea, still unformed, tumbled out in words: ". . . for you."

"Marvelous," Hoa exclaimed, running over to her husband. "Play it for me."

Tran Phuong turned his head away, smiling, and began to pound the keys of the piano. In a mirror suspended from the door, he looked up to see his own grin, his white teeth glistening.

8

L INH WOULD ALWAYS REMEMBER the fogs of her childhood. How the dawn light rose above the murky
swamps, the stillness of the air, the thin, reedy sounds
of solitude. Fog roaming over the earth like smoke. Why had
her mother died so young, abandoned her like this? She would
never understand, never be able to forgive her. When she died,
Linh's life had become empty and desolate overnight.

"Come sit by me, my girl." Her father would always call
for her like this, his voice hoarse from alcohol. He had loved
his wife too much, leaving no space in his heart for Linh. He
too had abandoned his daughter to follow his wife into the
shadows. These disparate, fragile memories were now gathered, joined, illuminated by the light of the present, by the
power of her love for Tran Phuong. This life experience revived
the past. Vague feelings once shrouded in fog now took shape.
All the tangled, confused emotions that had haunted her as a
child, that she had never understood clearly, suddenly formed
into mature thoughts and passions that beckoned to her. She
remembered the fiery dawns of her girlhood; the magical,

golden sunsets that used to dust the rice fields and their garden. How her father had remained, silent at his wife's side.
Linh's mother had always been busy with her hands—with a
sweater to knit, a sock to darn, or dough to knead for vegetar-
ian buns. And her father had always just sat there, motionless,
like a shadow. At the time, Linh had thought it strange. Now,
she understood the passion that had given him that strange
intensity. Now, Linh too could sit for hours by Tran Phuong's
side, day in and day out, happily contemplating his sad, black
eyes, or stroking the wrinkles at his temples. Love was like that;
it gave the beloved an aura of mystery, a poignancy rooted only
in the shadows of the mind. And there was love's endless questioning, its irresistible attraction, its infinite mystery.

Autumn had arrived. After the long summer rains, the
leaves of the trees on both sides of the street had turned a
silvery gray. The first dead leaves fell in drifts of gray-green,
speckled yellow, and rust. Young girls just old enough to dress
up were the first to mark the change of season. Blouses
trimmed with lace, T-shirts with the names of rock groups,
Abba, Bonney . . . vanished and were replaced with sweaters.
Old people strolled down the streets, gazing wearily at the
trees, hearing in their green murmur the muffled passing of
time, the implacable silence of age. Now and then, gusts of
wind whistled over the rooftops. It wasn't yet time for the oppressive autumn clouds, but the vivid colors of summer had
already faded. Time shuttled between a youthful passion that
had barely spent itself and the gloomy solitude of old age yet
to come.

The painter strolled down the street. He spotted her, the
woman who seemed to have disappeared since their last encounter. She was walking toward a store on the opposite sidewalk with a little girl.

That must be her niece. He crossed the street and silently followed them. In profile, Linh's face still seemed unusually beau-

tiful to him—but a beauty different from the one he had noticed in the café. Linh stopped in front of a soda stand.

"Buy me some cakes, Mommy," said the little girl.

My God, that's her daughter. She's already a woman.

Linh fumbled in her pockets. "Next time, sweetheart, I don't have any money on me."

"Yes you do, in your pocket. I want some cakes, you have money in your pocket."

"That's for vegetables. Tomorrow. Tomorrow I'll buy you some cakes."

Huong Ly started whimpering, ready to burst into tears. Linh hugged her. "Okay, I'll buy some for you."

The painter admired the nape of Linh's neck as she turned toward the street vendor. Her hair, pulled up in a chignon, revealed ivory skin covered with tender down. The vendor, an old man with a stern face, turned toward his merchandise. The little girl stood on tiptoe, watching the vendor as he handed a bag to her mother.

"Mama, why do you buy so few today?"

Linh used to buy half a dozen cakes for her daughter. The little girl didn't understand what was happening to her family. But her child's mind was troubled by the disruptions to her daily routines. Once, her mommy and daddy had lived together; now, she only saw them separately. Once the box of candies at home had always been full; now, the box of sweets had only a few pieces of sesame nougat or a few packets of green *chè*. Her mother doesn't smile anymore, like she used to. There was less fish and meat at meals. And her mother never ate any; she left everything for Huong Ly. The little girl sensed that something was very wrong, but she couldn't understand.

"Give it to me, Mommy," Huong Ly said, stamping her feet. She grabbed a cake, gobbled it down. Linh looked at her daughter, her throat tight. Lately, she had learned to calculate every *dong*. Out of pride, she refused the money Nguyen had tried to give her through Lan or Kim Anh. Tainted money, she thought. And yet, slowly but surely, this young woman obsessed with the purity of her noble ideals had been humbled by the privations of poverty and material need. After she finished her day job teaching, she did filing for a library, even knit clothes to make ends meet. But these jobs earned her only a meager income. Her face had become gaunt, her eyes large, oddly luminous. On the days when Huong Ly lived with her, she had to go without food so that her daughter wouldn't be too unhappy.

"Mama, the cake is too little. Buy me another one."

Huong Ly swallowed half of the cake, then went right back to stare hungrily at the display case.

"Tomorrow, I'll buy you one. Tomorrow. Let's go home now," said Linh abruptly. She picked up the little girl again and hurried away, afraid of humiliation if they stood in front of the window any longer. As she crossed the street, Linh suddenly recognized the man with the scraggly beard she had seen several times at the café. She detected sympathy in his gaze.

Huong Ly had become too heavy for Linh to carry in her thin, frail arms. She put her down to catch her breath, even before she reached the intersection, and stood there, resting for a few minutes. The painter still followed behind them. Linh picked up her daughter again and headed off. When they reached the gate to the high school, she saw things spinning, silvery patches, black inkspots, first dazzling sparkles then shadows. Fireflies danced in the air, like flashes of lightning. The flame tree in front of the offices seemed to race into the distance, like some gaudy, hunchbacked clown. The ground in the courtyard rippled, then bent like rubber under her feet.

"Mamaaaaa!"

Linh heard her daughter scream. Distant tears echoed in her ears. Inky black waves rose in crests, submerging streets, rivers, lakes, fields, everything sank under cold, icy water. Haunting music played softly, echoing through this surreal, black ocean, resonating above everything, the infinity of the universe, there where human dreams mingled with the suffering they had borne in life.

"Darling, I'm dying."

From the other side of the black tidal wave, Tran Phuong replied: "You'll never die. My love will save you."

How many times had he promised that?

When Linh's students, playing in the nearby courtyard, heard Huong Ly's scream, they rushed over and carried their teacher inside. Kim Anh, working there with the math teachers, took Linh in her arms and laid her on a table. The girl students burst into tears, while the boys kept their distance. A teacher, who had run off to call the nurse, returned, out of breath: "Miss Khuyen is on her way. It's lucky she's here."

The nurse arrived with medication that she had just bought, and put her package down on a chair. "Give her room to breathe. Move away." The students moved out of the room. The nurse pulled a bottle of alcohol out of her first aid kit, poured it over the syringe box, and ignited it with a match to sterilize it. Her gestures were rapid and precise. Kim Anh touched Linh's nose and asked: "Is it serious, Khuyen?"

The nurse shook her head. "No, nothing serious. A shot of this glucose should revive her." She pulled the syringe and the needle out of the blue flame, broke a glass vial, and sucked the contents into her syringe. All eyes were on her hands. She turned to a teacher at her side, "Squeeze her arm so I can find a vein. Like that."

The nurse rubbed Linh's arms with alcohol and looked at her for a moment. In a flash, the needle entered the livid skin. Khuyen pulled gently on the syringe pump. A tiny drop of blood rose through the needle, dissolving in thin threads, like smoke.

The principal watched anxiously as the clear glucose was

tinted red. Someone tugged gently at her arm. A female student, one of the youngest in Linh's class, on tiptoe, whispered in her ear: "Someone is asking to speak to Teacher Linh."

"Who?"

"I don't know. But he's kind of strange looking."

The nurse finished the shot, picked up her first aid bag, and slung it over her shoulder. "Don't worry, she'll be fine," she said calmly as she turned to leave. Linh's face slowly regained color and her breathing became more regular. Kim Anh told the students to go out into the courtyard, then walked with the girl student toward the school gate.

"Why didn't you ask him to come in to reception?" she asked.

"I did. But he told me he had to leave right away."

"What does he look like?"

"He has a long beard."

"What does he want with Miss Linh?"

Kim Anh looked in the direction in which the student pointed. She saw a man with shaggy hair and a beard, carrying a ragged satchel. He's repulsive, she thought, scared for a minute. But the man was already facing her.

"Hello, miss." He greeted her with a nod of his head in a way neither modest nor arrogant.

"You have a message for Linh?"

The man's eyes seemed gentle, clear. Aside from his Engels-style beard and his Cossack mustache, there wasn't really anything frightening about him.

"I'm a painter," the man said, as if to explain. "I owe Miss Linh money."

"I see."

Reading the surprise in Kim Anh's face, the man continued, "Well, I asked her to model for a painting. But I wasn't able to settle my debt."

"She has time to pose for you?" Kim Anh asked, suspicious.

"Oh, just a few hours on Sunday."

Kim Anh said nothing. She knew he was lying. Tran Phuong came to find Linh every Sunday to take her somewhere in the suburbs.

The man lowered his head, fumbled in his pockets, and pulled out an envelope. "I'd be grateful if you'd give this to her." After hesitating a minute, he added in a shaky voice, "Please send her my regards, my best wishes."

Kim Anh reluctantly took the envelope: "Well, I'm only passing this along. May I know your name and the amount?"

"Ah, ah . . ." the man stammered, embarrassed. He was about to take back the envelope and count the money, but he changed his mind, mumbling, "Of course, of course . . ."

He looked at Kim Anh, contrite, shrugged, and laughed. "You'll excuse me. In fact, I don't know how much there is. I'm a bit scattered. It's money that some of my colleagues at the Painters' Union brought me. Please, just do this for me, I'd be so grateful."

"Tell me, sir . . ."

He turned, looked at her with his gentle, silent eyes. Kim Anh couldn't contain her curiosity. "Are you . . . a friend . . . of the composer Tran Phuong?"

The man's face suddenly grew somber. "I don't know the man." He stepped back and left. Kim Anh returned to her office before she sat down and opened the envelope. Inside, she found a wad of bills fastened with a rubber band, and a piece of paper folded four times, with something scrawled on it:

I went to the exhibit and picked up your money two days ago. I've looked everywhere, high and low, but you were nowhere to be found, you rascal. So I'm throwing this through your window. Where do you hang out these days to drink? The exhibit organizers were stingy; they only paid us 3,500 *dong* each. I can't bring myself to give them a piece of my mind. By the way, Thao, the handicapped guy, is going to be in Saigon on the seventh; don't forget to be there to drink to his health. Rendezvous at Bach's house. There'll be first-class dog's meat. Bring your old toothless pal, Dao Hung, with you.

Kim Anh mechanically counted out the money. Three thousand five hundred *dong*. She thought for a long time. Linh wouldn't accept any of it if she told her the truth. She was so proud it was almost pathological. Whenever Lan came to bring Nguyen's money for Huong Ly, Linh had always refused to take it, saying she wanted to feed her daughter with money honestly earned. But now she was in a difficult situation. Kim Anh put the money in a drawer and decided to give it to Linh bit by bit, in the form of a bonus or on some other pretext.

9

NGUYEN'S MEETING lasted until six forty-five in the evening.

"Need a ride home?" his colleague Trong asked, throwing a jacket over his shoulders.

"No, spare me the sympathy please."

Trong shook Nguyen's hand. They were preparing to leave when a group of colleagues joined them.

"Hey, sit down, Nguyen. What's your hurry to leave?" said Tao, a former classmate who worked at the Journalists' Union, grabbing Nguyen's shirttail.

Nguyen always treated his friends well, especially old friends from his university days, like Tao.

"Let me go home," Nguyen scowled. "I've got to work early tomorrow."

"You dare refuse my invitation?" Tao said archly, his eyes flashing in mock anger.

Nguyen laughed. "No, of course not, but . . ."

He couldn't tell Tao that he had no desire to go out in the company of Ngoc Minh, the woman dolled up in a fake leather coat trimmed with rabbit hair who hung on his arm. In fact, Ngóc Minh was a fine journalist; her articles had a certain impact on her readers. But the woman in her didn't attract him at all. As if divining Nguyen's thoughts, Ngoc Minh giggled and said to Tao, "Let him go. It's time for him to mourn his lost beauty."

Ngoc Minh's proud, sarcastic laughter made Nguyen flush. Ashamed, angry, he glared at her.

"I don't believe we've met. I'd ask you to be polite."

Nguyen's cold, stern face was ashen. Trong was speechless.

"Come on, don't be angry," Tao said, conciliatory. "And you, Ngoc Minh, stop your teasing. Not everybody appreciates it. Hey, Nguyen, we haven't seen each other for almost a year even though we both live in Hanoi. If it hadn't been for this ceremony, you'd probably have forgotten me. Come on, let's go have a drink over at that café. Like the proverb goes, you'll always be a friend with whom I share everything, even my grass skirt."

In Tao's words, his gestures, Nguyen found something warm, tender, a bit of the love of a mother or a brother. Tao must have known about Nguyen's troubles; he was probably trying to share his pain. Tao tugged at Nguyen's shirttail with one hand, and called over the waitress with the other. When she arrived, he ordered a bottle of *Lua Moi* rice wine and a plate of grilled squid and sliced meat.

"Have a seat."

Tao insisted Nguyen sit next to him, then turned to taunt his friend Trong: "If you feel like a second round, stay. If you're not up to it, pack your bags and go home to your wife."

Trong chuckled softly and announced: "Sorry, ladies and gentlemen, I'm going back to my wife." He walked toward the door. Nguyen remained seated, distraught, still angry. Ngoc Minh, still defiant, sat down next to Tao, who pushed dirty dishes and glasses aside until the waitress came to clear them away. "You were sick two weeks ago?" he asked Nguyen.

Nguyen was surprised. "How did you know?"

Tao pulled out a pack of cigarettes, offered it to Nguyen. "You bastard, always buried in your work. Not like me. I've always got time for friends."

Nguyen said nothing. Tao continued: "Did you know that I'm going abroad?"

"Uh-huh."

"I leave next month."

"Really?" Nguyen said, nodding. In fact, during the last Journalists' Union meeting, he had been the one to recommend Tao and defended his candidacy for a professional study grant to Czechoslovakia. But he didn't want Tao to know.

"I've got a favor to ask you," Tao said. "When I leave the country, I'd be grateful if you'd check on my wife and kid once every two weeks."

"He's learned from experience. You've got to hold on to your wife or someone else will grab her," Ngoc Minh quipped. Then she roared with laughter, as if she had just heard a dirty joke. Nguyen was about to get up to leave. But fleeing would be cowardly, he thought, so he just sat there, puffing on his cigarette and responded calmly: "A man's greatest joy is having a woman he wants to hold on to."

Nguyen thought his words might shame this woman whose brazenness had earned her the nickname "The Tartar." But she wagged a finger at him: "My God, you are so archaic, *unbearably* archaic. In this day and age, and you still think like an old man with lacquered teeth and his hair in a bun." Her eyes glinted under her blue eyelids. She was impulsive, utterly uninhibited. "You should kill the Confucian in you. Europe had a sexual revolution about a century ago and you're still poring over *The Analects*. How are you going to understand young people today?"

Nguyen glared at the journalist, seething. Tao pinched her thigh to get her to drop it, then asked: "You dance well, I hope?"

"Like a pro," Ngoc Minh quipped back, rapid fire. "Look at that young thing there, Tao, the little one with the Abba sweater. That cost her 550 *dong*. Pity she's so ugly."

Again, Ngoc Minh's confidence startled Nguyen. *She must think she's beautiful, a real knockout, to judge others like that. In fact, the young woman with the Abba sweater is far prettier.* He studied Ngoc Minh: an almost square face caked with powder; a short, stubby nose; eyebrows exaggerated by an eye pencil; and when she laughed, teeth so stumpy they looked as if they'd been filed down. Nguyen could no longer dislike her. Curious, he observed her carefully, this woman who had inspired so many rumors. *It's a good opportunity to get to know life a bit better.* The waitress came back with the rice wine, the grilled squid, and other piping hot snacks.

"Bring us three of those cream cakes too," said Tao.

"How are we going to eat all this?" Nguyen asked.

"Let's chat, it'll go fast. It's not often that we're together," Tao said, serving Nguyen and Ngoc Minh some of the pork sausage wrapped in banana leaves. "You have to eat them hot to really taste the flavor."

Nguyen wasn't hungry, but the sausage was delicious. Ngoc Minh also appeared to be enjoying them. Eating greedily, she smeared her red lipstick on the cakes. Nguyen had never hung out with this kind of woman, the type who lived to the hilt, completely in the present moment. When she ate she thought of food; when she made love she thought only of sex. She balked at nothing, couldn't care less about the consequences of her actions.

She's the type of woman who throws herself headlong into life, a woman in keeping with the times.

Friends of Nguyen's had spoken of her like this. He knew that Ngoc Minh had a five-year-old boy, that her ex-husband was a skinny schoolteacher whom she had divorced when the boy was just two.

"You're the man," she had declared to her husband. "He carries your family name, yours and not mine, so you raise the child." The boy had lived with the father ever since. Every so often, Ngoc Minh told her friends, "Enough dancing and going out. I miss my son."

So she would apparently spend all morning buying clothes, shoes, and sweets for him, then head for her ex's house. "Where's my boy? Come here, precious, come to Mama." The kid would get his face smeared with red lipstick, almost suffocated by his mother's avalanche of kisses. The boy was thrilled by the new clothes and shoes, but often he couldn't wear them since Ngoc Minh never knew his size. His father often had to give them to a sister-in-law to resell.

The little boy would stuff himself for a week on the goodies his mother brought him. But her shopping sprees were irrational. When she had money and when she felt moved by maternal love, she would rush to her son's side and spend the whole day with him. But when she was broke, and even more often, when she lost herself in one of her love affairs, the months went by without a thought of her boy. Her ex-husband struggled to raise the child, as he earned very little. Every time she made one of her surprise visits, the father and the son would jump for joy. She came and went on her Honda like a squall. She was totally unpredictable and you couldn't rely on her for anything.

"Not bad. Really not bad. I ate four and you guys each had three. That's fair. After all, I drink less than you do," Ngoc Minh joked, as she wolfed down the last hot sausage. She smacked her lips like a child, then got out her lipstick to freshen her makeup. Her gestures titillated Nguyen's imagination. He remembered the rumors about her appetites as he looked at this woman in flesh and blood facing him.

"Stop looking at me like you stare at a gibbon in a zoo," Ngoc Minh said tartly, without even looking up.

Nguyen started. *The witch! She read my mind.*

Ngoc Minh put her lipstick back in her bag and squinted at Nguyen. "Finish that slice of sausage, and I'll serve you something to drink."

She speaks to me so intimately, as if she were my wife, Nguyen observed, still silent. Tao filled their glasses. "Drink up, Nguyen. Remember our last bash?"

"Oh yeah."

"Hung was completely drunk. Remember how he bawled? Just like a kid. We didn't get it. I found out later that the poor guy was in love with Thu Thuy, who was in love with that Professor Kha. Hung came back to her when Kha dropped her to marry the Indonesian ambassador's daughter, the girl with the buck teeth. They were married two weeks after Kha's nuptials. Were you invited?"

"Yes, but I had to leave that day for Nghe Tinh."

"Come on, gentlemen. You're not going to weep over the past again? You're just a bunch of weary old geezers in house slippers. For so-called intellectuals, you guys are a big letdown," Ngoc Minh interrupted.

Nguyen realized that she no longer irritated him. Tao also burst out laughing and pinched Ngoc Minh's ear. Nguyen knew that Tao loved his wife, had as much passion and respect for her as Nguyen did for Linh. He couldn't be in love with this bizarre woman, could he? Any other woman who talked or behaved like Ngoc Minh would have been totally shunned. Why, Nguyen might have even left the table. But Ngoc Minh was intelligent and she had an almost childlike candor.

"Come on, change the subject."

Nguyen looked at her and caught himself smiling. Had a few glasses of rice wine made him more tolerant? The woman's face began to seem almost familiar to him. The elongated eyebrows and glistening red lips no longer disgusted him.

Have I been too puritanical all these years? Maybe life should be as simple and as earthy as this woman. Like a boat that drifts with the current, or a butterfly, carefree, living the brief time it has to exist.

"Come on, Nguyen, drink up. Empty your glass! Tao has drunk four glasses, and I drank three. You're only on your second. What a wimp!" She filled Nguyen's glass to the rim. Nguyen shook his head. The woman licked her lips like a cat. "Drink, get drunk. There you go lost in your thoughts again. Oh how boring to have to act that part."

"What part?" asked Nguyen, uncomprehending.

Ngoc Minh burst out laughing. "Don't play dumb with me. You know, the wise hypocrite. You look like a judge. It's so tiresome."

"What are you insinuating? I'm not playing any part," Nguyen said angrily.

"That's a pack of lies. Except for me, everyone here plays a part. Grandeur, earnestness, moral integrity, sincerity. All acting!"

"You're deluding yourself. What makes you think you're so great?"

The woman laughed, without the slightest anger. "Not at all, but at least I dare to live the way I want to. I don't put on the act of maternal devotion or conjugal fidelity. If a man pleases me, I go with him."

Her insolence completely disarmed Nguyen, deflating his anger like air from a leaky tire. Indeed, he did gape at her the way he would have stared at an animal in a zoo. Ngoc Minh howled with laughter. "Am I really so exotic?"

Nguyen shook his head. "Who could imagine that Vietnam would produce a woman like you?"

Ngoc Minh nodded in agreement. "Amazing, isn't it? The Vietnamese Women's Union expelled me a long time ago. Actually I had no wish to remain a member. I would rather join an association of Martians or Neptunians." She cackled gleefully, plucked another strip of grilled squid, and started to chew, smacking her lips noisily. Tao drank in silence. He was used to Ngoc Minh's antics. He was more preoccupied with ensuring his family's comfort while he was abroad. Nguyen remained silent faced with his full glass.

"Oh, would you stop moping, Nguyen," Ngoc Minh said. "Life is short. So your darling Linh stole my precious ex-lover from me. Would you have the guts to try me?"

The fear and panic on Nguyen's impassive face startled Tao, distracting him from his worries.

"You hussy! There's a limit to your joking!" Nguyen snapped, furious.

Ngoc Minh just chuckled. "My, my, aren't we touchy! Well, excuse me."

Nguyen said nothing, just got up and announced that he had a meeting the next day with a delegation of Japanese journalists and had to go home immediately to prepare.

"My God, I didn't think I'd provoke such rage. I did apologize, didn't I?" Ngoc Minh said, rising and extending a hand to Nguyen. He shook it coldly and turned his back to her.

"Wait for me," Tao said, running up to the counter to pay. "I've got to go home too. Loan is probably waiting up for me."

Ngoc Minh slung her bag over her shoulder. "Okay, so let's go."

In front of the hotel, the man guarding the bicycles grumbled: "You paid me to watch the bikes until nine o'clock. It's nine-fifteen."

"Here, here. Keep the change and stop your whining," Ngoc Minh said.

They left together on their bicycles. Nguyen felt sick, but said nothing. His temples were pounding. After a couple dozen yards, his legs started to shake and his head felt like it was spinning.

Damn it, I've got the flu. I've got to get back to the house and ask Professor Le to alert the newspaper.

Nguyen gritted his teeth, gathering his strength to keep from fainting. The further he went, the more his head spun. The streetlights whirled before him like a cloud of fireflies and the cars seemed to glide and career past him like strange, hulking beasts.

"Nguyen!" Tao shouted as he saw his friend crash right into an old Peking truck moving in the opposite direction. He pushed him toward the sidewalk. Nguyen collapsed.

Tao jumped off his bicycle and lifted his friend. Nguyen had fainted. Ngoc Minh frantically flagged down a cyclo and gave orders to the driver. "Bring him back to my house, quick."

Ngoc Minh lived just a few hundred yards away. Tao hesitated a moment, but then accepted the plan, for lack of a better solution. Nguyen lived more than six miles away and Tao almost twice as far. The old cyclo driver, as muscular as an athlete, jumped from his seat, lifted Nguyen up, and laid him on the seat.

"Pedal fast, please, oh my God..." Ngoc Minh begged, slipping the old man five times the ordinary fee.

Tao followed, pushing Nguyen's bicycle with one hand. When they arrived, he carried Nguyen to Ngoc Minh's bed and gave her his bicycle.

"Go home now, Tao, I'll take care of everything."

Tao helped Ngoc Minh massage Nguyen with a balm until they felt his body grow warm and his breathing become regular. At this point, Tao got up to leave. On the doorstep, Ngoc Minh said to him: "Go home. Don't worry. No one knows how to cure drunken chills better than I. All my lovers are drinkers, you know that."

Tao shook his head, not knowing whether to laugh or cry.

ONE MORNING, the old custodian came to find Kim Anh in her office. Someone was there to see her. Kim Anh asked him to show the visitor in. After a few minutes, a forty-year-old woman appeared. Plump, fat even, she wore a transparent blouse that revealed a lacy camisole underneath. She had the smug, self-satisfied bearing of one of the city's wealthier citizens. "Madame Principal, I am the mother of little Van Anh, who is studying in Miss Linh's class."

Having introduced herself, she sat down in a chair. While Kim Anh prepared tea, the woman drummed her plump, ring-laden fingers on the table. Three of the rings were set with huge stones that seemed to loudly proclaim her status.

"I'm the manager of the State Fruit and Vegetable Store. It's a model store, and has been awarded Hanoi's model socialist values flag. Are you familiar with our establishment?"

"Yes, yes," Kim Anh said hesitantly as she poured tea. She didn't want to disappoint the visitor, who was apparently very proud of her position.

"To what do we owe the honor of your visit?" Kim Anh asked, as she poured the tea.

"A rather important matter, Madame Principal."

Her voice slowed, deepening into a grave tone. She emptied her cup of tea in a manner that implied it was rather ordinary, and promised Kim Anh that when she found a free moment she would be sure to send her some of the high-quality lotus tea she was accustomed to drinking at home. Then she began to explain the reason for her visit. She had a cousin who lived in Linh's neighborhood and who had related the scandal involving Linh in great detail: Miss. Tong's visit to Nguyen to offer advice; the cautionary speeches she had made to all the families in the building to avoid this couple's bad example; how the Neighborhood Reconciliation Committee had gone to investigate the circumstances of Linh's departure. Nguyen had

had a fever at the time, apparently, and had rudely slammed the door in the committee's face. He even told them that he had no need for their idiotic advice and that no one had the right to interfere with his freedom.

"Linh's personal situation is much too complicated. We cannot entrust the education of young people to such a person. I fear they may be corrupted by this woman's influence. I am a leading cadre in a state enterprise, after all. And as you know, my husband is also an important cadre in the army. We cannot have our children educated by such a shameless woman."

The woman heaved a sigh and fell silent. The purple and red gems on her fat fingers glittered in the sunlight that streamed into the office. Kim Anh looked at the hefty woman seated opposite her—her self-important air, the rolls of flesh that swelled her chiffon blouse. Suddenly Kim Anh felt weary, overcome by the urge to escape, to hide in the corner of a dark room to sleep. Straining, she finally replied: "Please don't worry. We are studying the situation. We'll find a solution."

The store owner shook her head. "We must put an end to this, Madame Principal. A socialist high school must not tolerate teachers so lacking in morals. The same goes for our sector."

The woman launched into another long speech on her model store, how she trained her staff to guarantee their moral purity, how she reeducated those who lacked the proper values. Kim Anh felt her ears buzz. She listened, but was distracted by the sight of those plump fingers covered with rings. After a long fifteen minutes, the woman finally showed signs of preparing to leave. Kim Anh retreated to her office and lay down on a couch to rest. When she got up a half an hour later, she summoned Dung, the deputy director and secretary of the high school Communist party cell, to come talk. Dung was a kind, honest man. The same age as Kim Anh, he seemed nevertheless older, less well preserved. His wife had died of an ulcer of the liver. Since her death, he had raised their children alone. His mother tended a small garden and cooked for him and his kids, but Dung earned very little money. The teachers often had to help him mend his clothes and sew on buttons. No woman had chosen to share his poor, lonely existence. He accepted his lot with patience and resignation.

Kim Anh related to Dung the visit from the wealthy manager of the State Vegetable Store. He rested his chin on his hand, looking miserable. After a long pause, Kim Anh asked, "What should we do?"

Dung sighed, but still made no reply.

"Sooner or later, the parents are going to react. I knew it . . . I wanted to avoid this, but . . ." Kim Anh hesitated a moment, then continued: "That's no longer an option. If we don't transfer Linh out of here, the rumors are going to spread like wildfire. Our society is full of people like this store manager, and they never yield. But if we remove Linh from her position, it will be a tremendous loss for the school. Three quarters of the winners at the literary competitions are her students. Both solutions seem unacceptable."

Dung looked up at Kim Anh. "Something has been bothering me awhile now, but I've been reluctant to ask. Do you know why Linh's marriage broke up?"

"Generally, but I'll never understand problems in any marriage other than my own. Don't you agree?"

"Maybe," Dung replied. He seemed troubled, undecided. Then he continued. "It's complicated. The Ministry of Education inspectors are sure to ask for a report. The other high schools in the city won't spare us either. That composer Tran Phuong is too famous."

"But no one here has even raised that issue."

"Everyone here respects and likes Linh. Anyone else in the same situation would have rapidly become a laughingstock.

My dear Kim Anh, this is not just a matter of the high school's internal affairs, this involves public relations. We're going to have to defend our position against public opinion. Like it or not, we are responsible, you and I, for the reputation of this community."

They deliberated like this late into the night, and finally decided to hand over Linh's class to a new teacher and to transfer her to a library job. Kim Anh was supposed to announce the decision at the next teachers' meeting, but a colleague overheard their conversation. The next morning, four young professors were on the doorstep to see Dung and Kim Anh.

"We're here to protest your disciplinary sanction of Linh. No one asked for her transfer. None of us have ever condemned her. Why have you made such a radical decision?"

"The parents are demanding it. Our school has to protect its reputation."

This is how Dung and Kim Anh replied, but they knew their explanations rang hollow. The teachers only renewed their protests. Their arguments plunged Dung and Kim Anh into doubt and confusion.

"One or two, three or four, even fourteen parents don't represent the will of all the parents. And even the opinion of all the parents doesn't necessarily represent the truth. We're Linh's colleagues. This woman has proved her dignity through years of living and working together with us. If we judge her, we'll have to examine our own consciences, weigh our own actions."

Kim Anh and Dung could only sigh in response. They found that the young teachers were right. After the teachers returned to conduct their classes, the two remained alone in the large, empty meeting room. But then, the enthusiasm that had, for a moment, touched them, slowly waned. They started to fearfully imagine the lewd rumors, the jeering criticism from the other Hanoi high schools, the possibility that their school might lose its reputation if there were letters of protest or, even worse, legal proceedings.

Linh's transfer was announced at the professors' board meeting the next day. Linh was promptly transferred to the school library. She tried to show a calm face, to hide her shame. *You can sacrifice even your life for love.* This is how she consoled herself. Shocked, her best students flocked to see her at the library.

"Come back, Miss Linh. We're going to see Mr. Dung to demand it."

"We know you, a new teacher will just confuse us . . . Anybody can take care of the library . . . Why are you leaving our class?"

Linh just smiled in reply. The children only dimly understood their teacher's unhappiness. The boys hardly paid attention. The girls, more sensitive, more schooled in the ways of the heart, whispered in the corners, but their affection for their teacher made them discreet. Many of Linh's students prepared themselves for the inevitable investigation and questioning they would be subjected to by the authorities. But her students' compassion only wounded Linh's pride. Every morning, from her room near the library, she awoke to their laughter and games in the courtyard. Their gaiety only heightened her pain. Once, she had lived in harmony with this joyous, familiar noise. Now, she felt as if she would suffocate in this dusty space, filled with the drone of termites gnawing at the wood, the scurrying of mice, the curtain rustling in the wind, and every so often the flailing of an insolent cockroach.

No, she didn't want their pity, which seemed to stick to her face like some invisible glue, impossible to wipe away. *Nothing is worse than the pity of others, if you have self-respect. Like a beggar accepting soup.*

This feeling plunged her into a dark, sweltering hell. Pity opened her gaping wound, the one still bleeding, unable to heal—because human generosity was like a mute beast, a sweet little child that she couldn't turn away.

Sometimes, when Linh walked past the library, Kim Anh glimpsed the pain and mute rebellion in the young woman's eyes. She knew Linh was torn apart, and she felt like telling her to end her hopeless love affair. But the principal kept her silence, realizing words would have no effect. Instead, they chatted nervously about this and that. Kim Anh always ended the conversation, lowering her voice and murmuring: "Please understand me, Linh, don't be angry."

Linh replied in a strong voice. "No, no, of course not."

But they both knew that these were polite, hollow words. Kim Anh went home to her loving, happy family. But sometimes she caught herself imagining Linh's little room, the smell of old books, the gnawing of termites in the night.

WINTER HAD COME suddenly to Hanoi. The bark of the trees was already covered with moss. The wind howled through the streets of the city. The windows to the soda shops had suddenly stopped displaying mangos, pineapples, and speckled watermelons from the South, and the jars of pickled limes and dark yellow apricot syrup disappeared. The orange season was still far away. Customers only drank coffee, and bean or manioc milk. Lan loved to sit in the city's cafés. After twenty years, this woman was a regular at the more fashionable establishments. She didn't smoke, but she could sit for hours, a hot cup of coffee in her hands, watching the faces of passersby.

Lan had grown up on Dao Street. She was pretty enough and rich. She had only completed primary school, so she should have been happy with her lot: running her small cosmetics shop, cooking and caring for her civil servant husband and her well-behaved children. But she had too much leisure time, had read too many romance novels. She was convinced that her life would be that of the princesses or the noblewomen immortalized in the books she read. Her husband came from a good family, had studied at the Ecole des Travaux Publics in Paris, where he had lived as a child. A patriot, he had returned to Vietnam after Liberation. Thanks to his paternal aunt and her French husband, he had found a job in France that earned him 500,000 francs a year and allowed him to buy a luxurious old colonial villa back in Hanoi. He had quickly reintegrated. When he returned, it was with an ideal wife in mind, and he searched long and hard for a typical Vietnamese beauty. His betrothed would be a young woman with a turban shaped like a crow's beak, a green silk sash tied around a plain brown skirt, just like the illustrations in the books that celebrated "the Vietnamese woman." After four years of searching, he met Lan. Her nose was graceful, and neither too big nor too flat. Her face was round, with tiny dimples nestled in her cheeks. She had exactly the kind of beauty he had dreamed of and he found her just when his patience was running thin. He immediately fell in love with her, and asked for her hand in marriage. Naturally, Lan's family was overjoyed and accepted the match instantly, with great pride. Lan's wedding, held on Dao Street, was one of the most opulent Hanoi weddings of the time; it became legendary, the ideal, the dream that haunted the young girls on sleepless, spring nights. Days, months passed. And Lan's passion, once sated, went cold in her.

But other passions followed. Like the dream of becoming a famous woman. Her engineer husband, while rich, would never escort her up the steps to fame. He only fulfilled her vision of wealth, but her ideal of glory, her spiritual aspirations, were unfulfilled. He gave her material comfort, a sweet, affectionate tenderness, but he did not satisfy her spiritual aspirations. She wanted to be admired everywhere she went—to the Opera House, the cafés and cinemas. She wanted people to strain to catch a glimpse of her, to watch her thrilled, burning with curiosity, as they whispered her name. She wanted their stares, fixed on the halo of her face, to be filled with envy. So many ugly women had been lucky to catch men in high positions. She knew that they followed their husbands to the embassy parties, the gallery openings, the solemn state ceremonies, the exclusive film premieres. And she, so stylish, was in the end just an ordinary woman stuck behind the counter in a cosmetics shop, poring over the accounts or tending to the cash register. Her frustrated dream of glory grew until it was as insistent as an eight-month-old fetus demanding to be born. It was in these circumstances, her desire at its peak, that she met Tran Phuong.

Heavens, when did winter arrive? Lan shivered as she examined herself in the mirror. Wrinkles had gathered at the corners of her eyes. Age spots had started to appear on her skin. She had never scrutinized her unmade-up face for so long before. Somewhere, deep inside her, a barrier fell. For a long time, she had refused to look at herself without makeup. At dawn, immediately after washing her face, she would grab her powder and her lipstick. At night, just before going to bed, she'd wash off the makeup and spread a layer of cream on her skin. The image that the mirror reflected back to her always had to be dazzling. She was determined to preserve her beauty. For her, it was also another weapon in her battle to win back her husband. For the past seventeen years, since the day her affair with Tran Phuong came to light, he had never forgiven her.

This morning she suddenly realized that her artifice was beginning to wear thin. A stranger looked back at her from the mirror, a woman with dull, vacuous eyes. Two deep creases underscored her lips, which she now saw were crisscrossed with tiny wrinkles. Soon, they would sink and buckle, she thought.

In a half hour, after she had applied her makeup, she would still be able to fool men at a twenty-yard distance. But she wouldn't be able to fool herself. She had lost her last weapon.

"Good-bye, Mama, I'm leaving," her youngest son shouted up from underneath the window. He'd just finished breakfast and was running off to his painting class. Her second son was at the Polytechnic. Her eldest daughter, who worked at the Institute of Social Sciences, was married and came back to visit every two weeks. As for her husband, he had no doubt left for a friend's house to play chess, or chat, or even to find a woman to fill his solitude. Anything was possible. She had no right to reproach him.

Lan's fingers lay absently on the dresser, an old piece of furniture made of amboyna wood. They had beautiful furniture, real treasures for antique collectors. But none of this had any meaning for her anymore.

The wind stirred up whirls of dust in the streets. The branches of the linden trees were almost barren; a few pale pink flowers still clung to the creeper vines. Cars whizzed by every now and then. An old couple strolled down the sidewalk. Lan suddenly sat up to get a closer look. Probably sixty years old. Both handsome, silver-haired. The man wore a pale gray suit, the woman silk pants and a velvet Chinese padded jacket. They walked slowly, gracefully. From time to time, the woman bent to whisper something in her husband's ear. The old man smiled under his white mustache. So happiness was possible for an old couple, between two people who had traveled a long road strewn with highs and lows, through feelings hot and cold, through life's tempests.

If only, if only . . .

She too could have known years of happiness with her husband if she hadn't fallen into this trap.

The old couple disappeared into the distance. Lan had followed their silhouettes with her eyes. In ten years, her hair would be as silver as the old woman's. But there would be no gray-suited man at her side to smile at her, to talk to. No human shadow on which she could lean at the end of winter, in the final years of her life. What could she expect from her children? She had placed her hopes in them for years now. But they lived their own lives, had their own loves and hatreds, their worries and struggles. Where then would she take refuge?

Lan could hear a song playing on the neighbor's record player: *What dust has been reincarnated in me, that one day I shall return to dust?*

Her slender fingers sifted through the jewelry, the lipstick, the makeup pencils, the powder puffs. Regret stabbed at her heart. Looming behind this vague, foggy curtain was a chasm from which rose a cry of hatred—the grinning face of a Lie bobbed on the tide of illusions. A Lie with coal black eyes, thick eyelashes, and a proud, blasé smile.

For the first time, Lan found no thrill in going to her favorite cafés, the places from which people passing by might furtively admire her beauty, where customers might stare at her. Lan tilted her face to the mirror, took a second look. A woman, just a woman.

She sighed, spread cream on her face, and methodically began to apply makeup.

Twenty minutes later, she left the room in her most expensive suit. She walked resolutely to Tran Phuong's apartment, not to stir the embers of their love, but to ignite a volcano of jealousy in the heart of his wife.

10

T HE NIGHT Nguyen fainted left a strange mark on him. It was like a moment outside of time. Years later, just thinking of it, he would feel lost.

The following morning, Nguyen awoke at four o'clock, his head aching and stiff. A black object peered over the bed. Odd, he thought, since he and Linh had never attached anything to the bed, aside from the mosquito netting. He squinted, trying to focus his gaze on the object, but his eyes were still bleary, stinging. This time, he saw a strangely shaped bedside lamp, totally different from the one in his bedroom.

"Where am I?" Nguyen sat up, slightly propping himself on his elbows. To his left, snuggled up to him, he saw a forehead covered with curls. A woman. For a second, Nguyen's heart leapt; he thought she was Linh. But the thin, flat nose disappointed him.

"Who are . . . ?" Nguyen sat straight up, stared intently at the half of the face that emerged from the covers. He recognized Ngoc Minh's pug nose. Only then did he realize what had happened. What an absurd situation. In his wildest dreams, he would never have imagined himself ending up in bed with a strange woman, and even worse, the bed of a woman he despised. Ngoc Minh slept soundly, her breath still reeking of alcohol. Her permed hair brushed against his skin, stirring an odd sensation in him. Her leg was slung over his stomach. He felt like shoving it off, but he didn't have the courage to touch her. He wanted to get up and go home, but his head was heavy, his joints achy. Outside, the winter wind whistled through the trees, shaking the room slightly. It was freezing out there, but here, a warm, welcoming atmosphere surrounded him. Nguyen closed his eyes again, relaxed, inhaling the sweet, powdery smell of the covers. This scent and the warmth of Ngoc Minh's body held him back. Suddenly an idea occurred to him: *Nothing wrong with a man sharing a woman's bed if she wants it. What's more, it happened by accident. For too long now I've been afraid of what people will think.*

Desire, like an electric current, ran through his body. Nguyen had lived for too long without a woman.

Oh why isn't it Linh? Suddenly his heart twisted and he began to tremble.

Nguyen imagined her in the little room near the high school library, sleeping in a cheap single bed. He knew that she ate badly, made all kinds of sacrifices to be able, every Sunday, to be together with Tran Phuong, sneaking off with him to some distant suburb. Since Linh had fallen ill, Huong Ly had gone to stay with her paternal grandfather. Their bed was empty now. And here he was, stretched out next to a stranger whose arms would sooner or later wrap around his neck; of this, he was certain. He groaned aloud.

Ngoc Minh stretched and yawned, still unaware that Nguyen was awake. Motionless, her eyes still closed, she touched his wrist. "Your pulse is almost normal."

Nguyen froze, his heart racing. She turned toward him, her warm breath against his face. He couldn't feign sleep. He opened his eyes again. "Miss Ngoc Minh?"

Ngoc Minh sat up in surprise.

"Oh, you're already awake? Well done. I thought you wouldn't be up before noon. Brrr, you were as cold as a cadaver. Do you know what you said before collapsing on the bed? Fortunately, it was me; any other woman would have fainted."

She chattered away. The smell of alcohol mixed with her perfume titillated Nguyen. She was so close that her hair brushed against his cheek.

"Damn, it was scary to see you vomiting. Waves of it, all over my clothes. Luckily, I had already taken off my jacket. Otherwise, it would have been ruined. Anyway, they say that if you vomit after a drunken chill, you're as good as cured."

Mortified, Nguyen imagined himself heaving on a total stranger. "Please forgive me, it's the first time I've gotten drunk like that."

Ngoc Minh shook her head. "No worries. I've already washed everything up. A man's got to get good and drunk once in awhile to escape the monotony of life, no? It would be deadly boring if we all stayed lucid as jaybirds. I'd rather die than live that way. Tell me, Nguyen, you're an intelligent man, do you think the Europeans are more rational than we are?"

Nguyen smiled. He was beginning to appreciate her feisty temperament.

"Every country has its own values. What's perfectly rational in one culture may seem absurd to another."

"A conservative. You're just a conservative."

Nguyen was stunned. How could she, barely awake, plunge with such gusto into an intellectual discussion?

"Hey," she continued. "When you've slept in a woman's bed, the least you can do is be frank, tell her what you really think."

Nguyen laughed. He didn't feel like discussing anything. He looked at the woman's face beside him. Ngoc Minh shrugged and urged him on. "Say it, just say it."

Nguyen took her hand. "It's probably better to say nothing."

"No," said Ngoc Minh, shaking her head.

Her pug nose and her square face seemed more attractive in the dim light of the room. Without her makeup, she had the simple, earthy beauty of a peasant woman. Nguyen lowered his voice: "Actually the only rational thing would be to kiss you."

"I knew that much," laughed Ngoc Minh. "One day you'll end up living real life. You may even leave the damned theater altogether."

Nguyen didn't hear the woman's words anymore. She held him in her arms, sweeping him up in a terrifying storm of repressed desire. A million drums thundered out of the deserted regions of his body, merging into one wild, irresistible beat.

A FEW DAYS LATER, Nguyen attended a meeting on the country's new agricultural policy with the editor-in-chief. During a break, the two men went to the cafeteria to have a beer and munch on some peanuts.

"Meetings! My brain is mush. Is there any other country in the world where they love meetings as much as we do?" the editor-in-chief grumbled. He chose an out-of-the-way corner.

Nguyen pulled a piece of paper out of his briefcase to wipe off the table, sticky with some sweet soda.

"We may meet all day, call for model behavior three times a week, but this table is still filthy and sticky; the waiters throw food in customers' faces like a bunch of bad-mannered brats just waiting for the opportunity to rip people off."

They sat down. It was cold out, but for beer lovers, it was perfect weather. The editor-in-chief called out to a kid hawking

Chinese sausage and grilled squid. The waitress brought over four mugs of beer that she slammed down on the table as if she were filling a pig's trough. The beer overflowed, spilling onto the table. The two men shook their heads and looked at each other ruefully. They said nothing, just drank in silence. In the courtyard, people arrived for the meeting, locked their bicycles, and strolled around the garden in front of the building. The editor-in-chief glanced at Nguyen. "You seem better. You don't get all red when you drink anymore."

"Yeah."

"It's chilly out."

The editor-in-chief suddenly changed the subject, questioned him. "Say, Nguyen . . ."

"Yes?"

The old man's eyes seemed hesitant under his thick glasses: "You . . . you know?"

Nguyen said nothing, just waited. The man continued. "There's been a lot of whispering about you and Miss Ngoc Minh. People have even come to me to complain. I know they're jealous of your position. I've replied firmly that state organizations no longer have any right to interfere in people's private lives. I've told them to stop being so nosy. But between you and me . . ."

He stopped, choosing his words, weighing one last time what he intended to say. Nguyen continued to puff on his cigarette in silence.

"Why have you chosen a woman who . . ." The editor-in-chief stopped again, embarrassed. He watched the wind chase dead leaves on a path through the garden. Finally, he looked Nguyen in the eye.

"Why, Nguyen? I always thought a man like you needed a different type of woman. Aside from the fact that you are still legally married to Linh. That doesn't matter. But couldn't you have waited a bit?"

Nguyen threw his cigarette butt into a trash can and lit another. Now it was the editor-in-chief's turn to wait for him. He didn't smoke, just drank in small, nervous sips. The plate of appetizers slowly disappeared. After a long pause, Nguyen looked up. "I'm grateful for your concern. I myself don't understand how I got into this. Perhaps because I was drunk that night, when I left the hotel. Maybe because ... because ..."

The editor-in-chief cut him off. "Alright, alright, ... but let me ask you something—is everything going to be alright?"

A smile fluttered at the sides of Nguyen's lips. "How would I know?"

The electric bell boomed from the loudspeakers, calling them back to the conference room. Sitting down in his seat, Nguyen confided in his boss: "Don't you understand, I'm still not happy ..."

Nguyen was sincere. He had quickly lost all pleasure in living with Ngoc Minh. The morning after, Nguyen had wanted to call the newspaper to apologize, but he had gotten dizzy again and collapsed back onto her bed. "My God, are you alright?" Ngoc Minh had screamed.

Even dizzy, Nguyen had been moved, recognizing in her cry of terror the kind of worry that a woman reserves for her husband. When Ngoc Minh bent over his chest to listen to his heartbeat, Nguyen felt the warmth of her breasts against his shoulder. This contact felt natural, familiar, as if he had always known it. In the end, it had been Ngoc Minh who called the editor-in-chief to alert him. She had then bustled around feverishly, insisting he take medicine, filling a hot water bottle. She didn't even take the time to put on her makeup, just brushed her hair before dashing out to buy him a kidney porridge flavored with mint and scallions. She lifted him up and fed him spoonfuls, like a mother. It was then that he saw the beauty in her, her generosity and sincerity. In fact, she was devoted to her friends, and she had a natural, unself-conscious manner

utterly lacking in most women. During his convalescence, Ngoc
Minh spared no pains nor money; she went to the market to
find all sorts of nourishing foods for him.

"Tonight, I'm going to make you stir-fried beef with onions.
Crab soup is delicious too, but it's too much fuss. If that's what
you crave, we'd better go to a restaurant . . . Sick of caramelized
pork? We'll have dog meat, okay? Rice wine and dog meat,
that's my favorite meat. People who don't like dog meat are
idiots. Even Buddhist monks sneak out to eat it in back of the
temples."

Nguyen had tried to adapt to Ngoc Minh's unpredictable
lifestyle. A reflective person, he couldn't stand parties and
drinking that lasted all night, the spectacle of drunken men
vomiting on the floor, their raucous jokes, their earthshaking
laughter, the way they flattered each other as they served themselves another drink. One day, Ngoc Minh would force him to
fill up on dog meat and rice wine. The next, because she didn't
feel like cooking, she'd propose eating fried bean cakes. When
the money ran out, she'd take him to the *pho* vendor who let
her eat on credit. It was fun the first time, bearable the second.
But by the ninth and tenth, their little family life was hell. Ngoc
Minh, sensing that her lifestyle clashed with Nguyen's, tried to
rein herself in, but sooner or later, her old wanderlust resurfaced. Why sacrifice her pleasure to keep one man when she
could have as many as she liked? Only the drinking parties she
loved to host could give her back her energy, her drive. Dozens
of men from all professions hunched around a table overflowing with food and wine. She loved to serve the wine, this
liquid fire that gave a man the power to imagine himself a wise
man or a knave. She relished their praise, how they applauded
her sharp wit, her liberal ideas. And she loved their conversations, a critical source of important news that she would otherwise have had to waste time searching for in documents.
Living like this, she hadn't had to work hard, like Nguyen. But

now that they lived together, things were different. She couldn't just invite her pals over to drink and play cards while he slaved away at the office. She couldn't interrupt him when he was translating documents to go out to cafés. And she would never be happy listening to music in her empty room. No, a hundred times, No! She had to hear it in parks and cafés packed with people. She even found her quiet moments in the middle of the bustle of the crowd. Ngoc Minh was hot-blooded; she needed sound, color, light. But Nguyen's heart beat to a different rhythm.

One Saturday night, he finally left. When he reached their old apartment, he met Professor Le in the stairwell.

"Dear friend, it's been a long time," said Professor Le, swinging a bucket.

"The water doesn't run up there anymore?" Nguyen asked, taking the bucket from the old man's hand.

"There hasn't been a single drop for a week."

They turned and went back to the courtyard together to pump more water. "Let me do it, professor."

"I'm free today. Why not come visit with me?" the professor asked. Nguyen nodded, carried the bucket all the way up to the old man's bathroom. Nothing had changed since Nguyen's first visit years ago. Flowering creeper vines still framed the window, clinging to the roof. An old bed with a copper frame was topped with a round bar to hold the mosquito netting. A long worktable, black and shiny as a polished buffalo horn, a red ink pot, a calendar on the wall, a red crystal tulip next to an odd-shaped stone paperweight.

"Would you like a coffee?"

Without waiting for Nguyen's reply, the professor set the coffee filter on top of a glass. *This must be the most precious object in the entire apartment.* The professor measured out the coffee, placed it in the filter with a precise, experienced gesture, and poured water into it. He put the top on the filter, poured more water in a ceramic dish, then set a glass into it. Nguyen watched him. *The old man has lived this way since he was twenty. Day in and day out, month after month, he contemplates this same calendar, these creeper vines, this old bed, the stone paperweight. He lives like a monk.*

"Drink up, before it gets cold. Someone sent it all the way from Ban Me Thuot."

He lifted the coffee glass out of the bath of hot water and placed it and a bowl of sugar in front of Nguyen. He sat down opposite Nguyen and slowly lit a cigarette.

"I've already had a cup this morning. Excuse me if I don't join you."

Professor Le exhaled, and the aroma of tobacco mingled with the coffee smells put Nguyen at ease. "I envy the simplicity of the life you lead. Most people, ordinary mortals like me, don't have the courage it takes to live like this."

"Please, please," said the old man, waving his hand.

"No, I'm being sincere," Nguyen said.

"I didn't think you were flattering me. But don't idealize my life, or glorify my choices. People have different needs. For some, I must certainly be a real eccentric, absorbed in my numbers and dusty old books, meditating on abstract questions that are of no interest to anyone. Normal men dream of a roof over their heads, a beautiful wife, handsome kids. And material comfort, of course. One shouldn't look down on these dreams, even the material considerations. Everyone has the right to aspire to a better life."

"Of course. I just meant that it's thanks to people like you that a country or a culture really evolves, that civilization progresses."

"It's our duty, dear friend."

"And yet, no shopkeeper on Dao Street would trade his wealth for your fame."

"Naturally, naturally." The old man spoke with a hint of

surprise. A smile appeared under his mustache. "But when you're an adult, you don't have the right to complain about the consequences of your choices. Only children whine about ending up with a smaller piece of the pie."

Nguyen found this professor endearing with his teeth blackened by cigarette smoke, his merry laugh, and sense of humor. This man was happy with his life, while he still teetered on a bamboo bridge over a void.

Professor Le glanced at Nguyen. "You haven't been home for a while. Problems?"

Nguyen hesitated for a few minutes, then, without looking at the professor, said, "I'd like to ask your advice . . . about a personal problem. Do you . . . do you think a man can suddenly discard the principles he's built his life on and adopt entirely different ones?"

Professor Le took a long drag on his cigarette, slowly exhaled, then tossed the stub into an ashtray.

"I can't advise you on any particular aspect of your marriage. But I can tell you what I think. People are courageous when they set principles to guide their lives. But sometimes it takes even more courage to abandon those same principles. Ideas are just milestones along the road. Humanity progresses precisely because new ideals sweep away those of the past. Of course, I don't mean we should make a tabula rasa of the past, of all we learned on our school benches. That would be naive, childlike."

The old man paused, coughed, and then continued. "Also, to abandon one lifestyle for another is natural. But man is a social animal. New ideas are only accepted if they respond to the evolution of the community, to the reality of people's lives. You have the right to smoke, but not to burn your neighbor's gas tank; you have the right to like oranges, but not to pick them from someone else's garden."

They fell silent. Then Nguyen changed the subject to talk

about the situation in the country, the turmoil sweeping the Middle East.

About a half hour later, he left for his own apartment. A slight, chilly breeze swept through the door, over his face. A fine layer of dust covered the room. Memories of days past stirred in him. He paced around the room. It was as if he could see her slender feet emerging from yellow pants, how she used to dip her head gracefully when she pulled the curtains. The carnations in the vase had faded, their petals scattered. This love pursued him, refused to let go. Nguyen thought he had forgotten her over the last few weeks. He knew some men who could love a different woman every week with equal passion. A few months later, they erased everything from memory. But he was bound by a single love. Nguyen knew that he would suffer for a long time.

What had Professor Le said? Something about it being alright to smoke but not to set fire to your neighbor's gas tank? Liking oranges but not to the extent that you went and stole them from someone else's garden? How simplistic. Morality had nothing to do with it. Ngoc Minh was no orange in someone's garden.

Nguyen felt powerless, incapable of changing. He had thought he could find a new kind of happiness with Ngoc Minh. He had tried to rid himself of old habits, let go of his former ideal of beauty and adapt to his new life. He had gone along on the nightly outings and parties, the long rambling walks down the streets of the city. He had grown accustomed to Ngoc Minh's booming laugh, to her whistling at all hours of the night; he was no longer shocked when she tossed off her clothes in the middle of the room. After all, she was a good person. She would give her last *dong* to some miserable soul, then go and beg a neighbor for a bowl of pickled vegetables for her own dinner. What's more, she was a good journalist, even if she did have gaps in her general knowledge. They shared a profession at least, the same ideas about their work, and that had created a fairly solid bond between them.

But one day, while Nguyen was correcting an article and Ngoc Minh was out shopping, a balding head with a thin crown of shoulder-length hair had popped through the open door to her apartment. "Ohhh, sweeeteee . . ."

Nguyen had looked up, surprising the fifty-year-old man.

"Oh, excuse me, Miss Ngoc Minh, is she at home?" the man laughed, embarrassed.

"Come in. She's out shopping, but she'll be back soon."

The visitor sat down on a chair. Nguyen poured him some tea. The man sipped it, slipping furtive glances at Nguyen. His inquisitive eyes searched the apartment; it was the look of an ex-master of the house. The visitor's look seemed to say: *I've known all this. There, where your jacket is hanging, was the place I hung my fur coat.*"

He pulled out a pack of cigarettes. "You mind giving me a light?"

Just then Ngoc Minh had returned, her shrill laugh echoing outside in the courtyard. "Hey, it's Duc's Honda."

She entered the room, greeting the visitor warmly. The man held out a hand, and his eyes lit up when he saw her. Nguyen noted that the man had restrained himself, held back from another, more affectionate gesture. Nguyen got up, went over to the coatrack, and took down his jacket. "I've got to do an errand. But please, you stay and visit with Ngoc Minh."

"Yes, go ahead, Nguyen," said Ngoc Minh, with barely concealed delight. "But don't be long."

Nguyen hadn't even made it out the door, when she said to her visitor: "Sit down, sit down, I want to hear *all* about your trip."

"Quietly, honey," Nguyen heard the man whisper. "Quiet, I'll tell you everything."

Nguyen cycled directly to the newspaper offices and

worked there until nightfall. When he came back, Ngoc Minh said reproachfully: "Well, you're going to have to eat cold rice. The pot is still half full."

Nguyen said nothing, just changed his clothes in silence. That evening they sat down together to drink tea Russian style, with a slice of lemon—Ngoc Minh's ritual since her trip to Russia. As soon as Nguyen was seated, she started to recount her day: "This morning, Duc told me so many funny stories. One really has to leave the country to see how people live in this world. We're just rotting away here in our hole. All the news we get is already old news. Did you know that . . ."

She launched into a long account of the man's trip. Knowing it would bother her if he remained silent too long, Nguyen asked: "What does he do?"

"Duc? He's one of the country's top biologists," she said, clucking her tongue in admiration. "A truly brilliant man."

Then she burst out laughing. "Ah, Duc, my dear ex-lover. What an eccentric. Do you know why he came? To ask if I would return a blender he gave me *years* ago as a gift. He said, 'My daughter's going to have a baby. We'll need it to make soup and juices for the kid.' Infuriating, no? I told him he could search the apartment his entire life and never find it. It's been *years*, enough time for me to sell off a hundred of those machines for money to eat! Why would I clutter up my house with that thing? He was stunned, left with his tail between his legs . . ."

She fell silent, lowering her head to serve tea. Seeing the tiny wrinkles that covered her forehead, Nguyen felt a pang of sadness. For her or for himself? Nguyen didn't know, but it felt like the ground under his feet would crack from this absurdity and the sheer weight of his humiliation. That night he couldn't sleep. In the pale blue glow of the bedside lamp, he contemplated the room he had lived in since the beginning of winter. The Impressionist print was hung carelessly, at an angle; at the foot of the bed, two blouses were slung over the back of a chair, just as they had been the night Nguyen had collapsed there in a drunken stupor. Underwear lay scattered on the floor. Like a cheap hotel room, everything was temporary, disordered, dusty. Everything spoke of restlessness, instability. A good hotel made you feel at home. Ngoc Minh's place made you feel like you should pack your bags; it was just a stopping place between two journeys. Here, sleep was intermittent, hurried, like a night aboard a freight train. No, no, this woman was not made to be tied to one man. Even if she remarried ten times, she would one day end up returning to this way station. At that moment, Nguyen knew he had to leave. He suddenly felt an immense tenderness for this woman whose bed he had shared. He propped himself on his elbows and observed her. Ngoc Minh was sleeping soundly, her face blurry in the dusk. He could still hear her carefree, easy laughter.

But Ngoc Minh's face was blurred now, an odd image drifting away, toward a faraway bank. The days they had spent together had scattered in him like flotsam and jetsam on waves.

The next morning when Ngoc Minh awoke, she realized he had already left for work. "Well, isn't he getting on his high horse," she grumbled to herself.

At noon, as usual, she prepared lunch. Nguyen had meant to call, to tell her he wasn't coming back. But late that morning, his footsteps led him mechanically back to her house.

"What's gotten into you?" Ngoc Minh reproached him as he walked in. After lunch was over, while Nguyen did the dishes, Ngoc Minh hopped into bed for a nap. "Have a glass of water and come join me. Hurry up," she said sweetly, as if she were speaking to her husband.

Nguyen looked at her, found himself hesitating. *Why? Why?* He paced around the room, incapable of explaining his doubts.

That evening, Nguyen told Ngoc Minh that he had to stay late at the newspaper to draft a feature article for the review.

In reality, he took the old custodian out to drink beer until two in the morning. He slept in the man's little room, slipped under the filthy cover reeking of sweat and medicinal balms. The next morning, when he returned to his own house, he felt like he had returned to terra firma after a long, rough ocean voyage. Nguyen spent the entire afternoon cleaning the apartment, washing dishes, sheets, curtains, the mosquito netting, the reed mat, sweeping away cobwebs that had gathered in the corners. When everything was sparkling clean, he took a bath and made a meal to celebrate: pork sausage wrapped in banana leaves, a sesame salad, fermented pork from a familiar shop on Bông Street, and some pickled vegetables from across the street. He looked at his meal. *Whatever happens, this will always be home.*

11

T RAN PHUONG had waited almost a year for this morning. He had just been received by a high-ranking party cadre, his wife's uncle. Hoa had sufficiently built up her husband so that the leader was well disposed to like him. Immensely clever, the composer had, for his part, instantly sized up his interlocutor. *A kindhearted old man, but without depth or refinement. It'll be easy to win him over. It's the barbed-wire fence of officials that surround him that will be the real obstacle. But thanks to Hoa, I've made it over the first hurdle.*

And Tran Phuong felt genuine affection for his wife.

The cadre received him warmly. Like all the old men who spent their childhood reciting poems by the great Chinese poets Li Bai and Du Fu, he admired scholars and wanted Tran Phuong to know that his artistic sensitivities ran deep, but that he had more important, political responsibilities.

Recite a few poems, tell a few amusing stories, a few witty remarks about some secondary player—that should be enough to entertain the old man. Tran Phuong knew that all men, whatever their rank, needed to confide in someone. He also knew that the longer a man repressed this need, the more likely it was to gush forth whenever an opportunity presented itself.

I've got to push the right buttons. The key is to hew to the middle road: be open but reverential, lighthearted but prudent. Say the words he wants to hear.

The cadre served tea to the composer and chuckled with pleasure. Their conversation was a rare moment of relaxation amidst the constant stress of his life.

"What do you think of young Hoan?"

"Why, he has all the zeal and intelligence of Don Quixote," Tran Phuong quipped, lowering his head. A lock of jet black hair hid the twinkle in his eye. Hoan was an idiot, whose construction projects had ruined countless historical sites in Hanoi. It would take years to restore what his dictatorial power and crass ignorance had demolished. But Hoan had once carried this cadre wounded on his back, forded a stream to escape an enemy roundup. Tran Phuong knew that this was the opportunity to score a decisive point, if only he could dispel the doubts that still encumbered this old man's sentimental heart.

"Yes, yes, you're quite right," the man jubilantly exclaimed. "He's like that Spaniard who fought windmills. You're very observant. I've lost so much sleep over that Hoan. Charges are piling up against him."

"That's life, people make snap judgments about others without really getting to the bottom of problems."

"Yes, that's true," the cadre sighed. "You have to know to see to the core of things. Did you know, once, during the resistance, that young Hoan . . ."

Some deep emotion flickered in those weary old eyes. He was probably thinking of days gone by when Hoan, still a trooper, had carried him on his back, grilling manioc roots to feed them under some rickety jungle shack. No doubt, the memory of this young, innocent soldier and his devotion would be forever engraved in his heart. In the meantime, Hoan had become a forty-year-old man with a mustache and power, known for his ignorance and cruelty to his subordinates.

"Now, now, don't be too hard on yourself," Tran Phuong said. "Think of your health. The ignorance of the masses is unfathomable. If the majority were always right, you'd never see an entire village rush to a Buddhist temple to scream for punishment of that hussy, Thi Mau, like in the legend."

"Ah, yes. Our ancestors were truly insightful. 'Rumors will kill even a monk.' This Hoan incident has bothered me for a long time. Now I feel at ease."

Tran Phuong smiled. Thanks to him, that bastard Hoan had been spared. But what use was keeping score? Only individual human lives were real; the masses could always be reduced to numbers.

A servant brought out a tray of cold *chè*. The cadre started to recite a poem by Du Fu. Tran Phuong matched him by reciting a couple of Tang dynasty poems. From time to time, the cadre's wife, seated in a nearby room, glanced into the living room. She had never heard her husband laugh so hard, with such gaiety. The conversation went on for five more minutes beyond lunchtime. Finally, Tran Phuong took his leave. The city seemed to smile at him again. Even the streets teeming with vendors, the dilapidated sidewalks with their open sewers under repair, seemed beautiful to him.

Success, failure, the outcome is so arbitrary.

He made a detour to Hang Da Market to buy flowers for his wife. *In the end, she's the one who loves me most, who is most devoted to me.* The composer imagined his wife's flat face, but it didn't annoy him as it ordinarily did.

He climbed the staircase, determined to be especially kind, to express his gratitude. The door had been left ajar, and he saw her seated in the living room, her hair disheveled, her nose red, her eyes swollen.

"Liar!" she screamed at him. Her jealous scenes always

started with the same refrain. Tran Phuong calmly set the bouquet of flowers down on the table.

"What's the matter? Stop screaming like that or you're going to be the laughingstock of the neighborhood."

Usually, by the time Hoa found out about her husband's affairs, they were history, the accused having already flown far, far away. Sometimes, Tran Phuong himself didn't even remember them. So he thought that his wife had discovered one of his old lovers, long gone from his field of gravity. Laughing, he placed his hand on his wife's shoulder. "Rumors again, I suppose?"

Hoa turned her swollen eyes to her husband and snarled, "Lan just came by."

Tran Phuong jumped. *I'm finished. This will be war.*

Hoa studied her husband's face, guessing his fears. "So, you don't deny it anymore?"

"Deny what?" Tran Phuong replied mechanically.

"Oh, so you're going to play innocent, is that it?"

Hoa choked back her sobs. She had wept her heart out that morning, in front of Lan, her former rival, a woman who had once been a conquering beauty. She had cried alone in their huge living room, alone with the dolls arranged in glass cabinets, the vials of medicine, the fancy hot water bottles, the electric massagers. All these material objects could not help her overcome her loneliness.

Tran Phuong stole a glance at his wife and sensed that he must stand firm. *This was the way women were. They strangled you when you yielded, yielded when you resisted.* He approached her, his face stern and haughty: "I forbid you to speak to me in that accusatory tone. How many times have you already made jealous scenes? And what have you gotten out of it aside from public ridicule and contempt?"

Tran Phuong had always known how to cover his tracks,

appearing stunned when confronted with facts, then ridiculing her. But she knew from long experience that a tiger lurked inside him. She knew that he had banished her, that there had been lots of others. But she loved him, still wanted him. It was only under the shock of these blows that she regained her lucidity.

"I know you're innocent," she said, in a calm voice, after a silence. Pain had made her shrewd; she glimpsed a new tactic to attain her goal. "I've been mistaken more than once about you."

"Yes, it's a good thing you realize it. It's a beautiful day. I brought you some flowers. I wanted to take you out." He untied the package and handed her the flowers. Hoa wiped away her tears. "I'll put them in a vase. But tell me, who is this Linh?"

"Who mentioned her?" Tran Phuong asked, his temples pounding.

"Lan."

"Oh, that woman—you know what the story is with her, don't you?"

"It's an old story. I'm talking about the other woman."

"Lan hates me because I rejected her," Tran Phuong continued, ignoring her. "She has delusions of grandeur. I have no respect for people who can't use their own talent to gain fame, who latch onto others to gain it." Then, Tran Phuong thought he should remind his wife of her rare, privileged position in society, how she owed it solely to his talent. Like so many times before, Hoa's pride was flattered and she calmed down. But this time, she was more lucid. Her face didn't budge; it remained stony. She spoke up again, determined. "Don't talk about Lan anymore. Who's this Linh woman?"

Tran Phuong shrugged, turning away. "An ordinary woman, like many you know."

"So you have no designs on her?"

"Of course not, you should know that."

"So you have absolutely no interest in her, and she loves you without any hope of your affections?"

The composer felt his ears burn. But he quickly repressed his anger and glared threateningly at his wife. "If you had married an ordinary man, you wouldn't have these kinds of worries. But you are a composer's wife, and you should consider the passion I inspire in women as a kind of glory."

"Alright, alright," Hoa said, conciliatory. "I just want to know if you're in love with her."

Tran Phuong turned toward the window. A pair of birds floated past, tufts of grass in their beaks. "No."

"What proof do I have?"

"She's just an ordinary schoolteacher. You should know that if I wanted to, I could easily find more beautiful, more elegant women."

Sparrows darted past the window again, their eyes glinting like fake pearls. Linh's face, her sparkling brown eyes seemed to flash for a moment against the screen of the sky.

Hoa continued. "So she doesn't know the disdain you feel for her?"

"Not many women would be intelligent enough to discern that," he snapped, pursing his lips into a contemptuous smile. At the same time, a thought screamed in his brain. *You witch. Why are you torturing me like this? I should have thrown you into a pit long ago, during the Resistance.* But he knew he didn't have what it took to kill her, that he had neither the courage to leave her nor the decency to live with her.

"Take me to see her," Hoa said imperiously. "I'll warn her not to chase after a hopeless, unrequited love, to stop pilfering from other people's rice pots." She glared at her husband as she spoke, saw him pale.

"Have you gone mad? Why would you do that?" Tran Phuong stammered.

Hoa was seething, trembling with rage, but she went on in a low voice. "There's nothing strange about that. Didn't you just say you hadn't done anything wrong?"

Tran Phuong had never lost his composure like this. His stammering belied his fear, his guilt. Hoa knew that her husband was afraid of the opprobrium that would fall on his beloved. But she was obsessed. *If that's the way it is, then I won't let you go until I've brought this affair to light.*

"You must take me to see her," she announced coldly.

Tran Phuong tried to stay calm. "You'll regret this. She's just one of thousands of schoolteachers in this city. You are a woman of a certain standing."

"I don't care. Take me to see her."

"Don't do this. I swear to you that she is a perfectly common woman. We should not ruin our reputation."

"No," said Hoa, her voice steely. She had always been an impulsive, flighty woman. But at this moment, she seemed driven by a rare tenacity. Tran Phuong began to tremble. His wife's eyes seemed to him to reflect all the sorrows of the world. On the other side of her gaze, there was a garden in a provincial town, his childhood, a young man, hungry for life, a man whose ideal of love was still unfulfilled. In his mind, he called to Linh, swooned into her sweet, passionate soul. He dreamed of the glow of her eyes, her smile, each word that came off her lips. He swallowed, a bitter taste in his mouth.

Hoa continued: "You know that what I do I can also undo. I have done everything for your success. I can destroy everything you have achieved."

"Shut up! How dare you threaten me?" he screamed. "I live for values completely beyond your ken. Without me, you'd be just a brainless, impulsive woman, incapable of earning your living. As for me, I'll always be a composer. People will always play my music!"

The blow was violent, but precise. Hoa burst into sobs.

"You're nothing but a brute. My whole life I've lived only for you, but you've never been true to me, not once."

While she wept and fell into recriminations, Tran Phuong regained his composure, hesitated, weighed the pros and the cons. The white Moscovic glided across the courtyard. The idea of giving up his car with a chauffeur for a motorcycle or a bicycle terrified him. *You've been climbing the tree for so long, why give up just as you are about to pluck the fruit?* He moved toward his wife and touched her shoulder. "Come, stop crying."

"Oh my God, I'm so miserable."

"Come now, nobody's hurt you. I swear to you, there's nothing between her and me."

"So why won't you take me to see her?"

"We'd make a laughingstock of ourselves. It's madness."

"No, you must take me to her."

Her heart beating fast, Hoa risked this last demand. Like a Chinese chess move, the sacrifice of a chariot clinched her victory. Tran Phuong sighed. His shoulders slumped and he turned aside. "Okay, if that's what you want . . ."

A FEW DAYS after Nguyen had left her, Ngoc Minh paid him a visit. It was dinner time, and Nguyen was snacking on some bread, reading a pile of old news articles. True to form, she banged loudly on the door. "Are you in there, holy man?" she shouted in her mocking voice. Nguyen set the bread down on the table. "Have a seat. I'll make tea."

Ngoc Minh took the bread, and raised it in the air. "Well, well, bread for dinner? Not as industrious as I thought you were. Too lazy to cook?"

"Yeah, too much trouble."

Ngoc Minh looked at him inquisitively. Nguyen rinsed the teapot out, put in some tea, slowly poured the water, then sat down across from her. "You just got back from the newspaper?"

"You must be joking. I spend three quarters of my life partying, three quarters sleeping, and the rest writing stupid articles for your newspapers."

Nguyen glanced at the tiny wrinkles on her forehead, visible despite a thick layer of makeup. For some time, without knowing why, every time he thought of her, he saw those tiny wrinkles.

"What are you studying on my face? The traces of my deep, moral dilemmas?" Ngoc Minh laughed defiantly. Her scarlet lips feigned a pout. Nguyen chuckled. He poured the hot tea into two glasses, sugared it, and added two thin slices of lemon. "There, that's how you like it, isn't it?"

"Exactly. This just proves that my lifestyle is superior to yours, that I prevail."

"No doubt."

Ngoc Minh bit greedily into Nguyen's half-finished piece of bread. "I'm starving. Today, I've got cash. Let's go out to eat at Ta Hien."

Nguyen shook his head. "No way. I've still got a pile of clips to read."

Ngoc Minh laughed. "You're afraid of rumors, being seen with me, aren't you? Come on, the damage is done. It's going to take more than that to make your wife leave her famous composer and come back to you."

Nguyen felt a growing irritation. He didn't reply, just sipped his tea.

"Or is this your hour of prayer? The moment you meditate on the great ideal?" she taunted.

Nguyen continued sipping in silence. Ngoc Minh champed violently at the bread, furious.

"I shouldn't have eaten this," she exclaimed as she finished it off. "It just whets my appetite." She leaned her voluptuous body across the table and grabbed Nguyen's hand. "Okay, I'll stop teasing you. Get changed and come with me. Hurry up."

Nguyen gently pulled his hand away. "Please understand, I can't go," he said in a sad voice that discouraged all joking. Ngoc Minh pulled back her arm and slumped back in her chair. "Why so stern?"

Nguyen looked her in the eye. "Everyone has to live with his choices. I've tried to change, but as you see, my capacity for self-transformation is limited."

"Nguyen, what's the point of slaving away, day in and day out?" Ngoc Minh asked, exasperated. "For what? Life is short— when you finally wake up, it's going to be too late."

Nguyen covered Ngoc Minh's hand with his. "When it comes to existentialist philosophy, I've read more than you have."

"I don't give a damn about philosophy. People have to live their own lives, that's the only thing worth discussing."

Nguyen nodded. "Point taken."

Ngoc Minh stood up and extended her hand. "So, let's go."

Nguyen didn't budge; he just laughed. "I can't."

Under the ceiling light, he still looked like a schoolboy. With his high forehead and fine straight nose, Nguyen was handsome, but a delicate kind of handsome.

Ngoc Minh slumped back into her chair, defeated. "Why, Nguyen?" she asked weakly.

Nguyen shook his head. "A woman only has power over a man who loves her. Forgive me . . . I just don't love you."

After a silence, he continued: "You may say, 'Ah, Love again, that stupid old myth.' You may say, 'Love no more exists between two people than Fidelity, or Perfect Harmony. All lies,' you'll say. I know all your arguments by heart."

"That's right." Ngoc Minh nodded her head, provocatively. But she was disarmed, troubled.

Nguyen continued. "For you, living together is like some kind of contract, with a guarantee of mutual gratification. When one party breaks their promise, the contract should be broken.

If that was the case, do you know how many days I'd have stayed with you?"

Ngoc Minh looked at him and asked sincerely. "No, tell me. How many?"

"Four. Exactly four days. Remember the Thursday morning when that basketball player showed up at your place? How he put his arm around your waist, right in front of me? Remember?"

She squinted, straining to recollect. "Oh, yeah, I remember now. You mean the fat guy, Quynh."

"No self-respecting man would find that normal."

Ngoc Minh pouted. "So we're still talking possession, stinking feudal laws—"

"But I continued to live with you ..." Nguyen cut her off. He didn't care what she thought, wasn't listening anymore, "because I thought we could each smooth down our rough edges, get along. Because I was grateful for your devotion when I was sick. Because you're a good woman who never tries to take advantage of others. You live by your instincts. But you're so liberated that you put yourself in danger. It's self-destructive."

Ngoc Minh shook her head. "There's no danger, I don't care."

He continued, gently, modestly: "One day you'll pay the price. A woman should want to protect her happiness, like a bird protects her nest. You, you flit from one nest to the other."

"And you would have me smothered in love, like one of those silly geese who spends her life with feathers ruffled, guarding her nest, blind to her freedom. Never! I will never be any man's prisoner, even if he's the bird king!" Ngoc Minh screamed, spraying saliva in his face.

Nguyen wiped his face. "I can't stop you from living your life. But I can't be with you."

Ngoc Minh stared at him, stunned. Nguyen stopped speaking. Time dragged on in this suffocating space. Nguyen finally looked up. "More tea?"

Ngoc Minh didn't reply. Then she said: "You left me without even saying good-bye, like a jerk. That was despicable."

"Maybe it was bad," said Nguyen, "but I felt insulted."

"Why was that?"

"Even after I moved in with you, there were still . . . the way you behaved, without the slightest inhibition, continued . . . and . . ."

"God, you're old-fashioned. Your brain is chained to feudal clichés. That Quyhn is really nice."

Startled, Nguyen stammered: "And the biologist too?"

Ngoc Minh nodded, "Yeah, a man of rare intelligence. An incomparable brain, like I told you."

An idea crossed Nguyen's mind and sprang to his lips: "So that means that at the same time . . ."

"What difference does it make? Did it hurt you? Why stay chained to your stupid ideas? It's possible to love more than one person at the same time."

After a long moment of reflection, Nguyen spoke: "It's only now that I really understand you. A few years ago, if a woman had said what you just did, I would have walked out. Today, I can listen, even see your point of view. Maybe it's high time for me to acknowledge that life can be seen from multiple, even contradictory points of view. But I don't need to love many women at the same time, or to live with all of them."

"How strange," Ngoc Minh murmured.

"What's that?"

"Your ideas. I always thought men just played the morality game, but that you all secretly yearned to satisfy your deepest, most repressed fantasies. But you're in a class all by yourself."

Nguyen stopped, gazed at her attentively. "You think everyone, deep down, really thinks like you, has the same desires, just doesn't have the courage to live like you. You think everyone is cloaked in the hypocrisy of some virtuous role that they play out of cowardice. *That's* what's strange."

Ngoc Minh thought a moment, "Actually, I still find what you say suspect."

"That's your right. But if I am like you, then what invisible cord ties me to this cold room? What would keep a normal, single man from . . ."

The nauseating thought of their lovemaking stopped him from speaking. Ngoc Minh seemed to him like a gluttonous child, as if nothing else in the world existed but the cake she was gulping down. Nguyen still looked at her. Her uneven, patchy blue eyeshadow made her look clownlike. Suddenly moved, he said: "To love, we need passion, but also respect. Once, someone told me that all you needed to build lasting happiness was a woman who admired and respected her man. But now, I know that's wrong. Happiness is much more difficult to attain. It's like crossing a suspension bridge; it's fragile, shaky, and there's no guardrail. You have to find your own equilibrium. And for that to happen, it has to rest on two centers of gravity, on both partners."

Ngoc Minh flushed with anger and shame. "Useless rhetoric," she hissed. "Men like you just repeat old clichés . . . Real life, that's always elsewhere, elsewhere . . ."

She waved her hand toward the window that looked down over the city: "Your theories are a bunch of rotten cabbage!"

She stood up and swung her leather bag over her shoulder. "Well, good-bye. Of all my lovers, you are the best person. I wanted to take you out, treat you to some of my favorite delicacies, and all I get is another sermon. What a waste."

She left without waiting for his reply, pounding the stairs with her high heels. Nguyen jumped up and ran after her. The stairwell was pitch black. A cold wind stung his face. He went back to his room, walked toward the window, and looked out onto the street. The panels of Ngoc Minh's *ao dai* fluttered in the wind. Usually she drove fast, elbows in the air, head held high and whistling like a sixteen-year-old. But now, in the cold, deserted street, she looked abandoned, distraught. Her Honda pitched and swayed. Nguyen closed the window, quickly changed, and jumped on his bicycle to go after her. When he reached her apartment, he found her flung on the bed, her face buried in a pillow, bawling like a kid. Nguyen felt a mixture of pity and tenderness. He didn't care what other people thought; he forgave her for everything. But he couldn't forgive who she was. Behind the theories of freedom that she got from her books, and despite her considerable intelligence, she was a wild breed, a true, pure, earth woman of prehistoric times. Ngoc Minh was authentic to the core. Living with her, almost unconsciously, an image had taken shape deep inside him: A woman standing alone, naked, facing the sea. Strong, yet vulnerable. A woman who stood there, resilient, in the middle of the crashing waves, on a beach that bore no trace of male footsteps.

Buffeted by the wind, the shutters on her window clattered violently. Ngoc Minh sobbed, her body heaving to their rhythm. At the foot of the bed, on a reed mat, lay a few empty bottles, some roasted peanuts. The shells flew about, scattered everywhere. How many times had he cleaned up after her, swept away the debris of her parties? Early that morning, when the party was over, after the men had finished the booze and food and gone home, Ngoc Minh had felt sad and thought of Nguyen. Her loss was greater than she had thought. Nguyen's patient, kind nature had made her yearn for the peaceful, balanced life that she had never had time to explore. In her vagabond soul, there was still space for the yearnings of a normal woman. Nguyen wasn't a boy anymore. He knew that under her brash, provocative shell, she had a woman's heart. In her youth, Ngoc Minh had probably been as pure as other girls, her primal instincts still dormant. But she had met too many clever, manipulative, egotistical men who had used her lusty body. These men of the world had taught her that love was just a hypocritical myth, that life was short, as thin as a wad of bills, and that if you didn't spend it you'd end up with slips of paper with no value. That she was the goddess of freedom and free love. Now these men were gone, had evaporated like soap bubbles, and Ngoc Minh found herself alone in a room littered with peanut shells.

Nguyen suddenly felt the urge to console her, but he knew it would be useless. He stood there in the doorway for a long time, motionless, then left. A few days later, Ngoc Minh came back to find him. This time, she was no longer arrogant or sarcastic. "I love you," she told him frankly. "And I want to have a child with you, a boy with your face, your gentleness. It's useless to get married. One day, the state will recognize the rights of all children who come into this world."

Nguyen refused. Ngoc Minh burst into tears and hurled insults at him. Every day after work, she waited for him outside his office. She went on one of her shopping sprees and bought him five fashionable new suits, showered him with the attentions of a model wife. Nguyen still firmly refused. For Ngoc Minh, his indifference was like a stone wall that she had decided to charge, gathering all her strength to pull it down. But the cement was too hard. And anyway, another male wall would soon rise in her path. To prove her power, Ngoc Minh shifted her target, steeling herself to do battle with this new, higher, more imposing wall.

Two weeks later, Nguyen ran into her; she was accompanied by a tall, dark young man with all the presence of a film star. They were on their way to the Opera House to see a new play. Ngoc Minh waved from afar to Nguyen, shouting: "Good evening, holy man. How are you? Off to say your prayers?"

Nguyen smiled, nodded, and moved away to find his seat.

12

THE ADMINISTRATIVE DIRECTOR hurried over to Nguyen when he saw him arrive at the newspaper office. "Nguyen, I've got an urgent matter for you," the man announced, handing him a note folded in quarters. "This morning, before leaving for the airport, the boss asked me to tell you to make sure this gets out right away."

Nguyen took the letter and opened the door to his office. Two newly hired journalists had already prepared tea. Nguyen served himself a cup and sipped it as he read the letter. He recognized the editor-in-chief's handwriting, hurried, blurry, heavy with words thickly underlined.

> Dear Nguyen:
>   I can't go into detail about the Hien matter.
>   Go see Trong at his house. His brother-in-law works for Hien. He'll bring you up to date on *all* the details. Hien has been my buddy since the Resistance. *Help him.* It will be as if you were helping me. *I'm counting on you.* The articles are at the secretariat.
>
>   See you in two weeks.
>   Best regards . . .

Nguyen folded up the letter and slipped it in his pocket. He checked his articles one last time before they went to press. Then he left on his bicycle for Trong's house. It was nine-fifteen. The sun was out, but it was cold. It was winter, but the chilly, silver clouds were reminiscent of autumn. Usually, Nguyen was a hard worker. The editor-in-chief knew he could count on Nguyen to rapidly execute his instructions. But today, Nguyen felt oddly apathetic. He pedaled slowly down the streets of Hanoi, contemplating the smooth, familiar surface of Hoan Kiem Lake in winter.

"Nguyen! Nguyen!" A familiar voice interrupted his contemplation.

It was Trong, making a U-turn on his Mobylette, his face red, his coat open to reveal a ragged old wool sweater. "I've been chasing after you," Trong panted.

"But I was coming to find you," Nguyen explained. "What's so urgent that you run out dressed like this?"

Trong lowered his head and buttoned his coat. "I know the boss left you a note, but my wife and her brother were impatient. They made me come find you. I rushed over to the newspaper, then came back here. Hurry, everyone's back at the house waiting."

"Okay, I'll follow you," Nguyen said, continuing to pedal slowly. Trong stayed speechless for a moment, then accelerated and passed Nguyen.

Nguyen didn't feel like hurrying and didn't really know why. This morning, he felt indifferent, unaccommodating. He arrived at Trong's a half hour later. The house was the ideal Hanoi residence—two large rooms, a spacious verandah, and a courtyard big enough for a table and bamboo chairs. Cam, Trong's wife, had divided the kitchen in half to raise pigs and chickens. In a certain sense, Trong was both the happiest and the wealthiest journalist at the newspaper. He had never known poverty, or the nagging, daily worries that plagued his colleagues. He spent his income on cigarettes, trips, or theater tickets. From time to time, Cam would check his pockets and, if he had run out of money, she would slip in enough to cover his purchases. At home, there was always some snake liqueur, a few bottles of herb liqueur, Thai Nguyen tea, jasmine tea, coffee, and all kinds of cigarettes. Cam didn't stint on anything for her husband, including his newspapers and dictionaries. The only thing Trong didn't care about was his appearance. They jokingly compared him to the Tay Phuong genie who liked to eat but not to dress up. And Nguyen had reprimanded him several times for receiving foreign visitors dressed like a docker. One day, Nguyen had to explain the problem to Cam.

"What's the use of being a slave to fashion?" she asked. "To pick up girls who spend their time partying?" When Cam finally did make her husband a suit, she only allowed him to wear it when she was sure it was for work.

Nguyen pushed his bicycle down the verandah. Trong and Cam rushed toward him. "My God, we've all been waiting for you!" Cam shouted, rushing over with a basin of hot water. "Here, wash up and have a drink. We've kept the food warm."

"Oh, Cam, you shouldn't have." Nguyen saw the dining room table piled with food, four bottles of wine, a vase of peonies, wine glasses. Everything looked so formal. A man in a white shirt, seated behind the table, jumped up when he saw Nguyen.

"Let me introduce Liem, my brother. This is Mr. Nguyen, Trong's director at work," Cam said, her voice excited, but deferential. The man moved toward the door and bowed his head low. Nguyen shook a small, cold, bony hand. He could see that Trong was nervous, waiting for a cue from his wife.

"Come on inside, everyone," Cam said. "There's no reason to stay outside."

"May I come in too, Cam?" Trong asked.

Cam was hanging a towel up to dry. She glanced at her

husband, exasperated. "Yes, of course, come on in and serve Mr. Nguyen a drink. Do I have to show you how to do that too?"

Nguyen smiled. "Don't be too hard on him." He entered the room, sat down in a chair. Liem and Trong busied themselves serving wine, cutting the squid and cold cuts.

"Why such a feast?" Nguyen asked, already sensing that there was something behind this. "Where are the kids?" he asked Trong.

Trong laughed nervously. Cam quickly replied for him. "The kids have already eaten, they've left for their grandmother's house. It's been a long time since you've been over to visit."

Nguyen said nothing. He guessed that this feast had something to do with the editor-in-chief's mission, but it would have been inappropriate to ask questions. Cam's brother looked up and rubbed his hands together. "Please, let's take up our chopsticks, it's a rare honor to meet someone as . . . important as you."

Nguyen didn't say anything. He looked at Liem's hands. They were trembling slightly. The man was trying to stay calm. He drank some wine, then lowered his head. "Well, *bon appétit*."

His hosts started to drink, sipping cautiously. They all ate the same way. This sumptuous meal was obviously a setup, an excuse for them to make some important announcement. Cam couldn't sit still; she kept jumping up and then sitting down again, warming up the soup, chopping more red chilies, peppering the dishes, scurrying off to get them cigarettes, or matches. The men just picked at the food with their chopsticks, raising and lowering them. Trong, a real gourmet, was the one who ate most freely and talked the loudest. "Eat up, Mr. Nguyen. Help yourself, everyone."

Cam served, urging Nguyen to eat. She noticed that many

of the dishes had been left untouched; the stew and the asparagus soup had barely been started. Her face creased with
worry.

Uneasy, Nguyen took a piece of asparagus with his chopsticks. "Come on Trong, Mr. Liem. We're men, after all. Like
they say, we're supposed to eat like tigers and women like
sparrows. Let's do honor to Cam's cooking."

Nguyen's little joke broke the ice. The two men emptied
their glasses, and poured more to drink. Nguyen stared at the
pink liquid. *The first time I got drunk it was at the Journalists'
Club. I ended up in Ngoc Minh's bed. What trap am I going to fall
into this time?* At the thought, Nguyen broke into a bitter, ironic
smile. Trong's plump cheeks and nose started to redden and
sweat. Nguyen glanced at the clock. It was ten forty-five. The
real conversation probably wouldn't start for at least another
hour.

He looked at Cam's plump wrists as she cleared the table,
and couldn't help remembering Linh's firm hands, the softness
of her skin. Cam was a housewife who had gone to seed early;
she was fat, with puffy eyelids and sagging cheeks. But she
was content with her life: her faithful, handsome husband and
her two well-behaved kids, her chicken coop full of eggs, and
her pigsty always stocked with meat. (Liem provided the feed
for the pigs and chickens, and one of his three mistresses, who
worked in the Ministry of Agriculture, supplied them with all
the necessary vaccines.)

"Have some fruit," said Cam, who had just peeled an orange. She pushed a plate toward Nguyen and slipped her husband a look, as if to let him know that he could broach the
subject. Trong poured water in Nguyen's cup. "Tea or coffee?"

"Neither, thanks, I had some this morning."

Nguyen lit a cigarette, took small drags, and waited. It was
time to get to the point. The alarm clock on the chest of drawers

indicated twenty minutes before noon. Trong began. "Nguyen, like the boss told you, he asked us to tell you the whole story."

"What's his full name again?" Nguyen interrupted.

"Nguyen Thanh Hien. He's a competent cadre, generous, trusted by his superiors and his staff. But his work isn't flawless. More specifically, in his relationships with women . . . he goes over the limit. What I mean is . . ."

Trong stammered, searching for words. Nguyen had rarely seen his colleague so nervous. Behind his glasses, Trong's beady eyes seemed riveted to the porcelain fish that held the toothpicks. His huge hands shook nervously. Liem stared at the face of his Orient wristwatch. The muscles in his cheeks twitched ever so slightly. Nguyen puffed on his cigarette. Cam returned from the courtyard with a plate of Hai Dong bean cakes. She set it down, surveyed the three men, and vanished. After an embarrassingly long pause, Trong continued: "Hien is currently in the middle of a lawsuit. People are denouncing him."

"Husbands?" Nguyen asked.

"No, the elder brother of a girl, fathers of other girls."

"Ah."

"In fact, Hien is in an extremely difficult situation. The public prosecutor and the court are taking this case very seriously. But Hien's department was quite heroic during the war. So, uh, the editor wants to know if you could write an article to support him. In support of the transport sector in general, of course, but even more importantly to help Hien in his current battle."

"Against who?" Nguyen asked, unable to conceal his contempt. But Trong and Liem didn't get it.

"Enemies, Mr. Nguyen," Liem piped up. "My boss is in grave danger. From the families of the girls, the public prosecutor's office, the court. They're all in league with one another."

"A united front," Nguyen quipped sarcastically. "Just like the National Liberation Front way back when."

Trong said nothing. Liem, his voice troubled, pressed further. "Help us, please. My boss is a loyal man. That's why he has always managed to find protection in difficult moments. Mr. Hien always remembers those who help him out. Even seven years later, he'll roll out the red carpet."

Nguyen laughed, feigned surprise. "You mean to say that my boss would take a real liking to Mr. Hien if they met? Or have they already?"

Nguyen watched Liem's face redden and twitch with fear. Unable to restrain himself, he slapped the man's shoulder. "I see, so your boss only remembers his debts for seven years? And if someone came to him in eight years, would his secretary throw them out?"

Liem gasped. Not knowing how to respond, he broke into a nervous grin, the muscles of his cheeks still twitching. Trong nervously served tea. The clip-clap of the water, flowing from the teapot into the cups, echoed in the silence.

"Mr. Liem," said Nguyen gently. "I'll give you my reply early next week. This week's issue has already gone to press."

"But that'll be too late," cried Liem, his forehead creased with worry lines. "Please, do us a favor. This is a crisis situation. Think of it as a forest fire; delaying a single day could be fatal."

"A crisis? I once wrote an urgent dispatch after the B52 bombings," said Nguyen. "They sent it directly to the printer's for the following day. But praise for the public transport sector doesn't exactly call for the same haste."

"Please, my boss has been praying for your article," Liem pleaded.

Nguyen continued: "In any case, to write an article I'll need documents, to examine the facts, reflect—"

"Of course, of course. My boss understands. He prepared everything for you." Liem jumped up, opened a black leather briefcase, and pulled out a folder.

"Here's the report on the year before last. Here are the official congratulations of the minister. Here's the dossier on our unit, designating it as a model service sector; this was presented to the National Congress of Road Transport four years ago. Here is the—"

"Very good, I'll take a look," Nguyen said, shaking his head. "My, your boss is really meticulous. A complete file, served up on a silver platter. Why, I won't even need to leave my office. I should thank him. But allow me to give you my reply later."

Then, nodding to Trong, Nguyen said coldly, "Your brother-in-law will give you my answer." He put on his jacket, pulling the zipper up to his chin. Cam appeared from the courtyard. "Stay a while longer, Mr. Nguyen. You come so rarely. Do you have to leave so soon?"

She slipped a glance at her husband's impassive face and at her brother's frightened one. She grabbed Nguyen's arm. "Why such haste, Mr. Nguyen? You're going to make us lose face."

Nguyen shook his head. "I've got urgent work to do. As a matter of fact, I need Trong to accompany me."

Cam frowned, thought for a minute, then turned to her husband. "Well, what are you waiting for? Follow Mr. Nguyen! Don't forget your wool sweater, the long-sleeved one."

Trong said nothing, grudgingly pulled on his sweater, and trudged after Nguyen onto the verandah. When the two men had crossed the courtyard, their bicycles in hand, they turned to wave good-bye to Liem. Seated on the edge of the bed, he followed them with his eyes. Cam stood next to him. As Nguyen and Trong reached the gate, she bent down to whisper something in her brother's ear, as if to console him. Nguyen didn't miss a detail, but he felt neither irritated nor curious. The two men pedaled absentmindedly down the streets, randomly choosing their path. After about a half hour, Nguyen said, "Let's go to my place. It's to the right, about five minutes from here."

"Okay."

They arrived at the foot of the stairs leading to Nguyen's apartment and parked their bicycles. Still not speaking, they mounted the stairs one by one. Nguyen opened the door.

"It's been a long time since I've been here, not since . . ." Trong stopped himself.

"Since my wife left me," Nguyen said, his voice cold, indifferent. Just then it sounded to him like the voice of a stranger, echoing from the other side of a wall. Trong didn't dare look him in the eye. He shifted on his feet, uneasy. Nguyen opened a window, then turned to his friend, his eyes inquisitorial, threatening: "Okay, now I want you to tell me everything."

Trong's red hands started scuttling across the table.

"What are you looking for? A cigarette?" Nguyen fumbled in his pocket, threw his pack of cigarettes on the table. "You never smoke, even though I noticed you've got every possible brand at your house. What else can I get you? Matches? I'm out of them. But here's my lighter."

Trong lit a cigarette and puffed greedily on it. Nguyen waited, still standing, his arms crossed. A long moment went by. Trong looked up and met Nguyen's eyes. "Cam's the one who set everything up. I was ashamed, especially in front of you, but I couldn't stop her."

"I know. Who is this Nguyen Thanh Hien character?"

"Never met him. But according to Cam and her brother he's a horrible man. He was an agricultural engineer. After he finished his studies, they assigned him to an institute attached to the Ministry of Agriculture. He was one of the first of the Resistance heroes to earn a university degree, so he was rapidly promoted. He climbed the ladder of the hierarchy in no time. As they say, he was destined to become an apparatchik: He found protection every step of the way. He was capable enough, but authoritarian and cruel. When Johnson launched the military escalation, Hien's section was evacuated to the countryside, about seventeen miles from Hanoi, in Ha Son Binh province. There, Hien raped a minor. The incident leaked out, and the girl's parents denounced him to the authorities. Hien forced his aging wife to retaliate with a lawsuit that accused the girl's father of being the rapist. It was a huge scandal in the city at the time. But as you know, Hien has many connections. Friends, family, Resistance buddies going back to the time of the anti-French Resistance. They more or less reprimanded him, but in the end, in the name of solidarity, respect for the past, they interceded on his behalf with the courts. Hien was given a six-month suspended prison sentence. But this criminal record didn't stop him. He didn't want to stay at his institute. His colleagues hated him. He might have escaped a prison sentence, but he couldn't save himself from public disgrace. So he pulled strings, and six months later he became director of a transport unit. He's been there for nine years."

"And during the past nine years, what crimes has he committed?"

"I don't know. But the latest scandal just came to light . . . involving a nineteen-year-old accountant who had a six-month assignment in Hien's office. She was orphaned at age five, but it turns out that her older brother is an army officer. He returned on leave to see his sister and discovered the truth when she locked herself in her room to sob. When she refused to come out, he broke down the door. He had to talk to her all night before she finally admitted that she'd been raped, that she wanted to commit suicide. Her brother went straight to Hien's office. He would have killed him on the spot if a group of Red Guards there hadn't stopped him. The officer brought charges against him with the court. The scandal got out, everyone was talking about it. Little by little, they discovered that Hien had abused every woman in his department. But they had all kept silent, either out of fear or out of shame, or because they didn't have a devoted elder brother courageous enough to confront the criminal. When they get to the bottom of this, Nguyen, I don't know how many rapes they are going to find."

Trong stopped. The two men were silent for a long time. Trong lit a cigarette. Nguyen stared at a point in space, then asked: "And your brother-in-law? What's this scandal to him that it would shake him up like that? Did the boss let him in on the leftovers of his plunder?"

Trong shook his head. "No, no. He's not the type. But he has other vices. You know, the war, it's been a magnet for foreign aid. Chauffeurs like Liem find it difficult to contain their greed. Hien quickly discovered Liem's petty theft. He summoned him, showed him proof, then put the goods into a leather briefcase to take them home. Liem lives in fear. He's become Hien's hostage, his lackey. Hien is a clever man, and he knows how to trap people. Liem now fears for Hien even more than he fears for himself. As long as his boss stays in power, Liem's theft won't come to light, and he'll continue to rake in the money. What he's really afraid of is that Hien's enemies in the department will search his files. What will become of Liem then?"

Nguyen smiled weakly, then said in caustic voice, "And you and Cam? You're a slave to Cam and Cam's a slave to her brother. Why, half of your house belongs to Liem. But he's given his share to your wife without asking for anything in return. In fact, he's a generous elder brother. What's more,

Cam's chickens and pigs bring him tens of thousands of *dong* every year. But that's also thanks to the bags of bran and corn he brings her. If something were to happen to Liem, your income would disappear, and that's not even consider-ing the worst-case scenario: if you had to share the house with your sister-in-law and her children. Correct me if I'm wrong."

Trong didn't reply; he continued to puff on his cigarette. Nguyen squinted and said sarcastically, "And here I am, given the honor of writing an article in praise of a criminal that will lighten his sentence, and if possible, transform him into a hero. Great. Well done. Do you know, by any chance, why our dear editor-in-chief has so much regard for this character? Why he would ask me to do this?"

Trong replied slowly. "I don't think the boss has a stake in this. Hien uses this tactic with all his connections. Gifts at Tet, loans for funerals or marriages, credit when someone needs to buy land or build a house. Using the pretext of public relations for his company, Hien distributes state goods to buy 'stocks' with men in power. But as far as the editor-in-chief is con-cerned, I think Hien was just counting on their friendship, which goes back to their youth. As you would say, it's just another case of our national illness of sentimentality."

"Ah yes, the ravages of sentimentality," Nguyen said, smil-ing. "But tell me, the banquet you just held in my honor, was that sentimentality or pragmatism?"

Trong looked up. The color of his already ruddy face deep-ened. His small eyes suddenly became hostile. "I told you. This whole story makes me sick, but I couldn't stop Cam from in-terfering. She's the one who rules in our house. I'm not obliv-ious to the fact that I'm the submissive type. But what about you? Don't you wonder why the editor-in-chief picked *you* to write an article to save Hien? Why didn't he ask me? Or Miss Tam, or Nam or Phuc? I'll tell you why. Because up until now, *you're* the one who has always jumped to attention, dutifully executing his every whim. He knows you'll be loyal to him, whatever the situation, like some kind of lackey!"

Nguyen, still standing, kept silent. Trong wiped his glasses after this angry outburst. Now that his rage had subsided, he regretted his words. For some time now, each time he had made mistakes, whether out of laziness or self-defense, Nguyen had come to his defense, protected him. Still wiping his glasses, Trong stuttered, searching for words to soothe his friend. Nguyen didn't give him the time. In a low, cold voice he said, "You're right . . . Why me?"

THE EVENING Hoa confronted Linh in a public scene of jealousy, Kim Anh went to find Dung at his house. Dung was at the dinner table with his elderly mother and his two daughters. Seeing Kim Anh lean her bicycle against the wall, Dung put down his bowl and went out to greet her. "Come join us for dinner, Kim Anh." Kim Anh looked up and greeted Dung's mother and his two daughters, who chimed an almost simultaneous greeting. "Please finish your meal," she said. "I'll wait. There's a problem we must discuss."

She poured herself a glass of water and picked a comic book off a shelf. Her simple, natural manner put them at ease. The family finished a simple everyday meal: a plate of duckweed greens and a few tiny freshwater shrimp sautéed with thinly sliced starfruit.

Dung got up to get some peanut nougat for Kim Anh.

"Please, no fuss, Dung, I'm not a teenager anymore." She shared the sweets with the two kids, who thanked her and withdrew to another room.

"What brings you, Kim Anh?"

"It's Linh. There's been a very unpleasant incident." She waited for Dung to question her, but he said nothing, just busied himself rinsing the teapot and preparing tea. After a moment, Kim Anh continued. "We were wrong to force Linh to go work in the library."

Dung said nothing.

"To be fair," said Kim Anh, "I made the decision. I was afraid of the pressure, the warnings from the district education department, afraid for the high school's reputation. Of course, you shared that decision, but I bear the lion's share of responsibility. We ignored the criticism and opposition of the other teachers. Now, I feel I was just cowardly. Who was I afraid of? What was I afraid of? Of that fat old lady, some manager of a state fruit and vegetable store? I was afraid of public opinion. I didn't want to lose the flag we had won for model behavior."

Dung lowered his head and stared into his cup of tea. He kept his silence. Kim Anh looked at him, exasperated, and continued: "Did I tell you? That fat lady with her Leninist speeches, the one who demanded that her child be taught by a virtuous teacher, was arrested last week. She teamed up with her sister-in-law, some high-ranking foreign trade official, to steal state goods to sell on the black market. In this incident alone, they embezzled a half million *dong*. A sum that we don't even dare dream of. And these are the people who come threaten us?"

"You've told me the story of the fat lady state store owner. But Linh's story is what we need to discuss. Tell me what happened this afternoon. Something serious, wasn't it?"

"No, nothing serious," said Kim Anh, her voice hardened. "Just another opportunity to understand what men are really like."

Dung looked up, fixed his gentle eyes on Kim Anh, and smiled. "You want to provoke me? But I've never been able to get angry, you know."

"Yes, that's right, and that's the worst thing about you," Kim Anh said wearily. "Someone who doesn't really know how to hate, doesn't really know how to love either."

Dung kept smiling. "That's theoretically accurate. But this is no time to be discussing theory. Tell me about Linh. What happened?"

Kim Anh sighed. Dung's patience had deflated her irritation. "A person's guilt often bears no relation to the act of wrongdoing. Linh's story isn't as simple as you think. We should let our hearts be the judge."

"You and me, we like Linh," said Dung. "The young teachers trust her even more. But feelings aren't the only thing at stake here. We have to be careful. If you hadn't proposed transferring Linh to the library, I'd have done it a few weeks later."

"I know. But we are teachers. And a teacher's ultimate duty is to give the best education to his or her students. Linh is our finest humanities teacher. Since she stopped teaching and tutoring students, we've started losing Hanoi's humanities competitions. But this is nothing when I think of the suffering we've caused her. So we acknowledge that our decision was wrong, but do we have the guts to retract it?"

Dung looked at Kim Anh. After a long pause, he asked, "Would you dare, Kim Anh?"

"Before, no. Now, yes."

"So, let's say that we admit we made a mistake to transfer Linh. Even if we try to justify our action, citing circumstances at the time, we won't fool anybody."

Kim reflected, then nodded energetically. "It doesn't matter."

"I approve of your decision," said Dung, "but tell me, Kim Anh, why now?"

"I . . . I . . ." stammered the principal, then stood up. "I must be going. They're waiting for me at home for dinner. See you tomorrow morning early, right?"

Dung accompanied her to the door. She was hiding something from him, but he didn't feel right questioning her.

A FIFTEEN-YEAR-OLD BOY, handsome, strolled by, hands in his pockets, singing. A passionate voice, dreamy eyes. Nguyen remembered being fifteen. He was still so innocent, more boy than man. Today, fifteen-year-old boys already whistled love songs. Once, at that age, Nguyen had wept at the foot of a guava tree because another boy had stolen a cake from him.

The waitress came over to his table. "You ordered coffee?"

Nguyen took the cup from the hands of a pretty young girl in white jeans and a red sweater. She looked more like an actress than a waitress.

"I'll have another piece of cake."

She brought it immediately. Nguyen pushed the empty plate to the side. He had already eaten two pieces of cake, but his stomach was still twisting. He hadn't had time to eat that morning. He had finished work and could have eaten a sandwich or a *pho*, but he had agreed to meet with Nguyen Trung, a young cadre working for the state prosecutor's office. Nguyen glanced at his watch. It was quarter to ten. The man was five minutes late. Nguyen guessed that he must have had a problem, since up until now, Trung had never been even a second late. "Three minutes early," he would say. "That's been my principle since college, whether it was for class or a date."

That's what Trung had told him when they first met, with a decisive, confident air rare in a young man of twenty-seven. He was thin, with a quick stride, twinkling eyes, and a full beard that covered his large, square jaw. In his way of observing everything around him, Trung showed an equanimity and a savvy that older men would have envied. His smile, his mischievous eyes—a gaze that could paralyze his interlocutors if necessary—everything about him appealed to Nguyen. He saw in this young man the image of himself ten years ago, more resolute, more aggressive, more profound.

Eleven minutes to ten. Trung still hadn't arrived. The young man passed in front of the café again, singing enthusiastically, as if he were alone in the world.

And the sky covers with clouds
The rain blurs
The silhouette of my beloved . . .

The silhouette of my beloved
Slowly dissolves in the rain.

The melancholy lyrics moved Nguyen. The boy sang in a hoarse voice, unaware of Nguyen's presence in the café. Then he sauntered off, hands in his pockets, his voice slowly fading. Nguyen pursued the boy's song in his mind, letting his memories drift. The smoke from his cigarette slowly unfurled, the ashes settling slowly onto his fingers. He suddenly jumped in pain from the burn and stubbed out his cigarette. Just then Trung entered the café.

"Please forgive me. Something unexpected came up," the young man said. Trung sat down, brushing away the thick cloud of cigarette smoke with his hand.

"I knew something had happened. You're usually so punctual. What'll you have?" Nguyen asked.

"Same as you, a coffee," Trung replied, pulling a small package out of his pocket. "Here, have a look. This is why I was late."

Nguyen fingered the package, expecting a precious object. He unwrapped two layers of paper. A small purple velvet box decorated with golden roses. All around the rim, a finely embroidered motif. A stamp still sealed the lid of the box.

"You haven't opened it yet?" Nguyen asked, surprised.

"Not yet," Trung said calmly, and took a sip from the cup of coffee the owner had just set on the table. "Open it. You'll get a thrill, just like cutting the red ribbon to inaugurate a building site."

The young man grinned sardonically, a devious twinkle in his eye. Nguyen smiled, peeled off the stamp, and carefully lifted the hinged cover. Nestled against the shiny, black velvet interior was a woman's watch mounted on a glittering gold bracelet. They both let out a whistle of surprise.

"I count fourteen precious stones. A gem reserved for the truly wealthy. As you can see, Mr. Hien doesn't skimp on his bribes," Trung said, emptying his cup of coffee. Nguyen offered him a cigarette.

"No thanks, Nguyen," Trung shook his head. "Your memory is going. I don't smoke. We've seen each other quite a few times now and you still keep offering me cigarettes."

"Sorry, my memory must be slipping."

"No, not yet. But you are preoccupied by something."

Nguyen didn't reply, but was startled. *This man is observant.*

"Let's get to the point. Twenty minutes ago, I find on my doorstep a tall, dark-skinned man, looking worried. I open the door to take out my bicycle. He enters and hurriedly closes it behind me. Without waiting for my questions, he introduces himself as the delegate for the colleagues and chauffeurs in Mr. Nguyen Thanh Hien's department. He tells me that all the employees love and respect their boss, and deplore the errors he has made, but that he's a talented man who did fight heroically for the Revolution, that his good qualities far outweigh his weaknesses, and that the masses are praying fervently to see him reinstated as head of the department. To finish, he offers me, no, he says he would like to offer my girlfriend, a gift. I protest and tell him to take it back, but he scurries off as fast as a mouse. I didn't want to chase the guy through the streets with this package, shouting, and, well . . . I wanted to show it to you. It's another piece of evidence. Hold on to it. Better that it be in your hands the day we reveal the truth about this man.

Now, about this Liem guy, do you know who he is, why he works for Hien?"

"He's just one of Hien's hostages. His livelihood depends on Hien's political survival. But he isn't a stooge. How far have you gotten, by the way, with the favor I asked? I'm in a hurry because my editor-in-chief came back from his trip yesterday morning. This morning, he's resting, but this afternoon, he'll go to the newspaper offices. I want to be sure what the story is before I see him."

"I've gathered all the documents and legal files for you. Everything is in a closet at my house. But now, I think you should come with me on an investigation." Trung glanced at his watch. "Let's go. We'll be early. I told my sister we would be there in twenty minutes. Wrap that watch back up and keep it. I trust there are no holes in your pocket? You lose that and we'll both stand accused of corruption with no one to defend us."

Nguyen paid the bill. They left on their bicycles, pedaling side by side in silence. When they reached the clock across from the Hong Ha Cinema, Trung stopped, "Let's wait here. In a minute, Hien's wife is going to leave the market. My sister checked her routine. When she shows, she'll ask her to come talk. Don't say a word. I'll handle everything."

Nguyen nodded, slightly nervous. Trung scrutinized the noisy, animated crowd, surveying the different multicolored clothes, haircuts, and bright scarves, the sea of faces.

"There's my sister, Trinh," Trung said suddenly.

Nguyen looked in the same direction and saw a very young woman, with Trung's features, but plumper. Trung had a sullen complexion, but his sister's was rosy, as if she wore rouge.

"She had a child eight months ago," Trung said, as if sensing Nguyen's doubts. Once again, Nguyen was startled by the man's powers of observation. As Trung watched his sister, his eyes were riveted to her, as if driven by a powerful, precise magnet. Suddenly, she stopped choosing vegetables, lifted her head, and signaled to Trung with her hand. She moved toward a row of people who were queuing in front of a butcher's stall, and said a few words to a woman in a blue blouse. A few seconds later, she led the woman out of the crowd in the direction of the two men. The distance that separated them slowly narrowed. Nguyen could suddenly see the features of the woman in blue more clearly. She was old, about sixty, or slightly less, with a long, sad face, and deep, taught lines around the mouth. She had an odd gait, waddling alternately from left to right, her head pitched forward.

"Hello, madame."

Trung's voice startled her and she looked up.

"Oh, hello sir, uh, gentlemen." Her murky eyes grew as frightened as those of a sparrow caught in a trap. Deep long wrinkles furrowed her cheeks. Nguyen suddenly felt his heart twist.

"We have a few questions to ask you. Would you please come with us?" Trung said firmly.

"I . . . I don't know anything," the woman stammered. "I don't know anything."

"We'll only ask about what you do know," said the young man, gently.

"Don't be afraid," his sister added. "You haven't done anything wrong, you have nothing to fear." She opened the door and entered the house. Everyone else followed. The house was near the market, but when the two wood shutters were closed, it became completely silent. Trinh prepared tea, served it, and withdrew into her room after saying a few more words of reassurance to the visitor. The old woman squeezed her hands over her stomach and stared at her cup of tea. Silence. Nguyen waited. Finally, Trung started to speak: "You get a lot of visitors at your place, don't you?"

"No," the old woman replied coldly, blinking her eyes as if

to shield her thoughts. This had to be a lie. Trung's face didn't move. He seemed accustomed to this kind of response, and continued in a neutral voice. "So, you don't have many visitors?"

"No, ah, yes, that's right, we don't."

"So no one comes to see the director of such a large transport unit?"

"No, I don't know."

"And friends? Mr. Hien has no friends then?"

"No, no. If he does, he must receive them in his office."

"Since his arrest then, no one has come to see you?"

"No one."

"Who brings food to your husband in jail? You, or your children?"

"My children."

"Which one takes care of this?"

"I don't know. They decide among themselves."

"No one discusses with you what takes place in your family?"

"No."

"When does your second son leave for Hungary to do his doctoral thesis?"

"I don't know. They decide."

"Your daughter Hoan has just built a lovely two-story house. Have you seen it?"

"No, no," said the old woman, shaking her head. "She's married, it's none of my business anymore." She spoke in a low drone, devoid of emotion, as monotonous as rain dripping off a thatch roof. Nguyen began to grow impatient. Trung, his hands on the table, looked suspiciously calm.

"Your son, Mr. Hoang, has just been promoted to chief of planning. Have you celebrated this promotion?" Trung continued.

"No," the woman said. Her voice had turned hard, stubborn, and her face was like a cave sealed off by huge black boulders.

"Your other son, Huy, managed to procure all the construction materials he needs to build his new home. Have you seen the blueprints for his new villa? They were done by a talented young architect who just finished his studies in Sofia."

"No, I know nothing about it."

"But you must know about this." Trung's voice changed, turning suddenly abrupt. The shift in tone disarmed the woman. Trung's eyes seemed to flash, bearing down on the woman. "You have a lovely villa in your native province in Hai Hung. The five rooms on the first floor are reserved for the altar to ancestors of your clan. Your mother and handicapped brother live in the three rooms on the ground floor."

The old woman remained rigid, impassive. Her stony, inert eyes seemed to see nothing in space. A statue's eyes in the shadowy half-light of pagodas, blind, lost in the deep waters of the void.

"You are a filial, pious woman. Thanks to you, your mother and your brother live comfortably. Was it for the eight-room house that nine years ago, to defend your husband, you brought charges against Mr. Tien, accusing him of raping his own daughter Vu Thuy Hong?"

The woman did not reply. Her face, her murky eyes were unfathomable.

"Five days ago, Mr. Hien summoned his nephew and told him to sell five rooms on the first floor of your house to get the cash he needed for bribes."

Uncertainty surfaced from the depths of the woman's eyes, flitting for an instant across the stony mask of her face. Wrinkles creased and deepened, circling the hollow orbs and her wizened lips. Suddenly, the haggard eyes seemed to ignite, shooting off sparks of terror and rage. "It's not true! You're lying, you're lying!"

Trung pulled an envelope of schoolchild's paper, sticky with glue, out of his pocket. The handwriting on it was shaky, awkward, like that of a child learning to trace the letters of the alphabet.

FROM: Truong Van Tuu
Hamlet of . . . village of . . . commune of . . . province of Hai Hung
TO: my sister Truong Thi Tuu
House # . . . street . . . <u>HANOI</u>

The word HANOI in capital letters was underlined. The woman's face paled. Her hands trembled, unable to open the envelope. The room sunk into an eerie silence, echoing only faint sounds from the street.

"Is this the price that Mr. Hien gave you nine years ago?"

The old woman didn't answer. Her face went as gray as ash, her eyes blurred.

"For this price, you accused an innocent man of a monstrous crime."

Trung stopped for a moment, lowered his voice, and said slowly, "Do you . . . ever think about that?"

"Yes!" the woman hissed back in a voice as hoarse as a tomcat's. "Yes, I've thought about it, again and again. But what could I do? It's been more than ten years since he's even looked at me. I'm just a slave in the house, just a maid to cook, do the marketing, laundry, prepare the holiday meals. My ungrateful children swear by their father—he has the power, the money, he gets them the jobs, the apartments, their husbands and wives, provides for their children. Me, what do I have to offer? But I brought them into the world, I must love them. At least, I've kept my family together, given my children and grand-children enough to eat, to wear. He would have thrown me into the street if I had turned him in . . . What can I do? There are only two people in this world who care about me, my mother and my poor brother."

Her bleary, bloodshot eyes brimmed with tears that spilled onto her cheeks and rolled down her chin. The old woman didn't move or make a sound. But her tears continued to trickle, one by one, down a familiar, furrowed path. After a long moment, she wiped them and raised her desolate face.

"Are they going to put me in prison? I don't care."

Trung stood up and replied politely but coldly, "You can go home now." He turned toward the back of the apartment. "You can come out, Trinh."

His sister lifted the screen between the two rooms, accompanied the old woman out, and then returned.

Trung looked back toward the middle of the apartment.

"Do you have anything to eat, Trinh?"

"Of course," his sister said dutifully. "I'll make some rice. There's none left in the rice cooker."

Trung turned back toward the table, poured himself a glass of water, and swallowed. "What do you think?"

"It's disgusting," Nguyen said. "Why hasn't this come to light sooner?"

"Because certain people haven't wanted it to."

The young man looked sad, his bright eyes clouding over for an instant, then twinkling again. Nguyen had never met anyone with such a commanding look. He puffed in silence on his cigarette, watching Trung admiringly. "Do you ever want to just give up?" Nguyen asked, putting out his cigarette.

"Yes, for brief moments. But not yet."

"But someday. Not tomorrow, but the day after tomorrow, or even much later?"

"It's possible. Human beings are the most sensitive, the most versatile of all animals. That's why governing a healthy society has to depend on principles and laws, not the goodness of people's hearts. Today, I'm honest, tomorrow I could be dishonest. Today we're friends, but tomorrow, in my own self-interest, I could be your downfall."

Trinh reappeared carrying a copious meal on a tray. Trung looked up and congratulated her. "You've turned into a good cook."

Trung laughed, flustered by his praise. "My husband taught me. Trung used to say that no man would ever marry a woman as clumsy as me."

Nguyen looked at Trung. "You're a bit of a patriarch, aren't you?"

Trung just laughed in reply. He passed his chopsticks to Nguyen. "Now this is a sumptuous meal, no? Pork sausage wrapped in banana leaves, stir-fried chicken, pickled shallots. My brother-in-law often goes on trips abroad, and he's got a second job. But you and I, we certainly don't dream of having such a feast every day, do we? Let's eat. Trinh, serve Mr. Nguyen some rice."

Trinh set two steaming bowls of rice down in front of them. "What are you waiting for to get married?" she grumbled. "Mama never stops complaining about you."

"Oh, it's not the right time," said Trung, half to his sister, half to Nguyen. "I'm afraid of the pressure. If I sell out, people will say that I did it for my wife and kids."

He's right. It was because of Linh and Huong Ly that I compromised myself. It's easier to defend your convictions when you live alone on cafeteria food and a canteen of water slung to the end of the bed.

Suddenly, Nguyen felt pathetic. Anger against Linh washed over him.

"Eat up, what are you brooding about?" Trung asked.

Nguyen just shook his head.

ON THE WAY BACK to the newspaper offices, Nguyen saw an exquisitely dressed woman call out to him from across the street. He stopped, squinted, and only after a long moment of concentration recognized her. It was Lan. In her journalist's outfit, her hair pulled up like that, she looked like some foreign correspondent who had just landed at Noi Bai Airport.

"Hello, Auntie Lan, are you out for a walk?"

"Not exactly. I'm going to the market. I just made a detour to go visit Linh. Huong Ly is sick, and she's asking for you. She said, tell my dad to come visit me for just a minute. She's a bright little girl."

"That's my daughter, alright," Nguyen said. He said goodbye to Lan and turned into the nearby office to call the editor-in-chief. He was going to tell him something urgent had come up that would take the afternoon. Then he went to buy the cakes and fruit that Huong Ly liked, piling packets wrapped in all sorts of different paper into his briefcase. The shopkeeper arranged everything meticulously so as not to squash them. The fruit might flatten the cakes; the sweets might ruin the cream icing on the custards. Living was as difficult as arranging different merchandise in such a narrow briefcase, Nguyen mused. Who could keep his youthful hopes and ideals intact through life's ordeals and crises?

By the time he reached the high school it was one o'clock in the afternoon. Linh had already gone to the library. Huong Ly was asleep. But she opened her eyes as soon as he sat down at the edge of the bed.

"Papa."

Nguyen leaned over her and pressed his cheek to her feverish forehead.

"What medicine did Mama give you?"

"Some herbs. It's very sweet, but it made the handkerchiefs and napkins black."

"I bought cakes and sweets for you. What do you want to eat?"

"Nothing, Papa. I just ate some rice porridge and milk. Just stay here with me."

Nguyen swallowed hard, looked at his daughter's face. The little girl looked back, her eyes intelligent and inquisitive.

"Papa?"

"Yes."

"Why doesn't Mama want to live at home? You don't hurt her or scold her."

"Big people also get angry for other reasons besides getting spanked and scolded. You'll understand when you grow up."

Huong Ly stayed silent, furrowed her little eyebrows, and creased her downy forehead. Nguyen felt his heart wrench. *Frightening how much she looks like her mother.* Huong Ly suddenly sighed, stretched, and put her burning hand on her father's: "Papa?"

"What is it?"

"Do you love Mama a lot?"

"A lot."

"I know you love Mama almost as much as I do," she said in a serious voice. "Why do the neighbors say bad things about Mama?"

"Because they don't know anything about her and don't understand her."

"They're mean. But I don't believe what they say. Our neighbors are like Lan in my class. He stole cakes from Hung to eat them, but he told the schoolmistress that he gave them to the pigeons."

Nguyen burst out laughing. "How do you know?"

"I saw him eat the cakes behind a closet."

"Did you tell the schoolmistress?"

"No."

"Why?"

"Because he'll hate me and pinch me. I'm just telling you."
Nguyen looked at his daughter's lips, as red as lacquer.
Those full lips also made her look like her mother. So she too
had known how to adapt to life, even at this early age, Nguyen
thought. He didn't know whether to mourn or to rejoice. He
looked at his daughter, and beyond her face he saw Linh's,
even more childish, more naive.

THE EDITOR-IN-CHIEF'S OFFICE wasn't very big, but his secretary had decorated it tastefully. A large, gleaming table, a soft
leather chair. Two white wicker armchairs for visitors. A closet
to store documents. On top of it, a crystal vase. A calendar with
a golden apple was tacked to the closet, and a single traditional
landscape painting hung on the wall.

Nguyen used to like this room. He had somehow always
been able to let go and relax in its light, peaceful atmosphere
when he worked with the editor-in-chief. But today, the sense
of familiar ease had evaporated. Seated in his chair, he glanced
at all the objects, the landscape painting, the calendar. They
looked strange to him, as if they had been imported from another world. The editor-in-chief didn't look at Nguyen. He fumbled in his briefcase. After a moment, he took out a pack of 555
cigarettes and a bag of raisins.

"Here's your gift. Sorry, I didn't have a free moment. I
couldn't find anything else," he said.

"Why did you bother? I'm used to smoking cheap tobacco."

The editor-in-chief said nothing, opened the packet of raisins, and poured them into a dish. "Have some."

"Thanks."

"Everything alright here?"

"Yes. Nothing I can complain about," Nguyen replied, uneasy. The editor-in-chief was putting on an act. His secretary
had probably told him everything. *Why is he beating around the
bush?*

The editor-in-chief lit Nguyen's cigarette.

"In capitalist countries, the value system, the mores, are totally different from ours. But I have to say, as far as journalism
goes, they are really intelligent, observant."

"True."

"And that goes for other professions too. Everything is based
on one supreme principle: Individual performance is the linch-
pin. You don't judge people by their connections, but on their
own merits. Even in a Japanese bank, before a director's son
can become his father's deputy he has to earn two degrees in
economics and law. Then he has to work seven years in various
branches to learn the profession."

"Mmm."

"An individual selected like this can survive on his own
merits. Then society is built on healthy foundations. But I've
told you this, I believe."

"Yes, I remember, quite well . . ."

Nguyen felt immensely sad. *When would he get to the heart
of the matter?* He looked at the editor-in-chief's fleshy arms, the
quivering wrinkles at his eyelids, beginning to droop under the
fat. This was the face of self-satisfaction and contentment, of
old age. Courage and willpower were now buried under the
weight of months and years of discouragement.

The editor-in-chief heaved a long sigh and shook his head.
"But here, well, everything is complicated, difficult."

Nguyen suddenly felt bored, impatient, claustrophobic. He
couldn't stand this atmosphere of hypocrisy, these self-serving
theories. He spoke up abruptly. "The day you left, you sent me
a letter."

"Yes," the editor-in-chief replied nervously, unsettled by
Nguyen's brusqueness. He took a long drag on his cigarette,
leaned back, face to the ceiling, and exhaled. Nguyen went on:
"I understand Hien's cronies were waiting on your doorstep

when you came back. I hear that they've been scurrying around here lobbying for support, banging at other doors."

"Hmm . . ." the editor-in-chief grumbled, neither agreeing nor disagreeing. Nguyen noticed that he was troubled but trying hard to feign indifference.

"Why did you choose me for this little assignment?"

"What?" the editor-in-chief asked, surprised.

"Why me? Why not Tam, or Phuc, or Trong?"

"What gives you the right to even ask that question?"

"You trust me, isn't that it?"

"Yes, I always have."

"Up until now I've always done your bidding, never done anything to give you cause for concern. I have always been your right-hand man, as they say here. So that's why you gave me this assignment, then, because it must involve you personally?"

"No, not personally. But it involves a friend. Okay, take it however you want to. But in reality . . ." The editor stopped speaking and looked anxiously at Nguyen. He seemed odd, enigmatic today. Nguyen lifted his cigarette to eye level, pondering the way its incandescent tip, covered with ash, slowly ate into the tobacco, as if straining to formulate a thought. After a long silence, he raised his head and said slowly, "Thank you for trusting me, but now I'd like to ask you a question: Has it ever occurred to you that this kind of trust does me no honor?"

The editor-in-chief blinked, visibly embarrassed. But age and experience helped him reply tactfully. He shook his head, as if amused. "Come now, you're starting to get complicated. Perhaps you've been living alone for too long?"

Nguyen remained stony-faced. "This has nothing to do with my personal life, or my psychological state."

The editor-in-chief just chuckled. But he felt his face heat up. Irritated, he took out a handkerchief and wiped his forehead, but there wasn't a drop of sweat.

"Do you know all the details on Hien?" Nguyen asked.

"He's an old friend. We go back to the days we did time together in the Son La prisons."

The editor-in-chief blinked again, his puffy eyelids twitching violently. He lowered his head, tapping his cigarette nervously into the ashtray.

"So you're aware of his heinous crimes?" Nguyen continued.

The editor-in-chief winced. "Of course, it's horrible, appalling."

"But because he's your friend, you don't really find it horrible or appalling, do you? That's why you asked me to defend him."

The editor-in-chief sighed and lowered his voice discreetly. "What else could I do? No one can betray bonds of friendship, even if it puts them in difficult situations. If we break these bonds, there's a sense of remorse. It's hard to explain, but the old principles are still valid. As our ancestors used to say: 'When you love, even a water chestnut seems round; when you hate, even a soapberry seems square.' "

Nguyen laughed. "Ah, yes, I know all about that. My father used to tell me stories about the village—the paternal side, the maternal side, the marriages, the funerals, the bandits, the corvée labor, the taxes. Our village was famous for its traditions of solidarity, mutual aid. When someone was attacked by a stranger, the entire village would rush to their aid, whether they were right or wrong. Once, a real bastard from our village stole a buffalo from an old man who had just moved to a neighboring hamlet. The old man chased him with a flail. The thief cried for help and the villagers, who were returning from a market fair or harvesting rice in the area, jumped on the old man. They broke his spinal column and gouged one of his eyes with a pole. This story was engraved on my young memory, like some unbelievable, horrible nightmare. Once, I doubted that it had really happened. Now I believe it."

Nguyen stopped and looked at his boss. His cigarette had burned out. He threw the filter into an ashtray.

"In villages in an underdeveloped country like ours, clan spirit is commonplace. But coming from you, it shocks me. We are more or less intellectuals and, in this profession . . ."

The editor-in-chief sighed and ran his fingers through his hair. "Nguyen, put yourself in my place. Hien shared my worst ordeals. We shared everything, even a wad of tobacco for the water pipe, grilled manioc. A man of honor must never forget debts of gratitude contracted in times of misery. To Huu wrote some beautiful verses on this subject. I still remember them:

> *Friends, let us share everything*
> *Manioc roasted on the fire*
> *A bowl of rice. Bedcovers.*

"In 1949 it was so cold it would have split your gut. I came down with malaria; I lost all my hair. I used to drool over a bowl of rice after surviving for a month on cornmeal gruel and boiled roots. Hien had charmed some traveling saleswoman, who brought him baskets full of French medicine, cookies, Guigoz milk from the occupied zones. Without that food, I'd be buried under the green grass now. Thanks to him, we lived like princes in the middle of the jungle. My God, what misery. Why did it all go so wrong?"

Nguyen smiled. "So, you did lend a hand to the people who got him out of prison? This time, you'll probably get him that job on the state farm. And next time? I suppose they'll make him head of a livestock-raising venture?"

The editor-in-chief turned away, avoiding Nguyen's sarcasm. For a second, Nguyen felt a pang of pity, but he had more to say. "I understand a man's need for loyalty. To cherish a common past is perfectly normal, but to save this man from prison is not. To put it bluntly, it's counterrevolutionary. Thanks to male loyalty, he went on to rape seventeen young girls *after* that nine-year-old girl. We could set up an equation between your loyalty and those eighteen victims."

Nguyen wanted to stop, to regain his composure, but the thoughts churning in his head suddenly poured forth in waves.

"An old proverb says: 'Be humane to the wolf, and you're cruel to the sheep.' The most horrible thing is that we betray our principles. We know what is right, but we act in self-interest. Is it true that in the name of honoring the past, you and your buddies are covering for this rapist? And don't tell me that a man who builds five lavish villas pays his debts with flattery alone."

The editor-in-chief looked at Nguyen and murmured, "Yes, there have been bribes for others. It's true. But not for me. If ever I have received a gift from him, its just been symbolic. Believe me."

Freed of his former reserve, Nguyen continued. And though he glared at the editor-in-chief, he was talking to himself.

"People can make a habit of compromise, submission. But we can also change, fight back. You've always trusted me to do your bidding. I didn't even think about it; I considered it a means of survival in this society, something I simply had to accept. Now, I realize I was a slave. My loyalty to you stripped me of my dignity. This time, I have to refuse. Thanks to the state prosecutor's office, I've gathered all the evidence related to the two trials, even though they were nine years apart. And we're going to make our findings public."

Nguyen stood up and left. Without even turning to look at his boss's stunned face, he crossed the garden. Shaking from sadness and shame, he strode quickly out the front gate of the newspaper offices, turned at the intersection, and walked like a sleepwalker through the streets. He felt as if he had shed his skin, lifted himself above the tide of compromises and cowardice that had already sucked so many under. He had almost said what he would have said five or ten years ago. That would have been normal behavior for any self-respecting person. And yet, he hadn't. It had taken all this time for the fruit to ripen. *My God, did I have to suffer so to find myself?*

13

THE NIGHT was calm, eerily silent. A blur of lights reflected on the creeper vines gave them an odd, lifelike shiver. Tran Phuong contemplated these vines, fumbling in his memory for a lost image. He saw just how closely the paths people took in life resembled their winding, sinuous curves, their random detours. These wild plants grew blindly, heedless of any particular goal or destination. It had been a month since he had last seen Linh.

The image suddenly surfaced: A grove of apple trees in full bloom. White flowers as far as the eye could see. In the background, Linh. She had inspired a love in him that his hastily made, twenty-year-old marriage had destroyed. Linh's naiveté had captivated him, and her innocence had earned his respect. Her modesty and integrity had humbled him. More than once, he had felt the urge to throw himself at her feet, to offer her the youth and the tenderness of those apple blossoms.

Tran Phuong turned around, oddly emptied. These painfully detailed memories tortured him. He remembered the passionate moments that he spent with Linh, her seductive young body, her luxuriant hair; the soft glow that filtered through her eyes, like sunlight through the foliage of trees. He saw it again—the indigo beauty mark the size of a kernel of corn on her left shoulder; the little mole on her slender wrist. He could almost smell the scent of her hair. Everything tortured him, panicked him. Tran Phuong tugged the hair at his temples to release the nervous tension. *Come now, let's forget life's vicissitudes. For a man, love is just one of many feasts.*

The voice of reason. But his heart wouldn't stop screaming, and its screams drowned out this voice of lucidity. His blood seemed to throb violently against his flesh, through each cell of his brain. The wound opened wider with each memory. Incapable of holding back, he went out and walked toward Linh's high school.

When he arrived, he asked the custodian, "I'd like to see Miss Linh, please."

The custodian stared at Tran Phuong, hesitant, as if he had seen him somewhere. He searched his memory, trying to remember this tall man with the handsome beard, but he gave up. Instead of his usual brown checked shirt, Tran Phuong wore an expensive leather jacket, the kind worn by younger men.

"Please come in," said the old man.

"I have to leave right away. I just want to give Linh some news of her family. If you wouldn't mind."

The old man watched the students that ran through the gate as if they were going through customs at an airport.

"Hey, hey, Van Thanh, come over here, please."

A young girl in a red coat with black buttons turned around. "What can I do for you, sir?"

"Go look for Miss Linh," he said. "There's someone here who has news of her family."

The girl glanced furtively up at Tran Phuong. She smiled and rushed out into the courtyard. The old custodian shouted after her: "Hurry up, you hear?"

His voice was intimidating. It was clear that the students both respected and feared him. The girl in the red coat crossed the courtyard and moved toward the two-story buildings with the sign Zone C. She disappeared behind a door.

Five minutes later, Linh appeared. Tran Phuong started to tremble. He pointed to the street. "Please, ask Miss Linh to meet me out there, where I've left my motorbike."

Without waiting for the old man's reply, Tran Phuong hurriedly crossed the street and stood motionless by his motorbike. Linh reached the reception office. She listened to the custodian and turned to look at the street. She stood motionless for a moment, then went and slowly crossed the street. Tran Phuong's heart was racing. He felt it freeze when he saw Linh was facing him. Now, her face was just a few feet away from his. The wind brushed a few locks of her hair onto his sleeve.

"Darling," Tran Phuong said in a choked voice. A shiver ran through the woman's body. Her face was icy, and the light in the depths of her eyes turned to shadow. Tran Phuong lost all self-control and moved to embrace her, to take her in his arms. He stopped, suddenly conscious of the situation, pulled back his hands, and let them drop by his side, swinging them like pieces of wood.

"Linh."

She raised her head and looked him in the eyes, her voice hoarse, indifferent: "Let's get out of here; this is not the place."

She turned her back and walked along the sidewalk. Tran Phuong followed her obediently, his motorbike in hand. They walked to the end of the street in silence. This was where the eastern suburbs of the city began. The flashy new villas and houses started to rise, helter-skelter, pretentious. Restaurants crowded the length of the streets, waiting for the trucks. They were ramshackle, as dusty as the provincial truck stop restaurants. At the intersection were rows of trucks filled with sand and lime. The drivers were noisily eating nearby.

"Let me say something to you," Tran Phuong begged, when they finally arrived in front of a sign: Stop, Slow Speed.

Linh turned to him: "There's nothing more to say."

But she stood motionless, gazing out at the vivid green carpet of rice seedlings that unfurled to the horizon. The wind whistled past them. Everything seemed withdrawn, huddled in the icy solitude of winter. A few roadside barbershops with wood signs, a few tea stalls, a few old-style black-tiled houses, *bim-bim* vines dragging in the dust. In the distance, trees arched over the road. Linh suddenly felt desolate in the midst of this landscape.

"I know I behaved like a coward," Tran Phuong pleaded. "I don't deserve to look at you, please, let me say something."

What did he say then? She couldn't remember. The bonds had been broken. They were just two solitary beings on the edge of a precipice.

"I know, I'm not even worthy of looking you in the eye. But, please, let me say something."

Anguished, Tran Phuong kept talking, supplicating. "He who recognizes his error is already half forgiven."

Some proverb he must have picked up out of a dictionary. His eyes are panicked, pitiful. Linh just kept walking. Tran Phuong followed, scrambling to keep up with her, his motorbike in hand. He was panting, and Linh suddenly took pity on him. *After all, he's suffering too.* She entered a café at the end of the street. Beyond it, there were no more houses, only the road that cut through the rice paddies. Tran Phuong parked his motorbike in front of the café and entered behind Linh. The owner set down two cups of tea. The bottoms of the glasses were stained black. After serving them, she retreated to her chair, whistling through her teeth from the cold. She pulled her knees to her chest, put her hands under her armpits, and closed her eyes to sleep. Tran Phuong leaned on the grimy, sticky table, and finally lifted his eyes to look at Linh.

"Insult me, curse me, hate me. Spit your contempt in my face. You have the right."

Linh said nothing. Tran Phuong lowered his voice and murmured, "But I know you never will, and that hurts me even more."

Tran Phuong lifted the locks of hair that fell on his forehead. Under his dark eyes, the muscles of his cheeks twitched uncontrollably. Despair had somehow lent his face a mysterious sweetness, an almost childlike fragility.

"Please, condemn me."

Tran Phuong dropped his head, and his hair fell back onto his forehead, masking the desperation of his face. His long, slender fingers awakened in Linh the memory of their caresses.

Who should be forgiven? The man who betrayed our shared ideals or the man who betrayed me? Who should be condemned? Who deserves my pity?

It was cold. The rice paddies spread their solitude to the horizon. The trees bent, hunched over the deserted road. From time to time, a convoy of trucks rumbled by.

Linh realized that these were just the clear, lucid arguments of reason. The blind cries of her heart would pardon Tran Phuong, lead her back to him. In the dark chasm into which she had fallen, she had only one thin, fragile vine to grasp on to: Tran Phuong's love. Her eyes swam with tears. She wiped them away in silence.

The following Sunday, at the same intersection, the composer waited for her again, filled with all the impatience and anxiety of a man on the edge of a second youth.

NGUYEN HAD BEEN WAITING for almost an hour. Under the drizzle, the bamboo leaves stuck to tiles in the courtyard. Outside, the wind howled, whirled through the room. The old custodian was seated in his chair, his hands stuffed in his padded cotton jacket.

"Only kids are happy in this kind of weather," he grumbled. "They can slip under the covers and sleep all day. No one to scold them."

"True," Nguyen said, laughing. "But all they dream about is becoming adults like us. Sovereign beings. When I was little, I thought adults were happy, that they did whatever they wanted!"

"Ha, ha, life is complicated. Why not go home?"

"I've got something urgent."

Nguyen glanced at his watch. "Are you sure the meeting will be over this morning?"

The old man nodded. "Positive. It's only ten-twenty. The way it's going, the meeting won't be over until eleven-thirty. Like I said, there's no point in coming so early."

"I'll wait."

That morning, Nguyen had tired himself out trying to convince Huong Ly to stay with her paternal grandparents. Separated from him for so long, she had clung to him. That night, she had slept with her arms around his neck. From time to time, her hand would slide onto his chest, patting it. "Mama, let me touch your breast."

Nguyen had pulled his daughter's hand away. Once, on this same bed, the child had slept between the couple. She had had all the love and tenderness of both parents. When she laughed, they both laughed in reply. Two pairs of eyes had followed her innocent games. Now, every day, she had to put up with this divided life, these divided feelings. Now ... now ... Nguyen couldn't sleep. He turned on the light to read. But the letters danced in front of his eyes, obscure signs. As soon as he shut the book it was as if he could just see Linh walking through the room, her figure reflected in the tiles, hear the clink of glasses and cups under her fingers. The windows, the air, still seemed to shiver with her carefree laughter. She turned and looked at him, the sky reflected in her lovely brown eyes. Was Linh really so beautiful? He had met thousands of women. Beautiful women weren't rare. Dazzling actresses in glittering costumes; sensitive, intelligent scientists; the young worker women, bursting with health, as juicy as ripe fruit. Beauty, in all its diversity—he had known it. But he had only loved Linh. Maybe he too was a fanatic? Perhaps, deep down, he was just a slave chained to the rock of his emotions, to the vision of his first love? All his wandering and searching hadn't been enough to make him forget her, to bind him to another woman. Since he had left Ngoc Minh his love for Linh had been rekindled a hundred times over. He had never stopped thinking of her or praying for the day she would return. That is, until the day that Kim Anh had brought little Huong Ly back to him and told him the whole story.

The old custodian watched Nguyen pace around. "Sit down," he urged. "It's less tiring to wait."

Nguyen shook his head. "Thanks, uncle, it warms me up." He took out a cigarette and lit it. Since he had left Huong Ly at her grandparents' house, Nguyen had smoked almost an entire pack. His mouth bitter, he didn't feel anything except the numbness that hardened the tip of his tongue. Nevertheless, his head was clear, lucid, even calm beyond what he had expected. He heard the sound of a motorbike braking. Trong appeared in the doorway, his shoulders covered with a nylon slicker. Rain streamed down his hair. "Well? I've been waiting for you for a while now."

"They're still in the meeting."

"Are you cold? How about going for coffee?"

"No, you go, I'll take care of the rest. Where's the key?"

Trong reached into a shirt pocket, pulled out a set of keys carefully attached to an anchor-shaped chain, and handed it to

Nguyen. "The children have left. Cam will only be back late tonight. I'm going to the newspaper offices."

"Thanks, you go and don't worry about me."

Trong peered at his friend with worried eyes from behind his rain-splattered glasses, then revved his motorbike. Nguyen sat down in a chair and waited. Thirty minutes later, the meeting ended. Tran Phuong left the Musicians' Union with a group of male colleagues. They all dashed across the rainy courtyard to a shed where they parked their bicycles and motorcycles. Nguyen left the reception office and walked as fast as he could, reaching the shed just before Tran Phuong.

"Hello, I believe you know who I am."

Tran Phuong looked up and fear flashed across his face. "Ah, ah, yes, hello," he stammered.

"We've got something to discuss."

Tran Phuong lowered his head and opened the lock on his bicycle. "Yes, yes, unfortunately, I'm busy today. Another time, if you like."

"No, you've got enough time, and I want it to be right now."

The look on Nguyen's face was enough to make Tran Phuong realize that he couldn't refuse. He stiffened and the chain on his motorcycle lock drooped in his hand. He glanced around nervously. The other musicians had gotten out their vehicles and were already hurrying toward the street. The white Moscovic slid across the courtyard. No one had seen this unpleasant encounter. Linh's husband was glaring at him, waiting. Judging from his cold manner, the cigarette firmly stuck between his fingers, Tran Phuong realized that Nguyen was prepared to wait for half a century if necessary.

"Okay. Where can we talk? I know a café near here," Tran Phuong said.

"That's not necessary. A few hundred yards from here, there's a place that will be just perfect."

Fear flashed again in Tran Phuong's gaze. Nguyen smiled. "There's no danger. I'm not a secret agent." His voice was sarcastic, contemptuous. Nguyen had known a fair number of adulterous men, but none as jittery as this famous composer. No doubt, without these twists of fate, he would never have met Tran Phuong, never learned his tics. "Follow me."

Nguyen led the way, pedaling in front on his bicycle. Tran Phuong followed on his motorbike. A few minutes passed. Trong's house was only about six yards from where they were. They lifted the bikes onto the sidewalk. Nguyen opened the gate and gestured to the verandah: "You can put your motorbike here."

The composer pushed his vehicle right up to the threshold, leaned it against the kickstand. He rubbed his hands to warm them.

"Come in," Nguyen said, passing in front. Once inside, he offered Tran Phuong a seat. The composer looked the room over. A homey place, peaceful, like so many comfortable lives. The room was large, airy, clean. The furniture was clean, no traces of dust. Trong had put a coffee filter, a bowl of sugar, and a Thermos bottle on the table. Nguyen made coffee, served it, and carefully sugared it. While he did this, he observed Tran Phuong. He thought he could see a wave of shadows floating across the face of this actor who was straining to appear calm, but who couldn't hide his distress.

An actor, that's all he is.

Tran Phuong had been an icon for his generation, for people who loved the arts. He was constantly surrounded by admirers who praised his talent as both a musician and a painter. No one knew better than Tran Phuong how to win over a young audience.

So this is the great man in the flesh.

Nguyen set a cup of coffee down in front of Tran Phuong.

"Please, drink while it's hot." He took a quick sip from his own cup, waiting for Tran Phuong. Only when the composer had finished and set his cup on the table, did Nguyen begin to speak.

"I didn't want us to meet, any more than you did. We're not the kind of people who like to expose ourselves to public ridicule—"

"Linh described the life she had with you," Tran Phuong said. "Frankly, from what she said, I realized that she was as unhappy as I was."

The composer stopped and winced. "That's the way it was. We were soul mates. We had both lost everything, so we couldn't resist, couldn't help . . . You're an intellectual, so you know people need to confide in someone, to share their hopes, their dreams."

Tran Phuong's words drummed rhythmically in Nguyen's ears. He still listened, but he gazed distractedly at the composer's hands drumming nervously on the table. Long, svelte, elegant hands, without a trace of cigarette smoke, without the calluses and tiny scars of hardworking hands. Nguyen suddenly thought: *These hands have caressed Linh.* He saw his wife, her smooth soft skin, her firm breasts, her slender neck. He felt a dagger of pain puncture his flesh, plunge into his body.

Tran Phuong watched Nguyen's face. But he couldn't detect the faintest reaction. He only saw patience engraved on a mask.

He's the kind capable of bearing pain and loneliness for years, maybe until death.

He suddenly felt pity for Nguyen. After a moment of hesitation, he said, "No doubt you aren't the brutal, unworthy man that Linh imagined. There must be some misunderstanding. I promise I'll try to help Linh see the truth."

Nguyen stared at Tran Phuong in disbelief, his lips pursing into a smile.

Why is he smiling? He doesn't believe me. Tran Phuong repeated himself with conviction. "You have my word. Man to man."

Nguyen's unfathomable smile continued to flit across his lips. He watched Tran Phuong attentively. *Who is he? Linh would never have said anything bad about me. It's not like her. Why is he inventing these stories? It's an insult to her intelligence.*

Nguyen's forehead creased. He gritted his teeth.

Linh, is this what you left me for?

The composer saw the mask fall as Nguyen's face sank into despair. He knew that Linh was Nguyen's whole life, with all its dreams, bitterness, and uncertainty. She was his vision of the future, both his hope and his pain. The composer was gripped by remorse and fear.

"Mr. Nguyen, I am in part responsible for your unhappiness. But there is some misunderstanding. I thought that Linh was unhappy. In fact, I was drawn to Linh more out of compassion than love. When an attractive young woman is in distress, her suffering often does irreversible physical damage. How many beauties have lost their youthful looks from some unhappy love?"

Tran Phuong stopped. He had actually begun to believe what he was saying. Yes, it was out of compassion that he had come to Linh, he thought, as her savior. He continued: "If a human being is crushed, she becomes cruel, more barbaric. But if she is elevated, she'll become better because the best of her will be free to develop. I wanted to pull Linh out of the ditch of despair. I thought that by loving her I could help her to . . ." Tran Phuong's eyes glistened with the intensity of these ideas that he so passionately declaimed. He was a seasoned actor, accustomed to performing for an admiring crowd.

Watching the composer's hands rise and fall, Nguyen was suddenly reminded of a gallery opening that Tran Phuong had presided at. After cutting the ribbon, he had taken a seat in the front row, letting his hands waft and settle in a graceful, care-free pose, all for the adoring eyes of the assembled crowd. This teenage idol, a hero for so many women and young girls, this man who had put him and his daughter through such misery, was he just a ham actor? If only Tran Phuong had smiled cruelly, said bluntly, *"You're just an idiot, Nguyen. A man who doesn't know how to hold on to his wife. Your wife is so sexy, how could I give her back?"*

Yes, if only the famous composer had flung these crass, but honest words in his face, Nguyen would have felt better. But this revolting lecture on human charity was too much to bear.

So he's the Savior, and Linh's just some lost lamb he's rescued from the pit of despair, the clutches of debauchery. The man who seduced Linh and then betrayed her is nothing but a mirage.

My God, Linh, why have you plunged us all into such unhappiness, for a man like this?

As Nguyen screamed these thoughts inside of himself, he felt a dagger of pain tear at his heart. He raised his eyes and glared at Tran Phuong. "And the day you brought your wife to insult her? No doubt that was for Linh's benefit, to help lift her from her despair?"

Tran Phuong remained motionless for a moment, still intoxicated by his own voice, then he stammered: "That's another issue, an entirely different matter."

The thin blade twisted again in Nguyen's heart, forcing him to double over. He didn't remember how, but suddenly, he let out a wild, broken cry. Tran Phuong gripped the table as if to steady himself. He turned toward Nguyen, his eyes terrified. He mumbled something Nguyen couldn't even remember. Nguyen tried to get up, his back still doubled over in pain. In a bizarre, hoarse voice, like that of a stranger, he screamed at Tran Phuong.

"Get out . . ."

14

THE DAY Linh went back to her teaching, her students threw a surprise party in her honor. They showered her little room and her classroom with flowers. The girls busied themselves with the decorating while the boys crowded around, chatting and laughing. A few began to restring the cords of their guitars and practice songs.

"We're going to play an entirely different musical program for you, Teacher Linh, entirely new songs. While you were gone, we didn't give a single concert."

"Teacher Linh, did you like the cakes? We went to get them on Duong Street."

The students' faces shone, radiating the soft light of deep affection. Linh was moved. Her class, the familiar blackboard, the affection of these students reminded her of the real values in life.

The party lasted until the evening. Linh returned to her room. For the first time, after many long, anxious weeks, she slept soundly. In the morning, she suddenly heard her daughter calling to her. "Mama!"

Linh thought she was dreaming and turned her face to the wall. But the child's cries still resonated insistent. "Mama, Mama, wake up!"

Linh opened her eyes. Standing at the head of her bed, Huong Ly tried to turn her mother's head. "Huong Ly, sweetheart!" Linh took her daughter in her arms, lifting her onto the bed into a passionate hug. "Did you miss me, my girl?"

"A lot."

"How much?"

"As much as the sky," Huong Ly said joyfully, stretching her arms.

"I missed you too, ten times more than the sky. How are Grandma and Grandpa? Are they well?"

"Good. Every day, Grandma gives me persimmons."

"When did Papa bring you back?"

"Monday."

"Where did Papa go after dropping you off here?"

"He didn't go anywhere, he's out there, sitting at the table," the little girl said, pointing to the library.

Linh sat up, startled, and saw Nguyen behind the curtain, seated in a small room adjoining the library. Her cheeks burned.

He must know everything. He's come to humiliate me.

At the idea, she slipped on a blouse, entered the room where he was seated, and said in an icy, defiant voice, "What brings you here?"

Nguyen looked up. Linh recoiled as if stung by an electric shock. His gaze was filled with love, anxiety, hope. This was the face of a man tortured by his thoughts. There was not a trace of irony or resentment.

Nguyen took out his pack of cigarettes. His thin fingers trembled. Linh gripped the edge of the table with her hands. She noticed again the white hair at his temples, the new wrinkles that creased his forehead. A call from the past echoed inside her, shaking the most secret corners of her soul. Memories of his kindness flooded back: "*Give me your hand, so I can bandage it. Why are you always in such a hurry? Don't read that romantic nonsense, it's a waste of your time.*" His warm, tender hand on her back. The cool of the university auditoriums, the well-worn paths bathed in moonlight around their dormitory. Young love tinged with something maternal, even fraternal. Golden, rippling rice fields in autumn. Lush green mountains silhouetted against the azure horizon. Shadows of their happiness flickered behind these familiar fingers. Linh's eyes blurred as these memories stirred in her, racing and crisscrossing each other at the speed of her feverish thoughts. Why? Why? From the scattered wreck of her life rose the image of a blue autumn sky over the place where they had once stopped along the road, in the rustle of the trees, to gaze into each other's eyes, intoxicated with happiness, and embraced the world for the space of a magical instant.

True or false, reality or mirage?

Linh suddenly screamed inside herself, torn between the perfection of her past images of happiness and the brutal uncertainty of her present, between dueling faces that confronted each other across a chasm. In her idol, Tran Phuong, Linh suddenly sensed something ephemeral, unstable. In her life with Nguyen, she now glimpsed a refuge that she had too hastily abandoned.

Nguyen lit a cigarette, held it between fingers yellowed by tobacco. Linh looked again at her husband's hands. She saw long, insomniac nights, solitary evenings, the torture of memory and undying hope. During that time, from the window of that room in the suburbs, she had watched sailboats on the Red River, listened to Tran Phuong's sweet words, his enchanting songs. But now, only shame and guilt churned inside her. Linh turned her head aside, trying to hold back her tears.

Nguyen still puffed on his cigarette. He inhaled calmly, then said, "If you want, I'll go now."

Linh couldn't speak. Huong Ly ran out from behind the curtain.

"Don't let Papa go. I want him to stay with me."

She put her arms around Nguyen's neck. He stroked her smooth hair. "If Mama wants me to, I'll stay."

Huong Ly turned to her mother. "You want him to, don't you Mama?"

Linh looked at the child in silence, biting back her tears. The little girl didn't wait for a reply, just turned to her father and said firmly, "Mama agrees. I'm going to sleep. When I wake up, you can take me to buy cakes on Trang Tien Boulevard."

She ran back into the bedroom and slipped a last, questioning look at her parents. Nguyen and Linh said nothing. It was Nguyen who broke the silence. "I shouldn't have come. But I was afraid you were still sick."

"Thank you, but I wasn't sick. I was never sick," Linh snapped, in a sharp, impatient voice. She didn't dare look at him. She knew that he knew everything, that he pitied her, that to him she was just a gullible, naive, lost woman.

Nguyen realized that he had twisted the knife in a wound that hadn't healed yet. Sincere, awkward, he always chose the wrong chess piece. Nguyen puffed silently on his cigarette, finished it, and said, "You may not be my wife anymore, but you're still Huong Ly's mother, it's my duty to—"

"You have no duty. I don't need anyone," Linh interrupted, tense, hostile.

Nguyen saw her lips tremble. He knew that she was reacting out of pride. He continued, conciliatory. "I've come to see you more than once since you've been here. It's true: I still love you. But people must learn their limits. If I hadn't learned to live with the idea and the pain of losing you, how would I survive? You took me for a saint, as pure as your imagination could mold him. But when you saw me in the harsh light of day, saw that your saint was just a lump of dried clay smeared with paint, you cast it into the street without even glancing behind you. But I'm no plaster saint, I'm a man who has to live the reality of a man's life. You were my dream too, my faith in this world, but I accepted you with all your shortcomings, your naivete, your illusions and mistakes. But you, you couldn't do that."

Linh didn't reply. She bit her lip, stubborn. But her heart was breaking. Nguyen was right. She suddenly saw things clearly as in a flash of lightning on a stormy night. In this moment she shuddered, saw the road she had taken, and the long, winding road that stretched before her. Regret churned in her with all the turbulent anxiety of the current at the bend in a river.

If only Nguyen could have read her soul at that moment. If only he knew that the moment he had waited for for so long, when he could regain his lost happiness, had alighted in the palm of his hand like a lark in the clear calm of dawn. But he couldn't. All he could see was her face, still as fresh and as candid as a sixteen-year-old's. He told himself that it was precisely this stubborn, naive self-confidence that attracted men, and that despite the love he still felt for her, he must break with her. For this face, in its drive to conquer, would never yield.

He lit another cigarette, "I came to see you today because I just met him."

Linh gasped, then pursed her lips.

Nguyen realized that Linh was still in love with Tran Phuong, even though she thought she hated him. He felt the urge to smile. It was as if he were standing outside himself, another man calmly studying the wretched pain in this Nguyen's eyes.

"I'm not going to relate our conversation. But I'd like you to have some facts. Maybe you'll judge things more clearly, fairly, if you do."

Nguyen paused for a few seconds, then lowered his voice. "The moments of weakness, the cowardice, the mistakes—they happen to everyone. What's important is to know why we made them, to see if we can forgive."

Linh looked at Nguyen. Her tendency to judge people brutally was suddenly rekindled, and it swept aside whatever other emotions had surfaced. She suddenly became stern, ruthless. "Don't try to cover your mistakes by calling attention to those of others. Tran Phuong treated me badly, but he's still faithful to his ideals. As for you, you turned your back on everything we held dear, on the values on which we built our life together."

"I'm just a speck of dust, Linh. I can't fight the world alone. It would have been futile."

"Maybe, but it also served your own interests."

"What would you have done, in my place?"

"I'd do what I thought was right."

"But we're just pawns, Linh, scribes, little hands that scurry over details."

"Your cries of alarm might have sent a warning signal."

"Solitary cries that would be drowned in silence like so many grains of sand at the bottom of the lake. You have to wait, Linh."

"Wait for what?"

"The day will come when truth will be valued."

"But that day, will it come if educated people like you behave like servants?"

Nguyen looked at Linh and smiled sadly. *You're always right, in theory, my girl.* And he felt a fatigue he had never known, as if he were dying of weariness. Invisible tears condensed in his heart. The sad memories, the evenings when, exhausted, he had left the newspaper for home, crossing the public garden still warm with sunlight, the bench where he stopped, lost in his thoughts, the scarlet flowers blooming in the twilight, the unspeakable loneliness. Why couldn't she understand this torment? Couldn't she see how helpless an individual was faced with the reality of power? Why was she so ruthless, so blind to life's constraints? Was it her passion for Tran Phuong? No doubt she had destroyed the memory of their former happiness, all capacity to comprehend him.

He inhaled his cigarette and looked up: "So, you must need a signature from me."

Before Linh had time to grasp what he was saying, Nguyen continued. "I told you that I could wait, one year, two years, three years, even longer. I love you more than anything a man could ever dream of having in life. More than fame, wealth, power. You haunt me even in my dreams. I thought I could wait forever for you to come back. But it's not necessary anymore. Give me a piece of paper."

Linh stiffened. She had urged Nguyen to sign the divorce papers many times. Now, the urgency had gone cold. If only she could have said: *Wait, calm down, I know I've been unfair to you . . . Give me time to think.* If only she could have said everything on her mind. But pride stopped her. She fumbled in her papers, pulled out a blank piece, and handed it to Nguyen.

"That'll do," he said, placing the paper on the table, facing him.

"You are the accusing party, so you sign in this corner. I'm the victim, so I sign in the opposite corner." Nguyen steadily drew a straight line across the piece of paper, dividing it in two. He wrote his name firmly and clearly at the bottom of the page. He stood up. "For the next few days, I want Huong Ly to stay with me. You're busy. And I need her more than you do."

His voice was calm, firm. Without waiting for Linh's reply,

he entered the bedroom and woke up Huong Ly. Linh stared at her husband, transfixed: *It's over.* No more hope of going back. Nguyen knew that she loved Huong Ly. If he loved her, he would yield. He would leave the child with her. For a long time now, she had come to depend on Nguyen's generosity, his kindness. She suddenly realized that he too could abandon her as any man can abandon a woman, even the one who had shared his life.

"Papa, are we going to Trang Tien Boulevard?" Huong Ly asked, as she woke up and slipped on her blouse.

"Yes, we're going to buy cakes."

"Then we're coming back to Mama's house?"

"No, we're going home."

"No, no, no, I don't want to, I want to stay here with Mama," the little girl cried, shaking her head from side to side. Nguyen looked at his daughter, then asked tenderly, softly: "How can you stay here? Tomorrow, Mama's students are going to come see her. There'll be lots of people. Let's go home, Mama will come later."

Huong Ly believed it. She ran toward her mother and covered her with kisses. "I'm going to Trang Tien Boulevard. When are you coming home, Mama?"

Linh's throat tightened. "Tomorrow," she stammered.

The little girl ran toward the door. Nguyen stopped for a moment to look back at Linh. "Sad, isn't it Linh? Here we are, both of us telling lies."

She didn't reply. He looked deep into her eyes, trying to see one last time, for his memory, the flame that burned there.

"Take care of yourself, your health. Recently, you look . . ."

He stopped. He had just noticed a blue vein pulsing on his wife's thin neck. He couldn't finish his sentence, and he left.

Huong Ly, once seated behind him on the bicycle, made hand signs to her mother. When father and daughter had disappeared, Linh broke down into sobs.

My God, I could have made peace with him, could have returned to our happy, peaceful life. Why can't I just forgive him? Why?

The street lamps flickered on. Nguyen pedaled, distraught, through the bustling crowds, Huong Ly still clutching his back. *Why, why? I came here to convince her to come back, and then I push her to divorce, to a final separation. Why?*

15

T ET WAS APPROACHING. Tran Phuong accompanied
his wife to the flower market on Luoc Street to buy some
peach tree blossoms. When they arrived, he told Hoa to
go ahead alone, that he'd wait for her at the corner. The Lada
was parked on a street far from the market, because the streets
leading up to it were closed to cars. The chauffeur stretched his
legs out the door and read *Journey to the West*.

Hoa had said she would be back in forty minutes. An hour
had gone by, and there was still no sign of her. His legs numb,
Tran Phuong wandered out in search of a café. But they were
all closed. Impatient, he returned to wait by the car. Suddenly,
he saw a woman headed straight for him. She must be about
forty, maybe more, he thought to himself. She's still thin. The
woman had a familiar gait and her complexion was still rosy
under violet-tinted glasses.

Who is she?

"Oh, Lan . . . hello, Lan," Tran Phuong stammered, stepping
back.

"Hello, why so fearful?" She smiled impishly and lifted off her sunglasses. "Steady there."

Tran Phuong lost his composure for a moment, then shrugged it off. "I'm fine," he said, noticing her scarlet lips. He scoured his memory for an image of those lips more than twenty years ago. She had been his first affair, at the time when he was still naive but already a rising star. He had been madly in love with her. But now she seemed like no more than a corpse shrouded in velvet and silk, embalmed with powder and lipstick. She would never be more than what she always had been—a shopkeeper, even if she was a Hanoi shopkeeper and not some wartime traveling saleswoman like his wife. After her, he had seduced more intelligent women. To his jaded eyes, Lan's flashy, unrefined beauty now seemed as banal as a plate of sticky rice. As these thoughts crossed his mind, Lan glared at him: "I've lost again. I wanted to take my revenge, but it fell on my poor, unhappy niece. You, you've escaped every one of fate's blows, just like a snake that hides itself in the mud. You must have protection from the gods."

Tran Phuong said nothing. *What does she want, this witch? I had better hear her out. No one is here to watch the scene.*

Lan continued to stare at Tran Phuong, her eyes fiery.

"Sometimes the heavens make a mistake, but they have eyes and ears. A vicious man like you always dies without heirs." She spat out each word, letting her hatred flow. "Because you would only bring snakes and scorpions like yourself into this world . . ."

She turned and left. Stunned, Tran Phuong followed her with his eyes. "What a witch!" he muttered. But he was terrified. A vague, distant world invaded his mind, hovering like a storm cloud. Lan's words reminded him of something ancient and elemental, of the promise of harvests, the vital, undying energy of the earth, the cycles of light and darkness. Back in the village, when he was a boy, his paternal grandmother had spoken like that by the flickering light of oil lamps. And even further back, in the distant past, some ancestor had no doubt muttered those same words in the broiling heat of the country afternoons, amid the lazy creaking of hammocks. Tran Phuong suddenly remembered the masklike faces of the Buddhas and demons in the temples of his childhood. Their faces, through the dense clouds of perfumed smoke and incense, had terrified him, left him breathless. These images, buried under the weight of the days and the years, resurfaced. *Superstitions. Am I already so old? Forget these superstitions.* But these chilling memories only grew clearer. Wisps of clouds gathered on the horizons, piled up into storm clouds. In these clouds pulsed countless other memories, other faces, and other facts. Life's highs and lows rose and sank like peaks and valleys, staring at each other, mirror images that bounced back and forth in a diabolical dance. Rising from this jeering gallery of faces, a painful, sickly face, with sunken cheeks and ash-colored hair, peered at him with bleary, desolate eyes. Underneath this visage lay a vast purple sea ablaze with a thousand sparks of twilight.

Tran Phuong shook his head and shut his eyes. When he reopened them, he found himself at the corner of the street. The crowd poured out of Hang Luoc Market into the surrounding streets. People scurried and bustled, some carrying potted kumquats, others a branch of peach blossoms.

Strange that she's not here.

For the first time in his life, Tran Phuong was impatient for his wife to return. He needed Hoa's presence to dispel this horrific daydream. But she was late. The skull rose again and bobbed on the ocean waves, staring at him. This time, the haggard eyes blinked.

Do you recognize me, Tran Phuong?

A body emerged from the wavy water. Bony shoulders, hunched back, spindly legs hugged to its chest. The ocean vanished. There was only an old man with a sad face sitting on a reed mat, a dirty bottle of rice wine and a few roasted peanuts by his side.

Do you recognize me, brother?

He bobbed his head. Tran Phuong turned his head away. He recognized the man, but he had aged and his face was horribly disfigured. They had been close friends during the war. Originally from Bac Ninh province, he had lived for a long time in Hanoi. When Tran Phuong arrived from his native village of Hai Dong, the man had offered him hospitality, letting him stay at his home. The two men shared memories, and their youth in the anti-French Resistance movement sprang alive again in the patriotic songs they wrote together. Oh, that beautiful time, the most heroic for the Vietnamese nation. The time when to stop the enemy people burned their own houses, and set fire to their family heirlooms and possessions with a calm smile on their lips. A time when in their zeal to resist the advance of enemy trucks they had thrown tea cabinets of precious amboyna wood encrusted with mother-of-pearl onto the barricades. A time when teary-eyed young men tore themselves from the arms of their loved ones to leave for the front, turning their backs on the capital in flames. Yes, the Vietnamese people had stood up and claimed their human dignity through noble tears.

Tran Phuong remembered, one time, in the Viet Bac jungle, he had gotten scabies. At the time, Tran Phuong even shared scarce clothes with this man, who used to recite verses from Quang Dung all day long.

> *We advance toward the west*
> *Blending, like tigers, into the green leaves*
> *Gazing beyond the frontier*

Once, when they were short of medicine and water to wash themselves, the man had scratched himself until his skin bled, wailing, "Those French bastards, you see what a state they've put me in." His buddies used to take turns rubbing his body with the sap of leaves rich in tannin, delousing him. He liked to drink, and he had a warm, seductive voice. The montagnards in the area often invited him to come play guitar and sing in their huts late into the night. The months, the years of the anti-French Resistance passed. When news came announcing the victory, the outcome of the Geneva Conference, they received an order to return to the plain to liberate the capital. Tran Phuong remembered how everyone had embraced, singing at the top of their lungs. The man had disappeared for an entire day; no one knew where he had gone. About three in the morning, he emerged from the forest, tears in his eyes. He began to strum his guitar, singing the song he had just composed. They had all thrown themselves on him, embracing him. Individual creation, at the time, was considered a revolutionary contribution by the entire community of artists. His song was by far the most beautiful and the most popular composed on that historic day.

They marched on the capital. Everywhere, troops struck up a chorus to his song, singing all the way to the gates of Hanoi. The singers themselves had been overcome with emotion; the spectators wept. Jealousy had bitten Tran Phuong's heart. Years later, when he had attained an important position, the party hierarchy put him in charge of the repression of a protest movement, *Nhan Van Giai Pham*, that was led by artists like his friends. Once Tran Phuong had accomplished this mission, he went even further by launching a campaign against sympathizers, even those who had vacillated, who risked being converted by the so-called reactionaries. Tran Phuong had personally classified his former composer friend—this frightened, incoherent wino—as a suspect "element." Tran Phuong knew the man was innocent, but he couldn't pass up the chance to crush this rival talent. Jealousy had grown roots, sprouted spines, burrowed into his heart. Envy had poured into his blood like poison, killing the memories of their days of struggle when they wore grass hats and ate manioc roots in jungle huts.

After the campaign, Tran Phuong had climbed to the pinnacle of his profession, while this man sank into a bottomless pit of despair, drowning his talent in alcohol.

Now, his ghost seemed to sit facing Tran Phuong, eyes bleary and cheeks sagging down a face that had once been so handsome, so animated.

You don't recognize me, Phuong the Bearded One?

The man blinked, surprised, repeating his question for the third time. "Phuong the Bearded One" was the affectionate nickname they had given Tran Phuong during the Resistance.

Tran Phuong shuddered. He couldn't go on keeping his eyes shut, turning away from the man. He saw a long road. At one end, the man was standing at his side, with a group of young people, their rifles slung over their shoulders, to liberate the country. At the other, where the road forked, they had each gone their separate ways.

What ridiculous imaginings. I must be getting old.

Tran Phuong shook himself, trying to dissipate the uneasiness that had settled on his heart, as oppressive as the air on the day of a gathering storm . . .

THE COUNTRY'S annual Communist Party Congress was over. People were ecstatic when they learned of the new faces among the elected. Everyone was talking about Tran Phuong's reinstatement to his former position. Those who admired him rejoiced. Those who hated him shrugged and shook their heads.

Linh, hearing the news, was secretly happy. After all, her life was now linked to Tran Phuong's. A week later, a meeting was held at the Music Conservatory to celebrate the outcome of the congress. Tran Phuong was to give a talk for the teachers and students. A cousin of Linh's, one of the composer's most loyal fans who was taking a course in music theory, had invited Linh to attend. The two cousins sat side by side in the auditorium. From their seats, by the window, they could see the five-colored banners floating above the gate to the conservatory. Large banners bearing slogans were tied to both sides of the gate. A red silk lantern bobbed in the wind in the middle of helium balloons. The bright *ao dais* the girl students wore gave everything a festive atmosphere. The chief organizer, stylishly dressed in a German fur coat with the collar pulled up, dashed about, nervously checking the loudspeakers and spotlights on the podium.

"Please, take your places and keep calm, comrades. The meeting will begin in five minutes."

A few minutes after this announcement, a white Moscovic rolled into the courtyard, turned, and stopped at the threshold. Linh could see Tran Phuong clearly in the backseat, looking lonely, irritated. The schoolteachers rushed down the steps to greet the composer. Tran Phuong himself opened the door and stepped out. How majestic he was! Fame was a terribly efficient weapon; it had endowed him with an extraordinary charisma.

Then Linh lost sight of Tran Phuong. He was probably seated in the front row. The music blaring from the loudspeakers suddenly stopped. The master of ceremonies said a few words of welcome. The director read a speech. Finally, Tran Phuong mounted the podium.

"Bravo!" someone shouted behind Linh. Thunderous applause. Tran Phuong turned his handsome face to the audience, smiling wearily. He waved a hand, half to greet the crowd, half to stop the frenzied applause. But the gesture only whipped up the crowd's enthusiasm. The applause grew, echoing from every corner of the room. The young people screamed. Tran Phuong bowed his head, shrugged slightly, smiled, and waited. The applause continued for another fifteen seconds before fading out. Tran Phuong started to speak. "Dear friends . . ."

Linh looked up. The world only existed for her in the face of this man, his huge, black eyes, his eyebrows traced in brushstrokes of Chinese ink. Hypnotic eyes that in intimacy could turn gentle, caressing. Tran Phuong's face now expressed strength and the desire for conquest. Linh was troubled, unnerved. She listened, more and more horrified, as Tran Phuong spoke.

No, it's not possible. It's only his style of expressing himself in public.

She struggled to concentrate, to grasp each phrase, each thought. But this time, there could be no mistake: Tran Phuong was proclaiming the exact opposite of what he had always said to her. His eloquent words resounded as crystal clear as notes from a brass trumpet. He expressed a respect for the authorities that was so exaggerated, and an optimism that was so hypocritical, that she wondered whether this was not some kind of sick joke.

Eyes gaping, she stared at the man gesticulating on the podium. But this was no magic show. This was the same Tran Phuong up there speaking. He brandished an arm and sliced the air with his hand in a stereotyped, heroic gesture. This was his voice, but so different, so slick.

It's not possible; it can't be him.

But the loudspeakers faithfully amplified his heavy breathing, the familiar cadences of his voice that hammered one word or made another gently hover, intoning warnings to the young people, respectfully repeating the advice of his elders.

Whose name did he just mention? She gasped, gripping the arms of her chair. Had he really just mentioned the name of the man who had stripped him of his position five years ago? Was he now glorifying the same name that Linh had heard mentioned with hatred so many times in his confidences to her? She herself had cursed this man, plotted ridiculous, crazy dreams of revenge. Linh lowered her head. Her face burned.

Her body tensed with shame. Something had just broken inside her. All the accumulated pain of months, like a stone fortress long battered by the sea, had crumbled into the ocean depths in a single blow.

Her idol had fallen. In an instant, Linh understood all the doubt and foreboding that had surfaced in her and that her passion had obscured. That day Tran Phuong had taken her, alone, into the concert hall of the Musicians' Union, when he had played for her, he had revealed the same cruel mask that was now holding forth under the spotlights.

Applause thundered in Linh's ears. *What did he just tell these young people? More sweet lies?* Tran Phuong laughed and bowed his head to the crowd's fervent applause. He looked carefree, spontaneous. With a dismissive gesture, he brushed aside the waiter who had just brought him a glass of water and stepped off the podium.

My God, he's Machiavellian.

Linh suddenly reared in pain. She had thought of him with such admiration, such passion for so long. How many days and nights had she endured humiliation, bitterness, for him? All this anxiety, her soul's turmoil, now showed its sad face. The great man she had loved and revered was nothing but a votive paper doll from Mã Street. Stripped of his layers of gold leaf, he was just a cheap bamboo skeleton.

How could I be such an idiot? This is supposed to be the hour of revenge and glory, the fulfillment of my dreams.

She would never be able to love Tran Phuong as she once had. The moment he mounted the podium was the moment she saw him as he was. He would soon find another woman to replace her. She would be just another flickering shadow in his memory, a face whose features would soon be shrouded in fog. She trembled uncontrollably, consumed by her desire for revenge.

Her cousin turned to her. "What's the matter, Linh? Are you feeling faint?" The young woman took Linh's arm. The loudspeakers announced the end of the meeting. The students piled noisily out of the auditorium.

Linh returned to her little room and collapsed on the bed. She lay there, motionless, until the following morning. In her fitful sleep, in her twisted dreams, she killed Tran Phuong a thousand times over. But when she awoke, she heard only the buzzing of a swarm of mosquitoes around her head. She saw a ray of silvery light spill across the ceiling. Her head was heavy and her limbs ached. But she massaged her temples, ate breakfast, and took some medicine. At eleven o'clock she gave her last course for the year.

The next morning, Linh went to the Musicians' Union and waited for Tran Phuong at the gate. Seeing her, Tran Phuong told the chauffeur to drop him off before parking the car. He strode toward her confidently: "Forgive me, I have been so busy the past few days."

When he saw the fire in her eyes he repeated softly: "Forgive me, there just wasn't a free moment to come see you."

She stared at him, taking the measure of the man who had been the sun of her world. Tran Phuong immediately sensed danger. He lowered his eyes and pleaded, "Forgive me, we'll see each other Sunday."

But Linh wasn't listening anymore. "You're an imposter," she murmured.

Tran Phuong glanced around nervously, and whispered, "Don't say that, get a grip on yourself."

Linh glared at him. "Liar! You're nothing but a miserable liar. You're not at all the man I thought you were."

The composer raised his eyes, a dark, misty look tinged with irony. He laughed. "You're crazy. Men like that don't exist."

Linh detected a glimmer of pity in his eyes. The pity of the charlatan for his victim, she thought, sickened. "You bastard!" she shrieked, choking back her rage.

Tran Phuong shot Linh an icy look. "Get a grip on yourself. Another shriek like that and I'll have you locked up in a psychiatric ward."

The color of his eyes had changed, turned to lead. He turned his back to Linh and entered the courtyard. A secretary hurriedly descended the staircase and rushed toward him. "Reporting, sir. They're waiting for you to start the meeting."

"Coming," the composer replied. He hurried off, taking large strides. Aside from a few passersby, no one noticed the scene between Linh and Tran Phuong. Curious, they stopped to watch. But a few seconds later, the man had disappeared up the staircase.

SPRING trickled by, as serene as water between two grassy banks. The rice fields were covered with young seedlings. All you had to do was leave the city limits to feel intoxicated by the beauty of the countryside. The sky had turned the strange blue that signaled the beginning of summer. The streets were littered with yellow pancovier leaves that swirled in the wind in thousands of sparkles, mixing with young sprouts underfoot. All day long the street cleaners swept these flaming yellow waves that poured into the streets. Summer was already present in the scarlet blooms of the flame trees and the poignant chant of cicadas. But for Linh, the last cruel days of spring still lay ahead. Around mid-March, a large sign in front of the Opera House announced a music competition organized by the Musicians' Union.

Linh paced around the sign for a long time, torn between the temptation to buy a ticket and the urge to go home. She didn't understand why today, after so many days and nights of suffering, she felt the need to see Tran Phuong. Was it curiosity or their shared past? She couldn't answer. For Linh, love and hate were no longer opposites: At the bottom of her hatred lay the rotting seeds of her passion. She had placed too much hope in her idol, and when he collapsed, he continued to haunt her.

Why?

Perhaps it was curiosity, after all. But it could also have been the regret that still obsessed her. Linh remembered Tran Phuong's sad, duplicitous words. The love she felt for him was fraught, laden with too many contradictions. She needed to see him one more time, if only to see the shards of her shattered idol.

Linh decided to buy a single ticket for the competition. That same evening, she went alone, arriving at the theater a half hour early. From the stairs, she watched the musicians climb out of a bus, their instruments under their arms, and hurry into the theater. Some of them were laughing, others grimaced, chattering with their colleagues. Linh reached the top of the stairs, entered, and found her seat. The bell announced the curtain in fifteen minutes. Tran Phuong still hadn't arrived. Twelve minutes later, at the moment she turned toward the door, a group of men entered. Tran Phuong walked in the middle. It wasn't cold outside anymore, but he still wore the expensive leather jacket so familiar to her. His hair, cut shorter, gave him a somewhat ascetic look. He had shaved off his beard. This man, whose body's every mark was familiar to her, exuded solemnity. Hoa strode proudly at his side, her arm linked to his. The crowd murmured their names. The couple seemed to burst with happiness; Tran Phuong with his elegant indifference, Hoa with all the pride of a conquering hen. They reached two rows from where Linh was seated. Tran Phuong suddenly lowered his head. No doubt he had recognized her. Panic and fear flashed in his eyes. His lip twitched. He turned away abruptly, quickly passing the row where Linh was seated.

He's afraid. Why, he's trembling from fear.

Linh's doubts and agitation evaporated. A coward—he was just a coward. Linh looked at the composer indifferently. He had taken his seat in the front row, where the spotlights illuminated a lock of his hair. The master of ceremonies solemnly announced the program and introduced the jury. Tran Phuong stood up and bowed first. Applause rang out as soon as the crowd saw him.

Linh couldn't hear anything but this wave of applause. She scattered the last ashes of her memories. She was just a nameless woman, a modest zero in the crowd. She suddenly understood the seduction of fame and celebrity, this magic that both elevated men to the summits of honor and then plunged them, smiling, into the depths of crime.

Tran Phuong was there, seated amid the spotlights. He had probably guessed what kind of a man she thought he was— one capable of understanding all that was noble, and yet of forgetting it all instantly.

The piano suddenly resounded. No, it was the entire orchestra beginning the overture to the first symphony of the evening. Linh didn't look at the stage, where the conductor brandished his baton with passionate verve, where the lights licked at the brass of the instruments like tongues of fire. She lowered her head. A blanket of sound covered everything as tenderly as a mother leaning over her child. The dim glow of twilight recalled the glow of childhood, when her father took her to the gardens in the suburbs of Hanoi. She remembered the murmur of water, the screeching of crickets, the clear birdsong, the rustle of leaves. There, among the golden *xuxu* flowers, the velvety carnations, the white snapdragons and scarlet peonies, even as a girl, she had searched passionately for life's secrets. How the hornet fumbled the heart of a trumpet-shaped flower, how a red-backed maybug crouched under the green leaves. For her, life would always be this passionate search. No fall, no failure deserved this despair.

Linh looked calmly in the face of her pain. For him, she had endured so much unhappiness. But it was from that point that she had matured, grown up. As long as she looked to others for her dignity, to gods haloed in stars and light, she would never become a woman. A woman must believe in herself, lead her own way to the meaning of her life.

The violins were hushed; now the piano raised its clear voice, pouring the infinite tenderness of life into her heart. Rain chanting on a lonely rooftop on a spring evening. Then, a sudden silence, as all the instruments exploded in a single voice, a single source, that of the tide. The sea rose and fell against banks left jagged by crashing waves. Streams of blue water, crested with foam, teemed with boats. All the storms and dawns.

Linh suddenly remembered the seaside town she had imagined the night she had left Nguyen. The stench of the oil slick on the water near the quays, the algae and dead fish that washed up on the shore. She would contemplate these shores from now on with the experienced eyes of someone who had lived and suffered. Nothing and no one would ever again inspire such bland fervor, have the power to make her suffer like that. She would measure her contempt and trust only after the test of time. She could never forgive Nguyen, but she would cherish the memory of their golden rice fields at harvest time, their lost gardens of ripening fruit, the gentle reflection of trees on water. She would be kinder, break with him forever. She would never again be able to follow anyone's path but her own.

Applause, again. Linh stood up. She needed to feel it fully, her happiness. The conductor bowed, his face drenched in sweat. Linh waited until he disappeared behind the curtains to leave. Tran Phuong turned to speak to a member of the jury seated in the row behind him. Seeing her, he lowered his eyes.

Miserable coward. She slipped between the seats and walked toward the exit. The young usher noticed her and asked: "Are you bored, elder sister?"

"No, it's very beautiful, but I've got things to do."

Linh nodded and left. She went down the stairs and walked nonchalantly down the street. A voice behind her back suddenly called to her.

"Hello, Miss Linh."

She turned around, recognized the badly dressed painter with the satchel. "Oh, hello."

He had followed her. "Mind if I walk with you?"

"As you like."

The man said nothing more. They walked down the street and reached the intersection. He seemed embarrassed, as if he wanted to ask her a difficult question. "How are you?"

Linh looked at him, burst out laughing.

"I'm fine, thanks."

He stopped, touched her sleeve. "Please, just give me a few days of your time," he pleaded. "I'd like to do a portrait of a woman. I've wanted to ask you for a long time, but never dared."

The painter looked at her, sincere, eager. Now Linh somehow trusted this odd man whom she had always avoided. She knew that for him, she was just the color of a cloud over the ocean, the hue of some wildflower, a trickle of light on a rice field at dusk. She was just another slice of the life he cherished, selflessly, without calculation.

"Okay, next Sunday. Come find me at school. Now, if you'll excuse me, I must go."

Linh walked toward her neighbor's house, where she had left her bicycle. She would return to her little room next to the library, but she was in no hurry. There was no urgency anymore. She needed silence. As she strolled slowly through the city, for the first time she felt the ground under her feet, no longer needed to lean on anyone. A soft, calm night. She could hear the rustle of falling leaves, and beyond it, another silent music, a chant that sprang from the secret storms of the heart. This was the music that rose from the place in every conscience where lucidity is paid in pain and loss, where hope springs from the ruins of illusion, and where life, like a creeper vine, twists and turns to reveal fresh new blossoms. In spite of the ruins. In spite of the lies.

Hanoi, May 27, 1986
DUONG THU HUONG

About the Author

Duong Thu Huong published this novel in 1987, the same year that the Vietnamese Communist Party called writers and intellectuals to freely and critically address the issues facing an impoverished and corrupt postwar Vietnam. A speech given by then Party chief Nguyen Van Linh opened up the floodgates of criticism, not only for Huong, who was forty years old at the time, but for a generation of writers and journalists who had been forced to speak only of glorious achievement and heroic acts, never of tragic error or personal despair. For almost three suffocating decades, Vietnamese writers and artists had yielded to the Party's rules of socialist realism and put their works in the service of the war effort. In the process, they were forced to sacrifice not only individual expression, but indeed all focus on private life or the fate of the individual.

Beyond Illusions broke this mold with its intensely personal yet lucid portrayal of a young Hanoi woman's disillusionment with and ultimate divorce from a man who bows to the Party apparatus and betrays their shared ideals. A divorced single mother herself, the author had taken an outspoken and very public stand on both literary freedom of expression and democratic reform. In 1982, Huong had stepped into the limelight by publicly protesting the censorship of one of her screenplays, indicting not just the Party, but the complicity and cowardice of ordinary Vietnamese intellectuals. As a result, from 1982 to 1985, her works were not published. Increasingly ostracized for her dissident views and stigmatized by her divorce—a rare act of defiance in Vietnam's deeply patriarchal society—Duong Thu Huong's own struggles were reflected in that of her uncompromising and indomitable protagonist, Linh.

But if this novel created a sensation among Vietnamese readers—selling out all 60,000 copies in less than two weeks—it was not merely because of its previously taboo depiction of private life and extramarital love. The novel's political dynamite lay in an explosive parallel between the heroine's disenchantment and the author's own sense of betrayal by the Party that her generation had spent its youth helping bring to power. As in her previous works, Huong made a point of endowing her main characters with the unmistakable traits of leading Hanoi artists and intellectuals. In *Beyond Illusions,* she singles out those who had betrayed their colleagues by joining in the Party's Maoist-style repression of a 1956 literary reform movement, *Nhan Van Giai Pham.* The most obvious example is the Machiavellian composer, Tran Phuong, who seduces and betrays countless women, while cynically using his loveless but politically astute marriage to regain his power and privilege within the Party machine. For Vietnamese readers, the charismatic composer's betrayal of his lovers and his fellow artists mirrored the Party's seduction and then abandonment of their generation.

These parallels were not lost on the Party hierarchy, which hastened to condemn and vilify Huong. But in 1988, she went on to write *Paradise of the Blind*—the first novel to denounce the terror of the Party's 1953–56 land reform campaign. The work was immediately banned and withdrawn from circulation after selling more than 100,000 copies. General Party Secretary Nguyen Van Linh, who had once personally championed the author, attempted to buy her silence with prizes and material privilege; when he failed, he turned against her publicly, referring to her as "the dissident slut." The indignities the author would herself endure in the years that followed—leading up to her expulsion from the Party in 1990 and culminating in her imprisonment without trial in 1991—is eerily anticipated in the public humiliation and isolation of her heroine, Linh. But Huong overcame this isolation in the 1990s when she went on to publish abroad, first in France and then the United States, two novels officially banned from publication in Vietnam—*Novel Without A Name* and *Memories of A Pure Spring*. In the space of a decade beginning in 1980—and during which her five novels and six short story collections established her as a major voice within Vietnam—Duong Thu Huong went from fame to ignominy, from Party protegée to pariah, from loyal dissent to internal exile. She also went from relative obscurity as a talented young writer in her own country to become the most internationally acclaimed, the most widely translated, and the most popular Vietnamese writer outside Vietnam.

NINA MCPHERSON